D1499071

MEXICAN
HEAT

MLR Press Authors

Featuring a roll call of some of the best writers of gay erotica and mysteries today!

Maura Anderson	Storm Grant
Victor J. Banis	Wayne Gunn
Laura Baumbach	J. L. Langley
Sarah Black	Josh Lanyon
Ally Blue	William Maltese
J. P. Bowie	Gary Martine
James Buchanan	Jet Mykles
Dick D	Luisa Prieto
Jason Edding	Jardonn Smith
Angela Fiddler	Richard Stevenson
Kimberly Gardner	Claire Thompson

Check out titles, both available and forthcoming, at
www.mlrpress.com

Mexican Heat

LAURA BAUMBACH
JOSH LANYON

mlrpress

Copyright 2008 by Laura Baumbach
Copyright 2008 by Josh Lanyon

Published by
MLR Press, LLC
3052 Gaines Waterport Rd.
Albion, NY 14411

Visit ManLoveRomance Press, LLC on the Internet:
www.mlrpress.com

Cover Art by Deana C. Jamroz
Editing by Judith David
Printed in the United States of America.

ISBN# 978-1-934531-05-1

First Edition
2008

Part I

He sauntered past the two shirtless, muscle-bound bouncers, the C-note he slipped the man on his right earning his passage through Club Madrone's front door — and a quick grope over his ass.

The air smelled like sex, sweat, and tequila, and the room pulsed with an intoxicating, driving Latin beat. Gabriel felt the pound of it in his chest, his heart picking up the rhythm. They were playing his song all right, and the name of that tune was danger.

He spared a grim smile as the vibration of the music tickled down his spine and made a playful grab for his cock. Another time, another place…yeah. But tonight he couldn't afford to lose focus. Literally *or* figuratively. The club's door swung heavily shut behind him. His sight adjusted to the dim lights and unfamiliar surroundings as he searched for Benny.

The little weasel better not have dragged him down here for nothing…

Gabriel shouldered his way through the crowd blocking his path. A couple of annoyed faces turned his way, met his level stare, and hastily averted their gazes.

He scanned the packed room. Not too many underage faces and nobody falling down drunk yet. Club Madrone had a decent rep for a bar rumored to be mob owned — though somebody should've whacked the interior decorator who came up with the idea of colored strobe lights and blue walls adorned by rough wooden crosses. The Frida Kahlo-like nude behind the bar wasn't bad, though. Not that Gabriel was much into naked chicks.

He pushed through another human wall — made up mostly of oblivious bare or nearly bare backs. This time the surprised looks turned flirtatious and inviting. He ignored them.

No sign of Benny's red-tipped rooster's comb at either of the long black bars located at each end of the spacious main room. There were a lot of bodies. But, none of them was Benny's.

Where the hell *was* he?

All that bullshit about Don Jesus Sanchez and the Mexican Mafia. Gabriel already knew about the big meet between Ricco Botelli and Sanchez, and what other information would a small-time grifter like Benny be privy to? Still, Gabriel couldn't take a chance. Once in a while Benny surprised them all with the things he managed to sniff out. It was worth a risk to Gabriel's cover if Benny really had ferreted out information Gabriel didn't have access to. But that was a big *if.*

Increasingly edgy, he scanned the crowds both on and off the dance area. The dark archways and thinly curtained alcoves half hid a variety of activities, from panting, pawing couples to group shared snort.

Yeah. Nice clientele here at Club Madrone. His lip curled.

Gabriel caught fragments of conversation as he made his way through the crowd to the bar on the far end of the room. Some of the talk was in English, some of it in Spanish. Several of the comments were addressed directly to him. He was used to it. His shoulder-length black hair and tanned skin allowed his Italian ancestry a free pass in this Latino crowd.

He ignored the challenging looks, the mutters, and the smiling come-ons alike. Sidestepping a giggling platinum-haired señorita, he reached the bar and ordered a Corona from the sleek, tattooed bartender.

"Nine bucks," the man said, sliding the glistening bottle down the bar.

Paying for his drink and pushing back the six dollars change in tip, Gabriel made eye contact long enough to let the man know he appreciated the fast service. The bartender returned his bold stare and gave him a slow, deliberate wink. *Ah. Message received.* Leaning back against the wooden rail, Gabriel surveyed the room, a faint smile touching his mouth as he brought the bottle to his lips.

Too bad he wasn't on his own time. He'd have liked to make the most of these few hours of freedom outside his cage.

On the slick center floor the dancers wriggled and slithered to the pounding music, a huge and coiling snake of mostly olive-skinned flesh and dark hair.

Gabriel's gaze moved on, automatically checking for faces he might recognize from charge reports, or outstanding wants and warrants or — God forbid — a previous bust. Nobody looked familiar. And nobody seemed particularly interested in him past the reason anybody in this dive was interested in anybody else — sex. Gabriel relaxed a fraction. Everything was cool. And that asshole Benny would show up any minute full of the usual bullshit excuses.

He took another pull on his beer. This bar, tucked into an out-of-the-way corner of the Latino neighborhood in a section of the city he had never worked undercover, was the kind of place he liked when he was off duty. It was difficult for an undercover vice cop to find a place to hook up for casual sex. And Gabriel liked his sex *very* casual — as in maybe even a little risky. Rough, hard and silent. Certainly never with the same partner twice. There lay the road to entanglements and complications. With his life on the line 24/7, he couldn't afford emotional attachments. Hell, he couldn't afford *emotions*.

Besides, even before he'd scored the long-term gig as one of Ricco Botelli's hired guns, he'd sort of been what was called "high maintenance." Never mind the brutal hours or the stress and strain of undercover work. Gabriel's aloof attitude and sarcastic mouth hadn't exactly endeared him to potential lovers.

Chugging the rest of his cold beer, he toyed with treating himself to some fine hombre tail once he and Benny completed their business. A smooth Spanish accent and a nice set of broad shoulders topped with a handsome face would be a start. *And big hands.*

He liked the feel of big, strong hands on his body — stroking his skin, pinching his nipples, cupping his ass, holding him still. Gabriel was always in motion: restless, impatient, edgy. *Little firecracker,* his mama used to say. *Hyperactive,* the old man used to say. Hell, maybe it was true. Even during sex he had trouble turning off — twisting, wriggling, squirming — fighting what he wanted, what he needed. It took a strong man, strong in will and physique, to contain all that wiry, crackling energy. Even if

Gabriel had been willing, which he wasn't, few guys were going to make that effort twice.

That's why God created occasional nights of knee-rattling, fuse-blowing sex with strangers, right? Gabriel had figured out a long time ago that was the best he was going to get. Hell, maybe it was all he deserved considering that he betrayed people — granted, not very nice people — for a living. By now he had to have collected one shitload of bad karma.

Turning to order another beer, he glimpsed a tall man moving through the crowd. Sleek black hair, white dress shirt, and black trousers — that described three-quarters of the guys present, but something about this man made it impossible for Gabriel to look away. He waited for a better view — and there it was — a tightly fitted white shirt unbuttoned to a lean waist revealing a nest of rich dark curls on a brown muscular chest. The ebony V dipped toward a silver belt buckle, emphasizing narrow hips and long legs.

Eyes fastened on the man's broad back, sexual heat blossoming in the pit of his stomach, Gabriel followed his easy progress through the crush.

Hungrily he watched as the man reached the far wall. And then his quarry paused as if somehow aware of Gabriel's regard. The man turned Gabriel's way. Their gazes locked.

The heat in Gabriel's belly coalesced into an electric sizzle that sent sparks shooting to his groin. He felt unable to look away as a wide, square hand reached up to rake thick, black hair out of the stranger's eyes. That grave, dark stare never wavered from his own.

The man raised an eyebrow. Just one elegant brow. The faintest smile touched his mouth. Heat flushed Gabriel's face, but he didn't look away — couldn't.

Still waiting for Gabriel's response, the man ran a blunt thumb slowly, consideringly over his full bottom lip.

And just like that Gabriel was rock-hard and aching for it. Well, hell. It had been a very long time. Too long.

A slender youth wiggled off the dance floor and tugged at the stranger's arm, forcing the man to break eye contact. Gabriel felt a surge of irritation. He watched the tall man talk to the insistent dancer, watched the shadow play of long eyelashes, the tug and tease of full sensual lips, a silent pantomime to Gabriel's hungry eyes. Gabriel was adept at lip reading, but in that bad light he could only catch enough to know the man was indulgent, amused by whatever the boy was offering.

Sighing, Gabriel turned back to face the bar, ordering another beer. The bartender provided it with a sympathetic smile, and Gabriel downed it in one long series of swallows, washing away the sizzle in his stomach, leaving only a faint queasiness behind.

If Tall, Dark, and Direct was up for a quickie with a pretty twink, he wasn't likely to be interested in going another round with a guy ten years older.

Gabriel checked his watch. Just where the fuck was Benny? He ought to know Gabriel couldn't afford to wait around here all night. He *did* know.

He risked another look across the room. The twink was near the dance floor talking animatedly with a squat Hispanic with a pockmarked face. There was something vaguely familiar about that ugly face, but Gabriel was unable to place him. He gave it up and looked back at where the tall, sexy stranger had stood.

He had vanished.

Gabriel scanned the room again. No. No sign of the man.

The disappointment he felt was out of proportion to…well, to anything. Even the twink had taken rejection with better grace.

This time he ordered tequila. Picking up the wedge of lime, he licked the curve between his thumb and index finger, flicked his wet skin with salt from the shaker, licked it, tossed back the tequila and bit into the lime.

Giving his head a quick shake, he pushed off from the bar. He'd have one last look for Benny, and then he was gone. The night was fucked — in every way but the one that counted.

Gabriel had already passed the roped-off staircase to the second floor with its curtained alcove balconies once when he decided to scope out the upstairs. After a quick check that no one was watching, he went up the steps two at a time. He wasn't looking for Benny by now — the snitch would have shown if he was coming — but the tequila was singing through Gabriel's system. He felt restless, strung out, and jacked up. He needed action, needed the night not to be another dead end, another waste of time —time being something he increasingly felt he was running out of.

Unchallenged, he found it seemed to be deserted, the club's other patrons more respectful of the velvet rope at the foot of the staircase. Gabriel made his way warily down the row of curtained cubicles. While the thudding bass of the music below concealed his footsteps, it also made it impossible to hear anyone else.

Down the hallway, a partially opened door led into what appeared to be a private office. And all at once the night was looking much brighter. Why the hell not? Why not take advantage of this unexpected opportunity to gather information about who exactly was backing Club Madrone?

In two steps he was in the doorway, brushing his knuckles against the wood. "Anyone home?" he asked softly.

Silence.

Gabriel slipped inside the room. He eased the door soundlessly shut behind him and felt for the wall switch. Light came on overhead revealing a mini-bar in one corner, a red velvet couch in another, and a heavy, antique desk, on which sat a computer. Gabriel considered it, grimly hoping that its secrets would prove more interesting than an inventory of glassware and booze receipts.

The office smelled of recent sex and marijuana. His body reacted to the scents — and the risk he was taking — his heart pounding in crazy time with the salsa rhythms insinuating their way through the floorboards.

Christ. Maybe it was true what they said about him. Maybe he *was* an adrenaline junkie.

When a couple of moments passed and nothing insidious or dangerous presented itself, Gabriel stepped further into the room and got a better look at two large oil paintings hanging behind the desk. They looked original, reminding him subtly of the Kahlo-style nude downstairs, but these felt more…authentic. Here the artist had copied no one, and the result was stunning.

For a moment even his cop's instinct took a backseat while his eyes feasted on the primitive colors and bold strokes. The paintings, companion pieces, vividly depicted sensuous couplings: two men and a woman, two women and a man. He'd never seen anything like them. The brilliant, rich hues of tawny skin and glossy hair, the way the men smiled knowingly at each other, hands brushing bodies in tender caress. He'd never thought of himself as particularly sensitive to art, but these were amazing, even moving…

Mesmerized, body swaying slightly to the throb of the music emanating through the floor and walls, his own sexual need tight and hot in his belly, Gabriel reached out to brush a fingertip over the surface of the nearer painting, as though trying to touch the indescribable, seductive emotions on the canvas, emotions he craved but had yet to acknowledge even within himself.

He was leaning closer to get a look at the signature in the bottom corner of the canvas when a scuffing sound jerked him back to reality too late. Beguiled by the exotic sights, the primal beat, and his own personal demons, Gabriel never heard the man behind him until he was seized and pinned face down over the broad oak desk.

He struggled, but alcohol and shock at his own carelessness slowed his reactions. His arms were twisted behind his back, his wrists painfully bent.

Belatedly, he remembered the semiautomatic pistol in the glove compartment of his SUV. He'd deliberately left his piece behind, expecting to be frisked entering the club. He hadn't really anticipated trouble that night. But that was no excuse. He'd been foolhardy. He deserved to get popped just for being stupid.

And the odds of that fate were good because he could feel the outline of the other man's shoulder holster and gun pressing into his back. The good news was he hadn't already pulled his weapon and blown Gabriel's head off.

In fact, now that Gabriel considered it, although the other man's hold was effective, it wasn't particularly…professional. It wasn't even genuinely threatening, although the full weight of his assailant had landed across his back, forcing the air from his lungs with an *oof*. The most immediate danger seemed to be to Gabriel's dick, which was trapped between his hips and the rounded edge of the hard surface.

Warm, tequila-laced breath danced across the cheek not rammed into the desktop. The scent of sandalwood soap and clean sweat teased his nose. Gabriel squirmed until the feel of a thick cock pressed against the back seam of his jeans froze him.

This was…different.

"Listen," he got out. "The door was open, and I saw the paintings. I'm not trying to steal anything."

No response.

Torn between the fear that he was really in trouble and the illicit thrill of being trapped and helpless in such a compromising position, Gabriel forced himself to remain still. When nothing further developed, he tried to turn his head to see his attacker, but a rough-velvet cheek landed on his own cleanly shaved one, immobilizing him.

"Hey, asshole," Gabriel managed. "You hear me?" He gave one angry heave, which the other man suppressed without much effort.

"Uh…something you want to say to me, asshole?" he inquired with an effort.

A genuinely amused chuckle rumbled out of the chest pressed into Gabriel's back and a low, honey-coated voice interrupted him just as he was getting started. There was a shift of hips and the thick rod riding the crease of Gabriel's jeans slid over him in short, slow strokes. Rubbing his bristled jaw over Gabriel's cheek, the man teased in a seductive growl, "Speaking of asses, *pequeño asno elegante*, I must say, *yours* is *very* fine."

That lean jaw moving against his own, those deep, smooth tones — that sexy trace of Spanish accent — vibrated through Gabriel's whole body, tingling all the way down his spine to his tailbone.

A tongue traced the edge of Gabriel's ear. His cock jerked at the touch, desire rippling from his groin directly to his brain, flooding out common sense, reason — self preservation — and Gabriel found himself pushing back, craving that increased contact. He closed his eyes, biting his lip, feeling the answering hard heat through their clothing — too much clothing.

The man chuckled, a deep, slightly breathless laugh. "So you want to tell me what you're doing in this private office, gringo? Besides offering up this pretty ass of yours?"

The laugh, even more than the words, recalled Gabriel to himself and his situation. His eyes snapped open. What the hell *was* he doing?

"I told you what I was doing. I was admiring the art collection. If you don't want people in here, then don't leave the fucking door open. It's a public place. An open door is an invitation to enter."

Unimpressed by this speech, his captor said softly, breath warm against his ear, "Possibly. Or did you think I was in here? Were you following me? I think maybe you were, gringo."

Say what? Gabriel made another attempt to free himself, but he could buck and pitch all he liked, he was just wearing himself out. Expelling a frustrated breath, he made himself relax once more on the hard surface. His breath fogged the glossy wood beneath his cheek.

"You're out of your fucking head…"

But of course he knew now. Only one man in Club Madrone that night had reason to think Gabriel might be looking for him. Well, two men counting Benny, but this powerful build and confident voice in no way belonged to that skinny, whiny weasel.

Gabriel renewed his struggles, nearly levering himself up from the desk, before giving in to the greater weight and strength forcing him back down.

Body tense, Gabriel waited, ready for whatever the next move was.

And there it was, that honey-baked chuckle again. It drove Gabriel frantic.

"Whatever you're thinking, *dick*head, forget it because I don't know what the *fuck* you're talking about. I don't know who you are, and I wasn't fucking following *anyone*."

The hard shaft against his ass pressed closer, and Gabriel involuntarily flexed his hips, rubbing himself over the desk edge and then back against the bulge snuggled into his crack. *God. Please, please. Yes. Jesus, please some kind of release…*

Hot breath scalded his neck and cheek. The man said silkily in his accented English, "*Madre mios.* You, my ferocious little one, have a gutter mouth a demon would be proud of."

Little? *Little?*

"Fuck. You." Incensed, Gabriel tried to head-butt his captor, only to have a forearm bear threateningly down on the back of his neck. Face smooshed against the slick wood again, he found breathing increasingly difficult.

He jerked as teeth nipped at his nape, the sharp sting startling a shudder out of him. The man gave a satisfied grunt.

"I think" — there was a deliberate pause — "I'd prefer it the other way around."

Gabriel tried to remember exactly what he'd said, and hissed as he was unexpectedly hauled off the desk. Hands momentarily free, he lashed out, managing to land a couple of hard but largely ineffectual blows at the other man's head. A second later his arms were yanked behind his back, wrists pinioned by one large, capable hand.

Christ, this guy's strong. Gabriel felt a flicker of genuine alarm. Even if he really wanted free, he wasn't sure he'd manage it. Once again he was manhandled over the desk.

Fingers threaded his hair, caressing, curling through the long strands. "So soft," the big man murmured. "Like a kitten."

"K-kitten? I remind you of a goddamned *kitten*?" Gabriel stuttered his indignation. He didn't want tenderness, didn't want caresses. He tossed his head, but the questing fingers merely clamped in his hair, demanding stillness.

"Shhh." And the guy said it gently like he fully expected Gabriel to hush up now.

And appallingly Gabriel felt a melting in his gut, a desire to shut up and do whatever this prick told him to do.

The larger man deliberately shoved his hips against Gabriel.

"D'you…mind…" he gasped.

"I might," he was informed mildly. "I might be quite sensitive. You might have seriously hurt my feelings."

Once again the sonofabitch was *laughing* at Gabriel. He ground out, "Yeah, right. Okay, asshole. Fun is fun. Now let me up. I've got things to do and places to go. Not that this hasn't been a night to remember…"

A breath of tequila huffed against the side of his face, tickling his ear. "Is that what you really want, little tiger? You do not like my attentions?"

Gabriel shivered as the man plastered himself closer still, his stiff member rubbing up and down Gabriel's ass. "You do not want my warmth against your body?"

He shook his head, not trusting his voice.

"We both know you're lying, *mi gatito parvulo.*" A big hand slid between Gabriel's legs to grope the hard bulge there. "You desire me, *sí?*"

"No, I don't see," Gabriel gritted. But, oh God, the feel of that big hand fondling him through the stiff denim of his jeans. It was all he could do not to beg.

The exploring hand found his waistband, and worked the button fly of his jeans. Before Gabriel could do more than grunt out a protest, his Levi's were roughly dragged down. Cool air wafted over his bare cheeks as the jeans slid down his long, strong legs to pool at his feet. He was left standing there in his jock strap.

"Silk," the big man murmured approvingly. "Yes. That is you. That is perfect."

Perfectly embarrassing, maybe.

And the wisp of silk and elastic went with one swipe, freeing Gabriel's swollen cock to jut up against the polished wood of the huge desk. He started to turn, then thought better of it, tensing at the clink of a belt buckle. This was followed by the slide of a zipper. Gabriel stood frozen, the blood pounding dizzily in his ears. His cock was already leaking in excitement.

The big man said something soft in Spanish, something Gabriel couldn't quite catch, but the velvet growl of words nuzzled into his hair set his heart tumbling.

Long steely fingers wrapped around his shaft. The blunt, callused pad of a thumb slowly massaged the head, teasing the underside and tracing the creamy slit. Gabriel bit his tongue to keep from moaning, but as the edge of that thumb smeared the precum, a faint sound escaped him. His knees weak, he gratefully acknowledged the hard arm about his waist, only noticing then — distantly — that his hands were free. Good thing. He needed them to steady himself on the edge of the desk.

Hard fingers moved between his legs, exploring the tight sac and then leisurely moving on. A sliding caress of one angular hip and then the long, blunt fingers slowly traced the crack of Gabriel's taut ass.

Then came the delicate press of a thick fingertip on the hot pink hole of Gabriel's anus.

"Holy mother!" the man said huskily. "You feel so ripe, so ready for me."

Gabriel moaned again, shivering. "Oh…fuck!"

The fingers pierced him slowly, sweetly. Slickly. Slickly? *Lube? Where did this guy get lube?* Was he some kind of always prepared sexual Boy Scout or did he find it in a desk drawer? It wasn't hard to believe in this place. Tubes of KY dispensed with the bottles of Wite-Out.

"Is that a request?" The man pressed his lips next to Gabriel's ear. The hand holding Gabriel's straining cock in its callused warmth stilled. "Because if it isn't, I'll stop now." Though the voice was no less seductive, an undertone of inflexibility cut through the haze of Gabriel's lust. "I have no wish to take what is not truly desired."

Gabriel twisted, staring back at the stern, handsome face watching his own. The big man's cock was nestled hotly in the crease of his ass. His own shaft rested trustingly in the other's tight grip. And *now* the guy wanted to discuss it? Jesus fucking Christ!

Of *course* Gabriel wanted him. He wanted this man with every fiber of his being, but he *hated* being forced to admit it out loud.

Tall, Dark, and Perverse's moral soft spot was going to spoil the whole goddamned thing. It was part of the game Gabriel played with himself. He relied on the illusion that he was being physically forced, restrained against his wishes, overpowered by a greater strength and will than his own. He craved the pretense of his helpless submission — and this man with his hard hands and silken voice, his velvety kisses and brutal strength, was Gabriel's fondest wet dream come true. A man who instinctively knew it took more than just a thick cock to take Gabriel to the peak of sexual ecstasy.

But not if they had to *talk* about it for chrissake!

The blunt head of the man's cock rubbed over his asshole, and Gabriel deliberately pushed backward. The tip of the slick, thick cock nudged into his ring of tight, quivering muscle. Gabriel groaned and thrust his hips to gain more of the deliciously teasing shaft. But infuriatingly, the big dick didn't shove past his sphincter muscle.

Wet lips brushed over his ear and drew a line of moisture down his neck. "Yes, gringo?"

The words tore out of him. He couldn't help it. "Yes! You *cholo* bastard. Yes!"

In one long smooth stroke the stout cock sheathed itself to the hilt in Gabriel's taut body. The man whispered into the crook of his neck. "Spanish. Not Mexicano. Not Americano. You are conquered by a true son of Spain."

"Like I give a shit." Gabriel gasped fretfully, "Just fuck me blind."

"*Si, mi gatito, si.* I will give you what you most desire."

Slow, strong, thrusts jarred Gabriel's teeth and knocked his bobbing hard-on into the desk with a heavy thud at each languid stroke. He could have wept at that solacing mix of pain and pleasure.

"Harder. God…harder…"

The stranger's shaft was long, thick, and hot. Gabriel seemed to feel every bulging, pulsing vein that ribbed its surface. Distantly he wondered whether the lube the man had used heated on contact with skin. His insides blazed, his opening burned and spasmed, straining to accommodate that driving cock.

The broad, blunt tip unexpectedly changed angle and grazed over his prostate. Gabriel cried out and tried to slam his ass down on that rigid pole, but powerful hands kept him from doing any damage to himself. Instead, he had to be content with the slow, slapping, snapping movement of the stranger's hips and measured thrusts.

Gabriel whimpered. *Yes.* This was it. The feeling of being overpowered, mastered.

Another pass over his prostate sent a charge of electricity crackling up Gabriel's spine. His breath caught raggedly.

"So…g —" He changed it mid sentence. "Harder," he ordered. "What, is it your first time —" He swallowed on the words as another deep thrust followed, intensifying the burn.

A low growl vibrated through his body, and Gabriel shook with the intensity of his body's response. He felt like he was having some kind of seizure. He'd never felt anything as intense as this. As good as this.

Too good. He needed to end this soon and get away from this man. Because he could get addicted to this kind of sexual high.

But if he worked it just right, he'd never even have to look at the man's face again — never have to meet his eyes. Gabriel pressed his face into the grain of the desk and gave himself over to the blinding pleasure of the moment, savoring it.

Another deep thrust made bright lights dance behind his closed eyelids. His skin felt prickly and much too hot, the sparse hair on his lithe body standing up erect and stiff as his cock. A tight sizzle crawled up his balls and over his stretched asshole toward his spine — and suddenly his body was empty. *The bastard had pulled out.*

A strangled cry of protest escaped his dry lips. But powerful hands closed on his waist. He was on his back, supine on the desktop before he knew what was happening.

"What the hell —" To his astonished dismay, the big stranger hauled off Gabriel's cowboy boots and tossed them aside, then yanked his jeans the rest of the way down and off.

He smacked at the other man's dark head, his fist grazing a dark-shadowed jaw. But his "lover" put an end to that, grabbing his hands and pinning them over his head.

"You sonofabitch," Gabriel spat. "No!"

Powerful body poised over Gabriel's, the man waited, still and quiet. Unable to resist that silent command, Gabriel slowly raised his eyes.

Inches away, a pair of sooty-fringed dark-chocolate eyes stared warmly into his own. They were so close Gabriel could see the ring of the black pupils and the fine crystal-like black lines through the irises. The whites were clear, clean, and bright. Laugh lines crinkled at the corners of the lids. There was passion, yes, but intelligence and humor and tenderness in that look as well. Too much. Way too much. Gabriel averted his eyes, but after a moment he looked back into that worldly, knowing stare.

Firm lips brushed tiny silken kisses over Gabriel's chin and down his jaw, then the man murmured in a low, liquid voice. "Oh yes, *gatito*." A sharp nip stung the edge of his jaw. "I want to watch your face quiver as I take you. I want to see those cynical eyes roll up in your pretty head when I make you come." A wet tongue darted over Gabriel's mouth, tasting him — only to withdraw when he moved to return the touch. "I want to hear your soft, kitten purrs of contentment when I've fucked you senseless."

Gabriel laughed shakily. "Man, you are one crazy motherfu —"

The words strangled in his throat as the man licked then sucked at his Adam's apple. Gabriel heard himself give another of those helpless pleading sounds. Embarrassment flushed his face, and he closed his eyes to block out the man's amused smile.

"No, no. Eyes open." The rasped words brought Gabriel's eyelids flitting open. His gut clenched at the grinding rub of the big man's slick cock over his spread, eager, empty hole.

Gabriel watched the man's handsome, absorbed face as he once more invaded Gabriel's ass. Panting and dizzy with the speed of that sudden fullness, his eyes widened to meet the stranger's sultry stare.

Something in that gleaming, discerning gaze hypnotized him, held him captive just as tightly as his body was held prisoner by the man's physical strength. He felt suddenly, vulnerably naked. Naked from the inside out.

"Beautiful," the man murmured. "*Mi pequeño gato encantador travieso.* My wicked lovely cat."

"Christ, will you just shut up and *do it?*" He arched, forcing the cock inside of him deeper.

The man rotated his hips with great deliberation, thrusting deep inside Gabriel's channel. Somehow, the grinding angle of those lean, muscular hips forced the tight ring of muscle at Gabriel's opening still wider. He was stretched and stroked over and over. The dual sensation had Gabriel writhing on the desk, crying out helplessly.

And the bastard fucking him had the gall to whisper more sweet and soothing things to him. As though he were *courting* him.

A buzzing sensation started in the tip of Gabriel's cock, zapped down the aching length, blazing through his balls and flashing up his spine. For one dizzy, perilous moment Gabriel thought he was either going to black out or burst into tears. Now *that* was a first.

Against his will, Gabriel laughed, a breathless, giddy gasp.

And the other bent, licking Gabriel's parted lips. His chin bumped against Gabriel's and he licked at his captive's lips again, silently, unexpectedly asking permission to claim them.

Gabriel lurched up to seal their mouths together. The click of teeth and the faint taste of blood added a dangerous, dirty element to this kiss that should never have happened. He knew better. *Christ. Kissing!* But he was never going to see the bastard again. He might as well get all he could from the encounter.

So Gabriel made his mouth hard and his kiss grinding, rejecting the sweetness offered him. The other slid his tongue down Gabriel's throat, turning the kiss into plundering. And Gabriel relaxed into it. This he understood. He submitted to the hot, wet tongue rudely testing every inch of his mouth, exploring palette, teeth and lips, tongue dueling lazily with Gabriel's own.

The desk rocked and slid a few inches across the floor, as the thrusts into Gabriel's body grew more rapid and frenzied. Teetering on the brink of climax, Gabriel couldn't stop his cry of protest when abruptly the rhythm changed.

"What are you *doing* to me? You sonofabitch —" He was incoherent with frustration.

"Here. I am here." The other sounded breathless. "Mother of God, what a noise you make!"

The man pulled back far enough to look Gabriel in the eyes, beginning a slow, sensual stroke, thrusting deeply, making sure to brush over the sweet, swollen nub in Gabriel's stuffed channel. Gabriel bit his lip hard, straining to control himself as the other gyrated against him with finality, then slowly withdrew until just the tip of his cock rested inside the entrance of Gabriel's body.

He paused for an excruciating moment, then flexed his buttocks, jerking the shaft resting on the rim of Gabriel's asshole. Gabriel sucked in a sharp breath, his back bowing.

When his tailbone hit the desk, his partner thrust into him again, repeating the whole agonizingly pleasurable stroke.

By the fifth thrust, Gabriel was wriggling and mewling like the newborn kitten the man teasingly called him. The build of exquisite tension had Gabriel striking out, clawing at the man taking possession of his body, and secretly delighted when his hands were roughly caught, his wrists forced over his head. Now he was truly helpless, truly captive.

"Look at me," the other jerked out, and Gabriel obeyed, finding himself unable to free his gaze from the man's hypnotic stare. He realized that his face was an open book to this stranger; that his every thought and emotion were being absorbed and analyzed. It was terrifying. He had never felt so exposed, so vulnerable. He wanted to close his eyes, to look away, but he could do nothing.

Helplessly, Gabriel stared back, memorizing the proud, fierce lines of the man's face. The square jaw, the wide almond-shaped eyes, the full, sensuous mouth — smooth olive skin made for touching, for tasting. He mapped the creases of a forehead furrowed in concentration and effort. He longed to reach up and lick a trail along the cleft in the man's chin, to run his hands through the man's thick, wavy hair and follow its curls to the nape of his corded, powerful neck.

Yes, despite the danger he wanted to remember this one. In fact, he suspected he would never forget him — couldn't forget him even if he tried. And perhaps the memory of this face would make those lonely nights less empty. Those nights when it was just Gabriel and his hand.

The now familiar buzz started to form at the base of his cock and his balls pulled up tight. Somewhere near the pit of his stomach, a fluttering wave of excitement rippled through him, racing downward to crash into the sensations building in his groin.

Stars exploded in his head and from an enthralled and spinning distance he watched as the man above him grimaced, full lips pulled back in a soundless cry as his hips stilled and his cock emptied into Gabriel.

Aroused that a stronger man's cum filled his ass, Gabriel arched and spasmed, riding the crest of his own climax. His body wrenched against the weight pinning him down, fighting the grip holding him helpless — not to gain his freedom, but to intensify the moment. For the first time ever he had truly been reduced to utter helplessness, and it was as exhilarating as it was terrifying. For all his fantasies, he'd never imagined that *helpless*, in the right man's arms, was *good*.

With their eyes focused on each other again, the man swooped down and claimed his mouth in a sweaty, sucking caress as though it were their first kiss of the night, leaving Gabriel breathless and dizzy by the time they broke contact.

No. Too much. He was starting to think about the next time — and there couldn't be a next time. This couldn't happen again. Not ever, not with this man who understood him far too well.

Despite his resolve, Gabriel felt bereft when the warm weight of cock slipped from his body, and he was released. He heard the rustle of clothing, soft furtive sounds as the other man began to dress.

Gabriel stared at the ceiling, at the hundreds of tiny dots in the squares of soundproofed tiles. Absently, he began to count them. Let the other dress and leave first. He didn't want to have to look at him — let alone talk to him.

He was startled when the other man bent over him and pressed soft words to his lips. It took a moment to decipher them.

"*Enorme, mi gatito, muy enorme.* I have never met one such as you. Demon and angel." After the scorching heat of their encounter, the kiss was unexpectedly sweet.

Gabriel answered fiercely, leaving bruising teeth marks on the stranger's lower lip.

The man swore and pulled Gabriel away by his hair. The dark eyes, more soft than smoldering now, studied Gabriel's face quizzically. "Mostly demon, I think," he declared. "All boiling passion and dark, buried need. I would have more of you again, another day. If you like."

There it was. Exactly what he feared. Gabriel opened his mouth, but the words — no words — would come. He couldn't agree to this — and yet he couldn't seem to make himself say no.

When he said nothing, his companion released Gabriel so abruptly he fell backward on the desk.

"Jesus," Gabriel swore. "That's some technique, Romeo."

"Only because you like it that way, my friend."

A business card appeared in the man's hand like a magician's parlor trick. *A business card. Like, does he do this for a living?* The man held it between his thumb and forefinger, the creamy paper dwarfed by the large, square hand.

Eyes riveted to the card moving teasingly under his nose, Gabriel opened his mouth to say something sarcastic, but the words just wouldn't come. He stared as the card slipped neatly into the breast pocket of his open shirt.

For a moment he closed his eyes. What would it hurt to just see what the card held? A name? A phone number? Or maybe just a place to meet?

The paper was warm just like the man. It burned through the thin fabric over Gabriel's chest and branded straight through until it reached his heart. By the time he had yanked the card back out, the stranger was at the door, half-turned to watch Gabriel's reaction.

Pointedly, Gabriel ignored the writing on the paper, scrunching the card in his hand. He pitched it at the trash can beside the desk — mildly surprised when it went in, given the way his hand was shaking.

The man's mouth tightened for a moment, but he said nothing. Instead he gave a tilt of his head in acceptance.

"As you wish, *gatito*."

This thing was impossible. Even if Gabriel wanted it to be different — and he didn't.

The man held his gaze a beat longer. Then he said, "There's an old Spanish proverb. *Eyes that do not see. Heart that does not feel.*"

But before he could decide, the man was gone. The door barely whispered as it closed, but Gabriel flinched anyway.

CHAPTER TWO

Catching his reflection in the massive foyer mirror, Gabriel straightened his black bow tie, double-checking the perfectly aligned collar of his crisp white tuxedo shirt.

Not bad for a kid from the wrong side of the tracks. If the boys from North Beach could see him now, they'd believe he was the badass villain he pretended to be.

Maybe it was the mirror. It was ten feet tall and gilded in antique gold. It covered a third of the wall in the vaulted-ceiling marble foyer. The antique reception table and side chairs dotting the walls were equally ornate and oversized, grandiose — just like Ricco Botelli's drug lord aspirations. Gabriel's mouth curved in a faint, contemptuous smile.

Eyeing the lines of his tux one final time, his fingers lingered over the smooth satin edging of the collarless jacket. He wasn't one to pay a lot of attention to his appearance. Elegant cheekbones, long-lashed hazel eyes, and an unexpectedly engaging grin made up for a multitude of grooming sins. And, of course, you couldn't beat the best tailoring money could buy — or at least that you could afford. *That* much Gabriel knew. But then his mama had spent her life working in the San Francisco garment district.

As his fingertips brushed the satin trim, a tactile memory from the previous night's tryst with the nameless stranger flooded him with phantom sensation. The wet trail of a man's mouth over his bare, sensitized skin — that silky-smooth slide, branding a hot trail of pleasure into his flesh. He closed his eyes for a moment, remembering the feel of the stranger's large, sure hands on his body, dimly aware his cock was reacting, swelling to half-mast. Even his nipples hardened against the cool linen of his shirt. Heat rose in his cheeks.

Glancing over his shoulder at the catering staff busily taking care of last minute details for the evening's reception, Gabriel covertly rearranged himself in his trousers, thankful the tailored pants had pleats. He buttoned his jacket for added security.

"It looks better unbuttoned, G." Small, silver-tipped hands slid around his waist from behind and delicately popped the button open.

Gabriel caught the hands as they dropped lower, turning to face their owner. He smiled that killer smile and pointedly clapped Gina Botelli's wandering hands together, pushing her — not ungently — away from him before releasing her.

"Gina. I thought you were waiting to make your grand entrance. You know, sweep down the staircase like Scarlett O'Hara. Bowl over your future husband with your grace and beauty."

Or, failing that, the dowry she brought as West Coast crime boss Ricco Botelli's only surviving relative.

Gina offered a gurgling laugh, the naughty glint in her eyes warning Gabriel before she stepped in closer. Again he captured her hands as they dove toward his belt. "I'd *rather* bowl you over, *ragazzo bello*." She nipped his earlobe before he stepped back.

He murmured, "Now, now. You trying to get me killed, angel?"

Gina wrinkled her pert nose. "What my big brother doesn't know won't hurt him. And Jesus Sanchez doesn't *own* me."

"Ricco knows a lot more than you think he does." Gently, but firmly, he forced her back a few more inches. "And Don Sanchez will be arriving any moment. And even if he wasn't, you're promised to him, remember?"

"*Promised!* You mean like I had a choice?" She opened her mouth to say more, but Gabriel cut in fast. If she was smart, this was a conversation she wouldn't have with him or anyone else. Yet Gina continued bitterly. "This isn't a marriage, it's a business merger. That's all Ricco thinks about — expanding his empire. All he cares about is making new connections, forging alliances, building new supply lines and distribution channels."

Did she really understand what she was saying? Gabriel was never quite sure.

Gina gave a desolate little sniff. "He cares more for his money than for my happiness." Her velvety dark eyes welled with easy emotion.

Gabriel said evenly, "Don Jesus is a powerful, wealthy man, Gina. As Don Sanchez' wife, you'll have everything you ever wanted." Sure, Jesus Sanchez was a crook and probably a psychopath, but he was the most powerful drug lord on the continent. As the prospective bridegroom for a crime family daughter, that made him quite a catch.

Gina's stare grew a shade calculating. "Including you?"

Gabriel lowered his voice to a conspiratorial whisper. "Only if you want my head served on a plate, Salome, because that's what'll happen if either your brother or Don Sanchez thinks we're playing fast and loose."

"*Salome!*" She was smiling, unfazed by the picture he was trying to draw her, but then in her own way Gina Botelli was surprisingly sheltered and maybe even a bit naïve. Slyly, she added, "It might be worth one night."

"It might be." He winked at her, flirting back just enough to not piss her off. "But trust me, angel, I'm not your type."

"I think you are." She leaned in close and tugged at the bow of Gabriel's tie, pretending to straighten it under the disinterested glances of the caterers and staff. Her lips parted, her breath smelling faintly — disarmingly — of bubblegum, as she dropped her hand, relying on the positions of their bodies to hide her actions. Fingers skimmed the fly of Gabriel's pants.

"Gina!" At the shout from the other room, Gabriel took a prudent step back. Annoyance flickered across Gina's face.

Ricco Botelli's voice rang off the walls in the marble foyer. "Christ, here you are!"

Gabriel met his boss's unsmiling black look without expression. Botelli turned to his sister.

Gina lifted her chin. "What'd you think, I ran away?"

"Don't be a smart mouth." Botelli took Gina by the elbow and gave her a nudge in the direction of the sweeping marble staircase the dominated the back half of the entry hall. "Wait up in your room, *il mio piu prezioso*. I want to introduce you properly to Don Sanchez."

"It's a little late for that!"

"Hey, mind your manners."

"It's boring upstairs. Why can't I wait here? G and I were talking." Gina wriggled free of her brother's grip. Botelli pulled her away less gently this time. Gabriel moved clear of the wrestling match.

"G is coming with me to meet the limo." Botelli walked his sister to the bottom of the staircase. He shooed her away with his hand. "Go on. Brush your hair again or something."

Gina flounced up a couple of steps. "Oh, well thanks *a lot*! Maybe I just won't come back down."

"For God's sake, Gina. It's your engagement party! Your fiancé is arriving tonight."

Gina stopped in her tracks. "And I'm supposed to get all in a tizzy? Come on, Ricco. This is more your wedding than mine. You should be the one picking the cake and choosing the invitations."

Botelli said flatly, "Don't kid yourself, Gina. This will be a real marriage."

For a moment brother and sister stared at each other. Then Gina said tartly, "Great! To a man I barely know. Way to go, big brother."

Botelli said, "I heard Sanchez bought a rock the size of Manhattan for you." He touched the tip of her nose with his finger. "Won't that look nice on your hand?"

A greedy sparkle replaced the defiance in Gina's flashing dark eyes. Gabriel watched the transformation from spoiled, petulant kid sister to spoiled, calculating woman. Yeah, no point wasting a lot of sympathy on Gina.

Sighing dramatically, Gina's eyes flicked to Gabriel. Rubbing her bare ring finger thoughtfully, Gina said, "Well, maaaaybe a couple of carats could go a long way to helping me see things from the right perspective."

Botelli chuckled, evidently approving of his baby sister's mercenary streak. He swatted her pert ass as she turned away and sashayed up the stairs, with more wiggle to her hips than the effort required. But then Gabriel guessed it was hard to stomp off effectively in four-inch heels and that tight, black silk gown.

At the top of the staircase Gina paused. "Okay. Just give me plenty of warning. I want to knock my future husband's Gucci's right off his big, flat feet." She disappeared and an instant later there came the sound of a door slammed shut.

Botelli shook his head, and turned back to Gabriel, who met his gaze levelly. Botelli wasn't bad looking, but forty years of hard living had etched lines and creases into his dark Mediterranean features. His black hair was already receding. The nearly constant squint from refusing to wear the glasses he needed gave him a hard, suspicious look. But then, he was a hard, suspicious man. Crazy-ambitious and harsh to the point of cruelty. His only soft spot was his sister.

"Come here."

Botelli motioned to Gabriel. Gabriel crossed the foyer, deliberately relaxing his shoulders, staying loose and easy, ready for anything. Botelli had an ugly temper, and part of Gabriel's job — like all Botelli's hired muscle — was to take it and like it. When he was in arm's distance, Botelli suddenly slung his heavy, surprisingly still-muscular arm around Gabriel's shoulders and hauled him close. The effect was something like being swallowed whole by an aftershave-soaked shark. Gabriel lowered his head slightly, keeping his spine relaxed under the added weight, submissive but not intimidated.

"You know, Gio, I like you," Botelli said. With a sinking in his gut, Gabriel knew Botelli had finally taken note of Gina's attentions to one of the hired guns.

Gabriel said humbly, "I know you took a chance bringing me on board, Ricco. I appreciate it." He raised his eyes briefly, lowered them again. It was a fine line between appearing obedient or weak. Weakness of any sort wasn't tolerated in the Botelli organization. But neither was insolence. "I won't let you down."

Botelli stared at him with those reptile eyes long enough for a trickle of sweat to track its way down Gabriel's spine. The staff continued to move about the hall putting the final touches on the room. The waxy perfume of a garden's worth of floral arrangements filled the air. The musicians were already set up in the ballroom, and the periodic discordant note as they checked their instruments floated down the hall. Gabriel couldn't help noticing that the caterers all moved around him and Botelli like they were invisible, eyes shying away from the two men and their under-voiced conversation.

The spell was broken when Botelli playfully slapped his cheek. His restraining arm crushed Gabriel tight, then released him.

"Hey, I understand, *paisan*. Gina has a crush on you." Botelli grinned a wolfish grin. "My baby sister is used to getting what she wants."

Gabriel said, "She's a Botelli, Ricco. She doesn't like no for an answer."

Botelli winked. "But you tell her no, right, Giovanni?"

Gabriel relaxed a fraction. The wink was a clue that Botelli was actually in a pretty good mood; learning to accurately gauge the man had been a matter of survival during the past year undercover, and in fact Gabriel had pretty much mastered playing Botelli's expectations and emotions. When it came down to it, he found evading and distracting Gina the real challenge.

"Sure," he said. He tried to look suitably surprised, like he was only catching on now that Gina's behavior might present a real problem for him. In this case, seeming sort of thick was the safest move. He added earnestly, "Gina's a wonderful woman. I know she's not in my class."

"That's right," Botelli agreed. "But she's a kid. What does she know? You're young, brave, good-looking. She thinks you're just her type."

"I'm not her type," Gabriel returned steadily.

"No?" Suspicion glinted in Botelli's coal-dark gaze. He scrutinized Gabriel's fine features framed in silky black. "So what type are you, *cugine*?"

Gabriel looked Botelli straight in the eye. Machismo was like a religion in the testosterone-drenched world of organized crime.

"Hey." He offered his easy smile. "I'm a gunman for a mighty underworld kingpin. My life expectancy alone makes me lousy relationship material." He opened his dinner jacket, his hand unconsciously caressing the butt of the 9mm secured in a shoulder holster under his left armpit, and it wasn't just a line when he said, "I'm nobody's type, Ricco. Not for more than one night, anyway."

Giovanni Contadino was a phantom with no past, no future. Only the here and now had substance or meaning for him — maybe not all that different than Gabriel Sandalini.

Botelli laughed and winked again, good humor restored by that vow of an early death in the line of duty.

"Sanchez and his men will be here any minute. You stand beside me when I greet him." Ricco clapped a hand around the back of Gabriel's neck, and gave him a playful shake. "Let him know who my trusted soldiers are, *capisce?*"

"*Capisce.*" But Gabriel couldn't help asking, "You're going to let Sanchez' men invade the house? How many guns does he need to salute his engagement? You don't think we oughta confiscate their weapons when they arrive?"

"*Confiscate their weapons.*" Botelli mimicked Gabriel, amused. "Where'd you go to school, the police academy? You don't treat a man like Sanchez like he's a common crook. You treat him with respect. With dignity."

Unless you managed to kill him first, but Botelli had decided it was easier to join him rather than fight him. Luckily he had two things Sanchez wanted — a beautiful young sister — and oversight of several very efficient West Coast drug distribution networks.

"A couple years ago nobody ever heard of Don Jesus Sanchez," Gabriel pointed out.

"That was a couple years ago. Sanchez has taken over half the Pacific Northwest in the last eighteen months. Right now he's holding the high cards, he's the man of the hour, so we gotta bend the rules a little. We gotta accommodate him. Once he sees we're the best possible partnership for his organization…well…" Botelli spread his hands.

"Not much of an honor if he decides to take advantage of the situation and eliminate the middle man."

"*Paisan*, you got a suspicious mind." Botelli chuckled, not displeased. "Relax! Sanchez *wants* to marry Gina. He'll be family soon. Naturally he's going to check out our operation. And we want to check out his. But tonight…tonight we celebrate a marriage between two families with good wine and good food and good friends."

It sounded like an ad for the Olive Garden. Gabriel tried not to let his cynicism show, but he must not have been entirely successful because Botelli said, "The Mexicans have taken over the supply pipeline to the city — the fucking western United States, for that matter. Our old connections are gone. In jail or dead. We need to negotiate a new deal fast. It's that simple."

Gabriel stood steady. It was his information, from deep inside Botelli's business that had sealed the fate for some of those absent connections. For others, Sanchez' ruthless pursuit of empire could take credit. And now Sanchez was positioning himself to be brought down, the biggest coup of all for Gabriel.

Botelli checked his Rolex, frowning.

One of the bodyguards stationed at the front door signaled to them. "Boss, the Mexicans are here!"

Botelli grabbed one of the servers as the girl scurried past, and she nearly dropped her tray of crab puffs.

"You, blondie, send a housemaid upstairs to tell my sister our guests have arrived." Despite all his assurances to Gabriel, Botelli's voice revealed his true tension. The uniformed server nodded hastily, backing away.

Botelli turned his attention briefly back to Gabriel. "You don't worry about Gina. I'll take care of my sister. You just make sure she keeps her hands off you or Sanchez'll cut *your* hands off — or maybe something else."

"Got it."

Except that it was easier said than done. Gina had all the self-control of a Pomeranian in heat.

"*Capisce?*" Botelli said sharply, as though Gabriel hadn't spoken.

"Yeah, got it. I'll stay clear of her."

Botelli nodded once sharply, apparently satisfied. Gabriel stayed silent and followed the other man through the wide-open front door and outside. He thought Botelli seemed uncharacteristically jittery as he positioned himself with his lieutenants at the top of the steps.

Edging forward to stand on Botelli's left, Gabriel glanced at the impassive face of Bruno, the mob boss's personal bodyguard. Gabriel always liked to know where Bruno was in relation to him because stepping in between Bruno and the object of his interest could constitute a health hazard.

On Botelli's right stood Michelangelo Rizzi, Botelli's underboss, second in command only to Botelli. He was of Sicilian descent — as he never tired of telling people — tall, blue-eyed and blond, handsome, vain, ambitious — and more slippery than an eel in an oil slick. Michelangelo's blue gaze slid to Gabriel's and he smiled. Gabriel smiled coolly back. Michelangelo didn't like him — resented Botelli's interest in the younger man — and they both knew it.

Covertly, Gabriel reached up to touch the pistol beneath his arm. Unlike his fellow hired guns who liked stealthy .22 calibers, he preferred the big bang of his favorite Walther P99, a compact snub nose with a grip that fit nice and snug in the palm of his slender hand.

In addition to the Walther, he wore a double-edged boot knife in his Kenneth Coles. Despite their party finery, the men he stood beside were equally well armed — as no doubt were the men inside the limo.

Gabriel's heart beat faster. He had spent eighteen months charming, manipulating, and deceiving his way into Botelli's den of thieves, drug dealers and murderers. When he landed this undercover gig no one could have foreseen the alliance between the infamous Mexican drug lord, Don Jesus Sanchez and Ricco Botelli, the reigning king of cocaine distribution on the West Coast. In fact, when the word had first spread through Botelli's ranks, it had sounded too good to be true. But here it was unfolding right before his eyes, the makings of the biggest drug bust in history.

A long, low, dark blue sedan with heavily tinted windows glided leisurely down the shady circular drive, stopping just outside the formal entrance. In a couple of quick moves, the driver expertly angled the car to block and prevent any other vehicle pulling alongside.

The limo doors popped open, and several scarred and grim faced men wearing immaculately tailored dark suits — and grim expressions beneath sunglasses — stepped out onto the drive. The men beside Gabriel shifted imperceptibly, straightening shoulders. The Mexican crew fell into position, silently appraising Botelli and the lieutenants flanking him.

Another man — this one in a tuxedo — disembarked from the back seat of the limo.

The tall man unbent, eying his soldiers without expression and then turning his strangely light gaze on the Botelli faction. Gabriel would have known this was Don Sanchez just by the aura of power the man exuded. The Mexican drug lord was forty-five, heavy-featured, dark-jowled. His eyes were an uncanny light brown — almost amber. *Tiger's eyes*, Gabriel thought. Unlike Botelli, who went for the bling, Sanchez was dressed in simple, almost severe, black. No rings, no flashy cufflinks or shirt studs, nothing but a single pin gleaming like a tiny captured star in the man's exquisitely tailored jacket lapel.

Glancing about, Gabriel fixed a picture of Botelli's soldiers' positions in relation to Sanchez' outfit. They appeared to be pretty evenly matched. He turned back to the limo in time to see another man emerge from the vehicle and straighten, disconnecting the cell phone call that had delayed him.

The pavement seemed to shift beneath Gabriel's feet as he stared down into familiar dark eyes. *No damn way*. His heart leapt into his throat. He blinked. Risked another look. Eyes as rich as espresso met his own — and widened in mirrored shock.

Tall, Dark and Handsome from the Club Madrone was one of Don Sanchez' lieutenants!

It took Gabriel a moment to absorb it, like a body blow. He recovered quickly, though. Neither he nor Sanchez' man was in any position to betray the other.

Sanchez' lieutenant stared straight back, eyes narrowed, a twisted half smile on those sensual lips — and the memory of that sexy, hungry mouth on his body turned Gabriel's face hot. He stared through the other man as though he were invisible.

Gabriel forced himself to show nothing at the sight of the tall, lean, elegantly clad figure strolling beside Sanchez toward the stairs. He wore a shoulder holster so finely made that it barely disturbed the cut of his classic black tux. Botella boots and a Movado watch; it was no secret that Sanchez paid well. This man exuded a tough but suave confidence, a genuine presence. He could easily have passed for the real man of position and importance in that group of thugs.

The stranger leaned forward and murmured something into Sanchez' ear. Sanchez smiled, incredibly, making him even less attractive. And his lieutenant chuckled — that deep velvet laugh that Gabriel remembered only too well. It sent a shudder of pleasurable memory down his spine.

Sanchez' men fell into position around him as they mounted the stairs. Botelli's own men tensed, shifted, readying themselves. Botelli was smiling widely, but Gabriel could see the bead of sweat trickling down his jowl.

Gabriel glanced again at Sanchez' lieutenant and met a burning stare. Gabriel forced a cocky grin to his face. The other man's eyes flickered, and he looked away — and Gabriel relaxed a fraction, forcing his attention back onto the job.

Botelli had arranged the meet so that he would have the advantage of standing on the upper level with Sanchez and his men on the stairs below, but Sanchez and his men just kept marching up the steps, and Botelli and his crew were forced to fall back a few feet — and then a few feet further — until they were all the way inside the marble foyer.

"Don Jesus." Botelli planted his feet and held a pudgy hand out in greeting. "You honor my home." His black gaze ran briefly over Sanchez' lieutenants. "Gentlemen."

Unsmiling, Sanchez accepted the handshake. "Ricco. I've looked forward to this day." He nodded curtly to the tall, handsome man at his side. "My second in command, Miguel Ortega."

Ortega. Miguel Ortega. Why wasn't he in any of the files Gabriel had seen on Sanchez' organization?

Botelli inclined his head politely, but made no move to shake hands. He gestured to his own underboss. "Michelangelo Rizzi."

The two lieutenants sized each other up with impassive faces.

Sanchez' tawny gaze moved past Botelli and his entourage to the service staff milling in the background. He said abruptly, "Where's Gina?" A hint of color came into his face. "I'm…looking forward to seeing my future bride again."

Anxious was more like it, and abruptly Gabriel realized that Botelli did indeed have some leverage. Sanchez wanted Gina all right; regardless of what this marriage meant to the Botellis, it was the real thing for Sanchez.

And Botelli knew it, too. He ushered his guests forward, saying smoothly in what Gabriel always thought of as his snake oil salesman voice, "Gina will join us shortly, Don Jesus. You know girls. And this is a very special evening for Gina. She wants to look her best."

Sanchez murmured, "I do so like pretty things."

Botelli motioned for a server to approach, and Sanchez accepted a fluted glass of champagne. His men stood wordlessly by, refusing to even acknowledge the offer while Botelli's crew accepted the champagne with the air of men making a point. Gabriel took a glass and made an effort not to look Ortega's way.

Sipping his champagne, Sanchez smiled — at his own thoughts — and Gabriel thought that white flash of teeth was more chilling than the tiger's blank stare. He unobtrusively studied the man's scarred, walnut-dark face, his nose obviously broken more than once. His face bore the legacy of a violent life. The brutal face of a brutal man.

Gabriel risked a look at Ortega. The man was staring expressionlessly at him. Gabriel stared stonily back. He had to be good at reading people to stay alive. Yet, never in a million years would he have pegged Ortega as a murderer or a drug dealer. Despite the rough sex and domineering attitude, he'd shown…gentleness. Had been almost loving. He'd read Gabriel like a bedtime story, understood every single secret desire and wish — and granted them generously.

Gabriel swallowed a mouthful of champagne. It could have been battery acid for all he knew.

Strands of classical music drifted out the open double doors leading into the ballroom. Partygoers were arriving now, a line of expensive cars pulling up the long, shady drive and fashionably dressed guests entering the mansion, smiling pleasantly and vaguely at their host, though most of them probably didn't know Botelli from Adam. Botelli ignored them, his attention fixed on his guest of honor, who sipped champagne and looked around the gracious room as though taking inventory.

Giggles and high voices bounced off the marble floor and vaulted ceiling. Even Sanchez' posse turned a few unsmiling faces to see the new arrivals. Gabriel recognized several of Gina's spoiled and brainless jet-setting pals in the most recent wave of arrivals.

Botelli selected a canapé from another circling server, shoved it in his mouth, speaking through the crumbs. "Don Jesus, I thought we might take some time and discuss a little business before my sister joins us." He gestured down the Aubusson-carpeted hallway where his study was located. "We can —"

Without so much as a glance at Botelli, Sanchez broke the spell of congenial pleasantries by raising his hand and snapping his fingers. The sharp sound cut across the music, the light chatter of guests — and Botelli's voice.

"Miguel." Sanchez spoke with casual curtness that was shocking for all its quiet.

Though Ortega did no more than turn his gaze on Botelli, Gabriel had the impression of something sleek and dangerous scenting prey.

"Mr. Botelli," he said in that sultry, slow voice — like poured honey. How well Gabriel recalled that charming inflection. Not quite an accent, but exotic all the same. Ortega's eyes moved dismissively over Botelli's men, clearly discounting them all. Bruno, Michelangelo — but when his gaze reached Gabriel, he let it linger mockingly. "Gentlemen," he said, and the amusement in that single word made it an insult. Botelli didn't look any too thrilled as Ortega continued, "You may remember we spoke before, Mr. Botelli? Specifically, at your last meeting with Don Sanchez."

"Uh, right," said Botelli, casting an uneasy look at Sanchez.

Sanchez said, "Miguel knows my wishes. He speaks for me in all things."

That ought to make life interesting for Gina, Gabriel thought sourly as Botelli blinked without comprehension.

Ortega smiled again, but the smile didn't conceal the steel in his eyes. "Tonight, all business requests go through me, Mr. Botelli. I will convey your wishes to Don Sanchez, and further action will be dependent on Don Sanchez' frame of mind at that time." He paused for effect then graciously excused his employer's demands by offering Botelli a face-saving explanation, "After all, tonight Don Sanchez' mind is on more…personal matters. And this is as you would wish, is it not?"

There was a harder edge to Ortega's deep voice than the night before, but beneath the cutting tone was still a hint of that almost musical lilt. It unsettled Gabriel, disturbed him in ways he didn't want to analyze.

"It is indeed, Señor Ortega." Botelli's smile was frozen on his lips, but he looked Sanchez in the eye while he answered. "He *is* an honored guest in my home. *The* guest of honor. And I'm happy to grant any *reasonable* request any guest of mine asks of me."

Gabriel could just barely pick up the emphasis on the word *reasonable*. The hired guns on both sides shifted, hands reaching surreptitiously to unbutton jackets, waiting. Gabriel's hands were relaxed and ready at his side, his jacket hanging open. He picked his mark - Ortega. It would be a pleasure to shoot the sonofabitch.

As he watched, Ortega flicked a look at his boss. Sanchez was smiling a strange smile.

It was a long, tense moment. The silence between the factions couldn't be filled by music or the laughing babble of oblivious partygoers. Then Sanchez said mildly, "I will try not to request anything too unreasonable, *amigo.*"

Botelli smiled widely at this sop to his ego, and just like that the situation was defused. Everyone was smiling again — or at least not frowning so blackly.

Gabriel relaxed a fraction. But, he was startled out of his reflections as Don Sanchez sucked in a sharp breath.

Gina had appeared at the top of the staircase, tall and voluptuous in a black silk gown that looked like something Sophia Loren would have worn in her heyday. With an unexpectedly good sense of timing, she sauntered down the long, winding staircase in a slow, sexy descent that had every man in the place watching her. Gina had the body to pull off that kind of old-fashioned glamour: ample, firm breasts, tiny waist, and lush hips. Her long dark hair billowed around her shoulders in waves that framed her beautiful face, accenting her sloe eyes.

Eyes that were wide with an eagerness Gabriel could only attribute to her desire to see the engagement rock Sanchez had brought her — or maybe from the few lines of the coke he knew she did when she was feeling stressed. She'd probably be feeling stressed full-time once she was Doña Sanchez, but that wasn't his concern. People made their choices and had to live with the consequences. He was living with his that very moment.

"Here she is!" There was genuine pride in Botelli's voice. "Don Jesus, here's your stunning bride to be."

His expression held that mix of excitement and avarice it always did when the mob boss thought about his kingdom aligned through marriage to Don Sanchez' empire. Maybe Botelli did love his sister in his way, but that look told Gabriel that Botelli was willing to sell his baby sister for thirty pieces of silver.

And the fact was, Gina was just as willing to sell herself for the promise of unlimited luxury and wealth.

At the bottom of the stairs she paused, pouting her wine colored lips. "G, may I take your arm?"

Gabriel stilled as a shocked ripple went through the circle of men. What the fuck was she playing at? She was going to get them both killed. Gina met his stare defiantly, a reckless look in her eyes.

For a searing moment a grim-faced Botelli met Gabriel's gaze, then turned to retrieve his sister himself.

Gabriel didn't so much as glance their way. After a few seconds, he chanced a look at Sanchez. He was staring with molten eyes as Gina approached on Botelli's arm — or, more accurately, he was staring at her perky, partially exposed breasts — and right next to him, Ortega was observing Gabriel with frank fascination.

Damn him. And damn Gina, who didn't have the survival instincts of a lemming.

Botelli unpeeled his sister from his arm and scooted her over to Sanchez. And Gina pulled out her party manners and best smile, offering her hand. "Jesus," she murmured.

And astonishingly, Don Sanchez took her hand and kissed it. Gina blinked in surprise, wavering there on her skyscraper heels, blinking at him under her fake eyelashes.

Gabriel's own attention moved to Ortega, who maneuvered close to him. In a voice for Gabriel's ear alone he murmured, "I don't believe we've been formally introduced."

"Giovanni Contadino," Gabriel grated.

"Very musical," Ortega commented. "And what *exactly* is it you do around here, Contadino?"

So many possible answers. But Gabriel could not afford to draw any more attention to himself this evening. He said shortly, "Whatever needs doing."

Ortega's tone was ever so slightly mocking. "You must be indispensable. Señorita Botelli seems to think so."

Gabriel turned his head to level a murderous stare, but Ortega was already striding away, following the others into the ballroom behind Sanchez and Gina.

Gabriel gave himself a few moments to compose himself. Losing his temper would just be stupid. But between Gina and Ortega this was going to be one very long night.

From the ballroom doorway he could see Sanchez' second in command chatting with one of Gina's bosom buddies, a stunning blond woman in a skimpy red sheath.

Gabriel straightened his shoulders and joined the party.

The champagne was very good. Crisp and dry and appropriately chilled although Gabriel was mostly just pretending to drink it. He liked the way the tiny bubbles tickled the roof of his mouth, though, with a slight burn, almost like a lover's tongue.

He had spent three hours ostensibly trailing Gina around the crowded room, staying close enough so her brother was happy with her protection, but well out of arm's reach. His real target for the night had to be Don Sanchez, but he had to be very careful in how much attention he seemed to be paying the drug lord. Unfortunately, Gina had put him squarely on Sanchez' radar — the very last place he wanted to be. He could feel that tawny, narrow gaze following him. He made sure he stayed well in the background for the rest of the evening, taking sparing sips of champagne, silently watching everyone and everything.

Of course part of watching everyone and everything meant watching Miguel Ortega talking and flirting with women in the packed room. Women were going gaga. Gabriel had seen at least two notes slipped into the underboss' pocket, one placed there by a local judge's wife. Justice really was blind it seemed. Ortega had accepted them all with that sizzling smile and a boyish wink. Sophisticated women giggled like schoolgirls as he skillfully brushed them off. For some illogical reason, the brush-offs pissed Gabriel even more than if the man had taken advantage of all he was offered. But then maybe he *would* be taking advantage. Just because he didn't drag these bimbos off upstairs the minute they offered to put out didn't mean he wouldn't accept an offer or two later when he was off the clock.

Glancing around the room, wall-to-wall with black tuxedos and jewel-colored evening gowns, Gabriel located Gina in the center of a group of her fawning friends, waggling her newly acquired diamond engagement ring under their cosmetically-enhanced noses. The rock covered the entire segment of bone on her ring finger, a rectangular emerald-cut diamond so massive that it looked fake. Gina's friends oohed and aahed while Gina pretended to heft her hand like she was determining just how heavy a stone it was and how much she could get for it.

Gabriel snorted a laugh into his drink. She was fine. He could take a turn around the patio and get some fresh air.

He turned away and nearly careened into a woman standing too close behind him. Her companion's hand shot out, grabbing his glass before he dumped the contents down the woman's long, bare back. Instead, the alcohol sloshed down the front of his trousers.

"Shit!" Gabriel gasped at the cold liquid soaking into his clothes. An offended, overly made up face turned his way.

"Sorry, Mrs. Ross," he apologized quickly to the judge's startled wife. "Please forgive me. I wasn't watching were I was going." He tried to disarm that glassy glare with his best contrite schoolboy smile. Mrs. Ross peered at him, then tittered.

Gabriel glanced at her companion. Miguel Ortega held Gabriel's empty glass, which he tilted in a mock toast, though whether that was aimed at Gabriel or Mrs. Ross was unclear. He handed the glass off to a waiting server and took a fresh one for himself.

"You should be more careful," Mrs. Ross informed Gabriel severely.

"He should," Ortega agreed, studying Gabriel with pseudo gravity.

"We could all afford to be more careful," Gabriel retorted.

Ortega's eyes flickered. "That is true," he said. To Mrs. Ross he added smoothly, "In fact, I believe I must speak to Mr. Contadino about some of this evening's security measures."

"Oh, but surely…?" Mrs. Ross protested, her expression absurdly crestfallen.

Ortega, however, had already fastened his free hand on Gabriel's shoulder, making his excuses to the woman and steering Gabriel away.

Or trying to. As soon as they were safely out of Mrs. Ross's clutches, Gabriel attempted to slide from under Ortega's grip. Ortega's hand tightened.

Gabriel said shortly, "D'you mind?"

Ortega cocked an elegant eyebrow. "I thought you liked the hands-on approach."

Gabriel stopped walking. "If you don't want a broken wrist, take your hand off my shoulder."

The hand clamped on his shoulder relaxed, smoothing its way across his shoulder and lightly down his bicep. Gabriel felt that touch as acutely as though it were caressing his bare skin. "I'm sorry." Ortega took a sip from his own nearly full glass — not quite managing to hide his smile. "I nearly forgot. You're not the sentimental type, are you, Giovanni. Or do you prefer to be called G?"

"I'd prefer you didn't talk to me about anything that isn't business related." Gabriel smiled insincerely, pitching his voice as if he and Ortega were having a casual chat. "Now, say whatever it is you have to say because I need to go change my clothes."

Ortega's brows rose. "And here I imagined I was rescuing you."

"By dumping a drink down my pants? Wow. Did you think my crotch was on fire?"

Ortega choked on his champagne.

Gabriel lifted a hand in greeting to Gina, ignoring her peremptory gesture for him to join her and her friends.

Ortega, having recovered from his amusement, pretended to give his own question thought. "Hmm. Since I prefer *gatito* I think I will use Señorita Gina's endearment for you." He graced Gabriel with that twisted sardonic half smile again. "G can stand for so *many* things, don't you think?"

"Sure," Gabriel returned. "Get lost. Get out of my face. Gorilla. Goddamn you. So many words, so little time. And what do I call you? A for ass-wipe? B for bastard? C for —?" He grinned, laughed too loudly, and clapped Ortega on the shoulder, jostling his drink.

Ortega seemed to be ready for him, though, and Gabriel was unsuccessful in dumping the other man's champagne on him.

Ortega, not at all put out by the impromptu and covert tussle, continued the charade of pleasantries exchanged for any interested onlookers. "You threw away my card," he said regretfully. "You don't get to call me at all."

"Yeah. That's the bright spot in all this."

Ortega studied him, his gaze speculative despite his smile. "Which leaves me wondering what exactly brought you to the Club Madrone last night, Contadino."

Gabriel's heart thudded hard against his ribs with alarm. "Really? If anyone should know, you should."

"Yes," Ortega said slowly, "but why were you in that private office? And why *did* you tear up my card?"

Gabriel drawled, "Didn't you ever hear of a one-night stand? Don't tell me everyone falls in love with you at first fuck." It was hard to tell in that light, but he thought there was a tinge of red in Ortega's bronze face. He pressed his advantage, "I could ask what you were doing in that private office, too."

"I was following you," Ortega said.

Gabriel tried to think. Even if Ortega had followed him from downstairs at the club all he would have seen was Gabriel looking around, and the guy was clearly egotistical enough to swallow the idea that Gabriel had been hunting for him.

He said coolly, "Looks like what we call a Mexican standoff."

"And standoff is what you would prefer me to do, eh?"

"Just as far as possible."

Ortega chuckled. His eyes moved past Gabriel, and he nodded smiling acknowledgment to someone. Then his gaze fastened on Gabriel's once more.

"Very well," he said. "We will agree to forget our previous…encounter."

He waited for Gabriel's acknowledgement.

Gabriel nodded curtly.

And with a murmured apology, Ortega moved away.

Surprised, Gabriel turned to watch his broad shoulders move through the crush of people. As Ortega reached a half-circle of smiling businessmen, he clapped one of the men on his shoulder as though they were old friends.

Interesting. How was it that the second-in-command of a Mexican drug lord was apparently on hobnobbing terms with a Sonoma Valley vintner?

CHAPTER THREE

"I wanna go dancing!"

It was several hours later. The musicians had played "La Bamba" six times, the floral arrangements were starting to wilt, and most of the important guests — the indigenous ones at least — had departed.

Reaching out to steady his sister, Botelli found Gabriel's gaze. Gabriel straightened from the wall he had been propping up and made his way to Botelli's side, ready to do whatever Botelli needed doing, up to and including barring Gina from leaving the premises.

Gina swayed, leaning back on her brother's arm, and turned her much-practiced doe-eyed look on him. "Ricco! You hear me?"

He patted her cheek. "There's musicians here, go dance."

She pouted. "I want real music, Ricco, not elevator noise. I want to celebrate my *fabulous* engagement with my *fabulous* friends!" She made a sweeping gesture with one arm taking in the dozen or so offspring of the richest people in the city, expensively groomed twenty-somethings whose main purpose in life seemed to be keeping drug suppliers like Ricco Botelli and Don Jesus Sanchez in business.

"Yeah, but maybe your fiancée objects." Botelli darted a questioning glance at Sanchez, who stood silently to the side watching his fiancée's antics with that amber, unsmiling look. It was an easy guess what Sanchez thought of Botelli's method of handling Gina — which basically consisted of giving into her every demand and then making it someone else's headache. As he was attempting to do now.

Gina swayed toward Sanchez and batted her eyes at him. "You don't mind, do you, Jesus?"

Gabriel didn't get the impression that Sanchez suffered from insecurity, but he eyed Gina for a long moment and then studied the tipsy, giggling, clique of sleek sophisticates. Most of them were young women — and none of the soft young men in the group showed any undue interest in Gina. Gabriel had been keeping an eye out in case he needed to run interference for some poor slob.

Unexpectedly, Sanchez smiled that disconcerting, predatory smile. "Why not? Your brother and I have matters to discuss, *chiquita*. Perhaps it's best if you spend time with your friends."

Disengaging herself from Botelli, Gina sparkled brightly up at Don Sanchez. Her smile was full of promise and mystery — and about 100 proof in Gabriel's opinion. "I knew you wouldn't care." She threw a triumphant look at her brother. "You're a man of the world. You know a girl can't sit around… just…just…knitting while her man works."

Knitting? What was she playing at? She wasn't stupid, really, so why was she deliberately tugging the tiger's tail? He watched her absently stroke the creamy, satin skin of her half-bared breasts, the enormous rock on her hand glittering in the thousands of tiny lights strung around the ballroom ceiling.

"I think you're going to be a *fabulous* husband, Jesus," Gina murmured, batting those ridiculous lashes.

Gabriel didn't care for the faint curve of Sanchez' mouth. He suspected Sanchez had no trouble reading Gina, that the man understood how she hoped to manipulate him with her unsubtle charms — and was untroubled, even entertained by it. He watched her every move, every expression like she was something delectable on a dessert cart.

"Well, that's settled then!" Botelli said jovially. "Gina and her friends can go dancing while we talk." He jerked his head at Gabriel. "Gio, go tell Paulo to drive Gina. I don't want her getting in any cars with drunk drivers."

Sanchez interjected silkily, "That won't be necessary. My wife — my future wife — is under my protection now. My own men will escort her and ensure her safety."

Gina blinked at him, puzzled. "Paulo always drives me," she said. "Or G."

Even Botelli looked uncomfortable as Sanchez' wasteland gaze found Gabriel. The Mexican drug lord said nothing. Gabriel didn't move a muscle.

Shit.

Happily oblivious, Gina smiled brightly, reassuringly at her bleak-faced betrothed. "G's all the protection I need. He saved my life, you know? Last year this fricking maniac attacked me right outside of Gallery of Jewels, and G happened to be walking by, and he came to my rescue."

Poor gullible Gina. SFPD had staged that attack outside Gallery of Jewels so Gabriel could gain Botelli's trust, and the ruse had worked.

She couldn't really be that oblivious to the position she was putting him in, so she had to be drunker than even Gabriel had realized. Botelli must have seen it as well. He thumped Gabriel on the back, gripping the nape of his neck and shaking him lightly in a show of indulgent dominance. "Don't let his pretty boy face fool you, Don Sanchez. Giovanni is one of my best men. He can be trusted. He knows what would happen to him if I couldn't trust him!" Botelli laughed loudly. Gabriel managed a weak smile as the others — with the exception of Sanchez — belatedly joined in. It was clear that Gabriel was the last person in this room Sanchez was letting Gina out with. Which suited Gabriel fine, because a night spent babysitting Gina would be a total waste of opportunity.

"I'm sure he is." Unsmiling, unbending, Sanchez dismissed the idea of Gabriel. "However, as I cannot spare the time to accompany her, my wife will go with my most trusted lieutenant. Miguel!"

Gabriel hadn't seen Ortega approach — hadn't seen him for the last hour or two except from a distance — but suddenly the man was standing right next to him, that spicy hint of lime and aftershave alerting him even before he turned.

"*Sí,*" Ortega said. He turned his head. His eyes met Gabriel's coolly.

"Gina wishes to visit the dance clubs tonight. You will accompany her in my place, *amigo.*"

"It will be an honor," Ortega responded.

"Wow!" Gina giggled. "How about in that case we all go together?"

Gabriel glanced at Ortega, who returned his look.

Ortega said in that lazy, untroubled tone, "By all means, let him tag along if it will make the señorita more comfortable."

The compromise shouldn't have been necessary, but Gabriel spoke stiffly. "Whatever Mr. Botelli wants."

"What about what *I* want?" Gina complained. "I don't know these men. I don't know Ricardo Montalban here." She pouted at Ortega.

Feeling Ortega stiffen, Gabriel permitted himself the tiniest smirk.

"Gina! Behave yourself," Botelli snapped, the good-humored mask slipping for a moment. She glared at him, looked at Sanchez and giggled.

Gabriel wasn't sure what she found so funny. Sanchez was watching her, smiling that genial smile that sent ice down Gabriel's spine. Not because Sanchez seemed annoyed — because he didn't. Once again, he seemed faintly entertained by Gina's bad manners.

Gina swayed forward again, and Gabriel reached out to stop her from teetering right over. "I'm missing my party," she informed her brother. "It's supposed to be *my* night, isn't it?"

"Gina, you better show some respect to Mr. Ortega," Botelli said shortly. He turned to Gabriel. "Take the Ferrari, Gio,"

Gabriel nodded.

"Make sure she gets back here in the same condition she left in, *capisce*?"

Drunk off her ass? That shouldn't be a problem. Gabriel nodded again, touched the shoulder holster beneath his jacket in a sort of my-gun-is-at-your-service gesture. Botelli went for that kind of Hollywood crap.

Gina looped one arm around his and the other around Ortega's. "And what do I call you, Ricardo? O? The Big O?" She giggled again. Ortega murmured something smooth and noncommittal.

Oh yeah, it was going to be a long night.

Botelli laughed that oily laugh of his. "Italian women!" He handed Sanchez a fresh flute of champagne, raising his own glass in salute.

As Gina drew Ortega and him toward the ballroom doors, Gabriel heard Botelli saying, "My sister is a passionate girl, but she'll make you a good wife, Don Sanchez. Have no worries on that score."

And Sanchez replied, "I know Italian women, *amigo*. My first wife was Italian."

First wife? That was news. There was no mention of any wife in Sanchez' folder. Gabriel was too far out of range to hear more, but he made a mental note to check on it the next time he called his captain.

The front drive of the Botelli mansion was clogged with expensive sports cars and inebriated wannabe A-listers. A couple of morons had just discovered their horns and were blasting them into the foggy night. Exhaust fumes and alcohol floated on the breeze.

"Gina, come on! Drive with us!" shrieked the red-haired daughter of a prominent Snob Hill family waving from a yellow Lamborghini.

It was like a VC Section 23153 epidemic waiting to happen.

Laughing, Gina released Gabriel and Ortega, starting forward toward the open door of an Audi TT.

"No, no, Señorita Botelli," Ortega said, catching her arm, and drawing her back. "G has already called for your car."

"Huh?" Gina blinked up at him, and then at Gabriel. "Oh, yeah." She waved to her restless entourage and called out a few unhelpful comments.

Botelli's black Ferrari came roaring up, screeching to a halt a few inches behind a Mercedes that had its hazards flashing and windshield wipers going — to the hysterical amusement of its passengers.

The Botelli chauffeur jumped out and tossed the keys to Gabriel, who caught them one-handed.

"Are you sure *you're* not over the legal limit?" Ortega asked Gabriel.

Gabriel gave him the look that froze perps in their tracks. It seemed to have zero effect on Ortega, who lifted a dismissing shoulder.

"Don Sanchez frowns on the abuse of alcohol or the use of illegal substances within his organization."

Gabriel snorted. Don Sanchez was in for a rude awakening when he married Señorita Botelli. All he said was, "I don't work for Don Sanchez."

"No?" Ortega was smiling.

What a pleasure it was going to be to put this arrogant asshole behind bars.

Happily oblivious to any hostile undertones — or overtones, for that matter — Gina inquired, "Do you like to dance, Mr. Ortega?"

They were making their way across the velvety grass to the Ferrari, Ortega doing yeoman's duty keeping Gina from pinning herself into the lawn with those crampon heels of hers. "I do, yes."

"Because G *doesn't*." Gina sounded like this was one of the great tragedies of her young life. "You wouldn't think so, but he's actually very *shy*."

And right on cue, smoother than Dean Martin on silk sheets, Ortega returned. "Young men are often shy in the presence of such a beautiful woman."

"Then I'll dance with *you* all night." Gina smirked at Gabriel, who pretended to ignore the whole exchange.

He slid in behind the wheel of the Ferrari. Inserted the key into the ignition. The car purred to life beneath his hands as Ortega wriggled agilely into the backseat. Gina settled her skirts around herself.

"Belt up, Gina," Gabriel ordered.

She sighed, long-suffering, and obeyed.

"No one drives G. Ever," she informed Ortega.

"Never?" he murmured in that mocking tone that made Gabriel want to shove his teeth down his throat.

"Never. Gabriel always has to be in control."

Ortega laughed.

Gabriel opened his mouth, but before he could speak, the Lamborghini at the head of the line of cars took off, tires smoking. The Audi tore out after it. The other cars peeled out, rubber squealing on pavement.

"Christ Almighty," he muttered.

"Catch them, G!" shrieked Gina. "We should be in front!"

She wasn't wrong about that because the way her asshole friends were jockeying for position there was going to be a wreck before they even got out of the tall gates of the estate.

"Hold on," Gabriel said under his breath, and gunned the engine, shooting out after the line of weaving cars. He caught up to the last car within seconds, swerving widely to avoid the driver of the Mercedes who was all over the driveway, pulling briefly onto the lawn and safely passing the waving, screaming carload of idiots.

Downshifting, he passed two more cars and then sped ahead of the Audi, which showed signs of starting to fishtail. Gabriel punched the gas and they flew on.

From the backseat he heard Ortega's soft laugh.

"Now pass that bitch, Amaryllis," Gina ordered as they drew up behind the Lamborghini.

The tall, black iron gates of the estate appeared in their headlights a few yards ahead.

Gabriel floored it, rocketing ahead of the Lamborghini. Amaryllis accelerated, but Gabriel kept his foot to the pedal and they flew on, zipping out through the main gates safely ahead of the rest of the wagon train.

Gina was squealing her pleasure.

As they hit the main highway, Gabriel slowed to a respectable sixty, the Ferrari hugging the road's curves effortlessly.

"Where did you learn to drive like that, Contadino?" Ortega asked from the backseat. There was a different note in his voice.

"*Speed Racer*," Gabriel said lightly, and his companions laughed.

Gina Botelli was well known at Ruby Blue — but then she had been going there since she was an underage — but very rich — mob brat. That was the kind of club Ruby Blue was. The management was not above turning a blind eye to the sufficiently connected minor or the occasional line of coke done beneath the watered-silk wallpaper in its lounge. If you were rich enough — and well dressed enough — a multitude of sins could be overlooked.

It wasn't the first time Gabriel had accompanied Gina to the club, and the beefy bouncer hadn't batted an eye when Gabriel briefly flashed his shoulder holster and gun. In fact, the bruiser had actually smiled like he was looking forward to something happening to liven up his evening.

Ortega, on the other hand, received a brief but thorough pat down before Gina burst out laughing and informed the bouncer that he was part of her retinue. Unamused, the mob boss stared at Gabriel who stared blandly back. But the truth was Gabriel was shaken by the lurch of lust he'd experienced watching the bouncer's meaty hands trailing over Ortega's lean torso and hips.

Ruby Blue had three distinct areas: the main bar where buff and beautiful bartenders served signature cocktails, the dance floor where nationally known DJs offered an eclectic mix of music on the state of the art sound system, and the VIP lounge with its pale blue leather couches where the famous and infamous could relax and unwind with their friends and enemies in style. Forty-five hundred square feet of comfort and catering.

"G, come dance with me!" Gina and her pampered, pretty posse were no sooner inside the club than she was tugging at Gabriel's arm with both hands, a sexy pout on her lips and a demanding glint in her eye as she tried to drag him out onto the dance floor.

"Come on, Gina. I'm on duty. Let's get your table." He tried to shepherd her and the entire group through the crowded club, keeping Gina in the middle of the pack and using her friends as an unwitting human shield around her.

"You need a drink, G. You need *a lot* of drinks." Leaning in close, Gina breathed alcohol fumes and bubblegum scent in

Gabriel's face. He pegged her alcohol level at .3 and rising. If he got lucky, she'd pass out on the drive home. If he was unlucky, she'd throw up.

She swayed widely, and Gabriel reached for her. Gina reached back, winding her arm around his neck, bumping and rubbing against him in a seductive parody of dance that ignored the tempo of the music pounding out from the sound system.

"Let's dance, G," she whispered hotly into his ear. "I know you want to."

She let her full weight collapse against him, and Gabriel staggered back. Hands on his hips steadied him. Big hands. Male hands. *Shit.* He recovered his balance, putting Gina back on her feet. As he stepped away, one large palm slid appreciatively over his ass, cupping him intimately for a moment.

Well, he didn't think that hand belonged to any of Gina's pals, so that left one possible suspect, and Gabriel was not about to turn around and give that asshole the pleasure of a reaction.

Shoving his charge none-too-gently along the glass-slick zebra wood floors of the club, Gabriel put as much space as possible between himself and Ortega.

Which turned out not to be much, because getting Gina through that crush of people was like trying to maneuver a wheelbarrow. Ortega's breath was warm on the back of his neck as the other man said in a conversational tone that still managed to carry over the music, "It's easy to see she thinks of you as a brother."

Throwing a wintery look over his shoulder, Gabriel pushed Gina toward the stairs leading up to the VIP lounges, but she spotted a friend in the heaving throng of dancers, and twisted away, joining the party on the dance floor.

Gabriel let her go. That's why they were at the club, supposedly — although he was beginning to wonder if her real aim wasn't to get him killed. She was certainly going about it the right way. Slipping off to a respectful distance, he watched cynically as Gina proceeded to show her engagement rock to anyone who happened to glance her way.

An hour or so passed. Gabriel spent most of it scanning the surrounding crowd, picking out faces and automatically running them against his internal wants and warrants database. He noticed that Ortega was on the dance floor with the stunning blonde woman he'd spent a lot of time talking to at the Botelli mansion. Gabriel watched them moving in and out of the shadows, swaying to the sultry music, a slow, sexy tune that was all heat and sensual rhythm.

And annoyingly, he felt a wash of jealousy as the woman wound her arms around Ortega's broad shoulders, pressing close, molding herself against his body. For God's sake, this was one of the bad guys. Second in command to an infamous Mexican drug lord. He could only imagine what heinous acts Ortega had performed to gain that position of power.

Sanchez had a rep for employing the most violent and morally corrupt. Ortega's rap sheet was probably longer than his…well, it was probably long. And blood-drenched. The thought of reading it made Gabriel feel slightly queasy. He'd had no sense of the man's true nature during their sexual encounter. Not a hint.

But then that was the thing that civilians didn't understand. Only comic book villains were evil 24/7. Most people came in shades of gray, and even sociopaths had been known to feed stray cats and send Mother's Day cards.

Broodingly, he watched Ortega subtly maneuvering his partner away from his gun arm. The bastard even moved like a dream.

He watched Ortega guiding the blonde through some intricate steps. That graceful, loose embrace reminded Gabriel of old black and white movies with Fred Astaire and Ginger Rogers. He couldn't even imagine moving with that kind of flowing confidence around a dance floor. Somewhere down the line, Ortega must have taken ballroom dance lessons. Now what kind of vicious drug lord took ballroom dancing?

That was funny, right? So why didn't Gabriel feel like laughing? Bitterly he observed Ortega whispering in the blonde's ear while they danced. The woman nodded, and

Ortega whipped her around in some kind of tricky spin. The blonde threw her head back, laughing.

Gabriel wanted to shoot them both. It was like…Jesus. It was like high school again. Like being the skinny, frail, queer kid at the dance — wondering why the hell you were there. Or even on the fucking planet.

Gabriel forced his attention back on the job, scanning the dance floor for Gina. She wasn't there, but he spotted her quickly enough, twenty feet away in her usual circle of admirers, downing shots of Amaretto and bouncing to a beat Gabriel couldn't hear. Her engagement ring flashed in the spotlights like a lighthouse beacon, undoubtedly drawing every scumbag in five square miles.

He studied the crowd — and this time a familiar face caught his eye. Several faces in fact, and none of them belonged in these refined surroundings. Rocky Scarborough's crew was pushing its way through the exclusive doors of Ruby Blue, shoving past the clearly outclassed bouncers and knocking down the pretty people in their path. Scarborough was Botelli's major competition for the Sanchez alliance, and Gabriel didn't believe in coincidences.

He looked to the dance floor and, to his surprise, Ortega was moving his way, dark eyes finding Gabriel's own — locking on. And Gabriel realized his uppermost feeling was relief. He could use help.

"What is it? You look unhappy, Contadino," Ortega said, reaching him.

Gabriel was already moving through the crowd to where Gina stood oblivious to her danger. He threw words over his shoulder, "Rocky Scarborough's crew is here. And I don't think it's a coincidence. I think Scarborough is stupid enough to believe that if something happened to Gina, your boss might look on his distribution network more favorably."

"Then he truly is stupid." Ortega spoke calmly, his low voice slicing right through the thump of the music.

Stupid and vicious. That summed up Rocky Scarborough. Gabriel could feel Ortega at his back, feel the man's heat and solid presence, and it was reassuring. Ortega sounded calm —

even resigned — clearly no stranger to violence, and Gabriel knew if he went down Ortega would somehow get Gina out of there. That was all that mattered. Gina might have the brains of a parakeet, but she was the innocent here.

His eyes raked the room as he chose his escape route. One set of emergency doors led to an alley in back. Another exit, beside the bandstand, was closer but strobe lights and the moving crowd prevented him from seeing whether it was clear.

He unbuttoned his jacket, reaching up to ease his gun in its holster, making sure it would draw smoothly should the moment come.

"Frank Donald's here," Ortega said, and Gabriel spared him a quick look.

"Where?"

Ortega jerked his head in the direction of the side exit. Sure enough Scarborough's favorite enforcer was positioned near the door. Either Gabriel missed Donald the first time he'd checked, or Scarborough's men were stationing themselves around the room. Not good.

And he could see by the grim lines on Ortega's handsome face that he concurred.

Briefly, Gabriel wondered how a Mexican underboss knew a local enforcer by sight. Had Sanchez considered partnership with the unstable Scarborough?

Then he reached Gina's side and there was no more time for reflection.

"Time to go, party girl." He grabbed her arm, and she nearly toppled over.

"Whaddaya doing, G?" she slurred, trying to straighten herself. "We jus' got here!"

"Yeah, but it's way past my bedtime." He drew her forward, away from her disappointed cronies, and Gina picked that moment to be obstinate.

"Don' wanna go home. Wanna dance! Wanna dance with you, G." She smiled up at him with glassy eyes. "Love you, G."

Like things weren't scary enough?

"No, you don't. Don't say that." He threw a quick look around the room, and was disturbed to see that he could no longer easily spot Scarborough's men. Bad news. He tightened his grip on Gina's slender wrist, one of her jeweled bracelets cutting into his palm. "Gina — now."

With the unpredictability of the very drunk, her affection turned on a dime and went straight to anger. "I said, *I'm not ready*!" She tried to push him away.

Gabriel clamped her to his side and began walking toward the front door. Gina's heels skittered on the slick floor as she tried to get her footing.

Ortega came up on Gina's other side, taking part of her weight. His free hand rested lightly inside his tuxedo jacket.

Together they hustled her along, ignoring her slurred objections.

Gabriel pulled out his cell phone, flipping it open. It took a few precious moments to make himself heard over the din of music and voices — and then another few seconds to convince the dispatcher on the other end of the line that he wasn't kidding.

"Back exit," he yelled to Ortega over Gina's bobbing head.

Ortega wheeled Gina about, changing direction so smoothly Gabriel wondered if there wasn't some value to that ballroom dancing after all.

"Who did you call?" Ortega asked.

"A cab."

Ortega laughed.

"I'm not kidding. I called a cab company and promised a five hundred dollar tip to the driver who gets to the back of this club within five minutes."

The elegant brows rose. "If our friends are aware they were made, they'll expect us to use the back door."

"I don't think so. I think they'll stick with the Ferrari. Anyway, we don't have a lot of options."

Two of Gina's girlfriends, a blonde and a brunette, noticed the exodus and fell into line behind them. Briefly Gabriel considered using them as decoys, but abandoned the idea.

Replacing one innocent in the line of fire with another wasn't any solution, although Giovanni Contadino would have done it in a heartbeat.

An unfriendly face loomed to his right. His arm shot out, catching the thug under the chin with the heel of his hand, sending him to the floor. There were squeals of protest and angry voices behind them, but they kept moving.

"I'm tellin' Ricco on you, G," Gina was complaining. "You gonna be in soooo much trouble…" Her head lolled on his shoulder. He hoped she stayed on her feet long enough to reach the car. Carrying a healthy, adult-size woman would definitely impair his aim. He had no doubt that this night would not end peaceably.

The panic bar on the door popped and the heavy metal swung out into the mild night air and a long empty alley. No cab.

"Fuck!" Gabriel swore, drawing his gun.

He zeroed in on an archway ten feet down the alley and glanced at Ortega. The other man had already fastened on the same spot. He nodded to Gabriel and shifted Gina on his arm, taking more of her weight. They trotted down the broken asphalt, the heels of the two girls trailing them clopping like horses' hooves.

"What are we doing?" one of them asked plaintively.

Gabriel had nearly forgotten about them. "You need to go back inside," he told them. Ortega threw him a strange look.

"Why?" asked the other one. "What are you doing?"

"Reporters, I bet." Her friend nodded knowledgably.

"You don't shoot reporters," the first girl objected. "Not *before* they write the story."

"Look, there's liable to be trouble," Gabriel said. "Will you just go back inside the club?"

He caught up to Ortega, who had reached the brick archway and was trying to prop Gina against the wall. As flimsy a shelter as the recess provided, it was the only available cover as they waited for the taxi.

"You sure the cab company believed you?" Ortega asked grimly.

Gabriel shrugged. He wasn't sure of anything, but what were their choices at this point?

The two other girls, still bickering, joined them in the alcove.

"*Madre mios,*" Ortega murmured. His eyes gleamed in the sickly alley light as they met Gabriel's.

"You're not my G!" Gina giggled, twining her arms around Ortega's neck. "But you *are* a handsome one." Lacing her fingers through his thick black hair, she pulled Ortega's face down to within centimeters of her own. "Your boss is very ugly," she informed him seriously.

"Gina!" Gabriel said sharply. "Shut the fuck up."

Gina rolled her head in his direction. "We could have a threesome, G. Me and you and Mr. O. Mr. Big O. Mr. Big O is very nice. He smells *very* nice..."

"Great taste in men you've got," Gabriel muttered, his eyes searching the mouth of the alley. *Was that movement down by the trash dumpster?*

"Oh, I don't know, Contadino," Ortega said. "Not much worse than your own."

Gabriel bit down on his instinctive comment. Gina might be mostly out of it, but the two other girls were still sober enough to remember this conversation. Assuming they all survived the next ten minutes.

"If she passes out, you're going to have to carry her." Gabriel bundled Gina completely into Ortega's arms. Cell in one hand, he hit redial.

He expected Ortega to argue, but the bigger man said nothing. Grudgingly, Gabriel awarded him points for practicality.

The cab company picked up. "Where the fuck are you?" Gabriel listened for three seconds. "Listen, the tip goes down by a hundred bucks for every minute we wait here."

He hung up.

"Let's try to make it back inside. We'll cut through the club and make for the parking lot on the side of the building," Ortega said. "We're sitting ducks here."

He was right, but they were ducks in a shooting gallery walking back down the alley.

"I think we should stay —"

But Ortega had already swung Gina — who was now mumbling complaints — up into his arms and was carrying her swiftly down the alleyway, dodging holes and weeds poking up through the broken asphalt.

Gabriel went after him, gun at ready.

"Goddamn it! I said we should stay put."

"As I outrank you —"

"Out*rank* me? We don't even work for the same man."

"Whoever you work for, I hope you can shoot." Ortega hoisted Gina up onto his shoulder, hanging onto her with one arm, and drawing his gun.

Gabriel threw a distracted look over his shoulder at the two women clip-clopping along behind him. Beyond them, at the end of the alley he could see traffic cruising steadily up and down the cross street. Headlights flashed by, spotlighting fire escapes and trash bins — and picking out slinking figures moving into position.

"Move in front of me," he told the women, and they trotted past him, skirts rustling, heels clacking on the pavement.

As they retraced their steps, the thumping beat of the dance music filtered through the walls of the building.

Ahead of them a door opened. Gabriel and Ortega trained their weapons as a young woman stepped out of the club. She tottered there in the doorway, mascara-tinted tears streaking her cheeks.

Simultaneously, the men lowered their pistols. Gabriel expelled a sharp breath of relief.

There was a screech of tires behind them and a green and white cab came hurtling down the alley toward them — barely skidding to a stop in time. In two steps Gabriel had the back door open and was shoving Gina's protesting friends inside —

just as a black sedan rounded the corner of the alley and came tearing toward them.

"Get her in the car!" he yelled to Ortega, feeling that familiar thrill of dread and excitement. No running now. The moment was on them — and he welcomed it.

The men down the alley ran forward as the sedan angled across, blocking that egress. The sedan doors flew open. Gabriel threw himself flat and fired two rounds into the tinted windshield.

He sensed motion behind him but couldn't risk turning to see. Two men piled out of the sedan and began firing — joined by the men who had been lurking at the mouth of the alley. A body slumped out of the driver's side and spilled onto the asphalt.

Shots rang off the cinderblock walls and stucco buildings. Heart hammering in a rush of adrenaline, Gabriel fired steadily back, laying down a barrage of bullets. He was outgunned and the light was too bad to afford any genuine aim. His only hope was to make the direct approach seriously uninviting.

Fuck! A bullet hit the asphalt next to Gabriel and ricocheted off to the left, startling a shaky laugh out of him. *What the hell. Nobody lives forever…*

Next to him, a car door slammed shut and the cab took off in the opposite direction — a tire just missing Gabriel's foot. The cab fender scraped the cement wall, sending sparks flying. The next outlet was a block or so up, but unless they met oncoming traffic, Gina and her friends were home free. Some of Gabriel's tension eased. He relaxed into the business of trying to blow away anything and everything that moved. The receding squeal of the taxi's tires provided an almost soothing soundtrack to his efforts.

Narrowing his eyes, he sighted his target, squeezed. It felt good. The bullet shattered the glass of the sedan door.

Gabriel had taken it for granted that Ortega would go with Gina and the women. He was an important mob underboss, and Gabriel was a simple foot soldier. There was no question of whose job it was to cover Gina's escape. So it was with total astonishment that he heard what sounded like a Glock 22 open fire behind him.

He spared a quick glance. Ortega was flattened against the wall, firing with cool deliberation at the sedan. In the doorway behind him, the party girl stood frozen in place.

"Get back!" Gabriel yelled at her. "Go back inside."

Out of the corner of his eye, he caught motion beneath the sedan. He fired and heard a yell. A man pitched out behind the shielding door and sprawled motionless in the alley.

To the side of him the Glock continued to fire, steady and unhurried. The shots echoed up and down the alley in calm answer to the erratic blasting from Scarborough's thugs.

The nearest passenger door closed and someone scrambled over the body lying by the driver's side to climb behind the wheel. There were shouts and cursing. The shooters piled back into the car, the doors slammed shut, and the sedan reversed crookedly, tires burning as the car went racing backwards in a drunken zigzag down the alley, taking out trash cans and sending cardboard boxes flying.

The black sedan shot out of the alley — and just escaped getting nailed by oncoming traffic. Horns blared. The sedan reversed, lurched forward and went screeching down the boulevard.

An uncanny hush seemed to fall in the wake of Scarborough's departing thugs. Gabriel got to his feet, gun trained on the men he had shot. The driver was dumped on his face, blackness spreading in a pool beneath him. A few feet away the other man lay on his back, moaning. More darkness pooled around his shattered leg. The smell of gunpowder and burned rubber was strong.

Gabriel heard the click of Ortega putting the safety back on his pistol.

That was a relief. He wasn't sure what he would do if Ortega took it upon himself to summarily execute any survivors. He glanced around. Ortega's dark gaze met his levelly. Neither of them spoke.

If Ortega had left with the women it would probably be Gabriel now lying slumped on his face dying in an alley. He had no idea what to say. *Thank you* seemed inadequate. Or maybe he just didn't want to feel grateful to a guy he planned on putting behind bars.

As the silence stretched between them he could hear the tinkling charms of the bracelet on the girl shaking in the doorway behind them.

It was after five in the morning when Gabriel got back to the room he'd rented for the last two years in the Tenderloin district. He poured himself a drink and had a smoke, going over the night's events yet another time. Food was out of the question. He was still too strung up with adrenaline and anger for digestion. What he needed most was sleep, but that would have to wait.

Stretching out on the rumpled mattress of his bed, Gabriel dug a second cell phone out of his bedside table drawer. He dialed from memory, eyes closed, while he waited for someone to answer.

Somebody had tattooed Ortega's likeness on the inside of his eyelids because every time he closed his eyes he could see the man's face in every damn detail, those sultry, heavy-lidded eyes and that slightly amused twist to his sensual mouth…

Cold-blooded killer that he was, Ortega hadn't turned a hair over the violence in the alleyway.

"I suggest we take our leave, *amigo*," he had said as they listened to the sirens in the distance.

And, unspeaking, they returned to the Ferrari, and drove back to the Botelli estate to find that Gina and her friends had arrived safely by taxi a half hour before. Botelli was in a fury — as though Gabriel had somehow been responsible for their being jumped by Scarborough's men at the club.

Ortega had said nothing, standing silently while Gabriel got his ass chewed by Botelli. Don Sanchez looked on, impassive and unspeaking, like one of those pre-Columbian monoliths.

A gruff, harried voice on the end of the line forced Gabriel to blink and Ortega's derisive smile disappeared.

"O'Brien."

"It's me."

O'Brien said shortly, "It's about time. You're about four hours late."

"Tell me about it. There was a shooting at the Ruby Blue —"

"That was you?"

"Rocky Scarborough tried to take out Gina tonight. I think the plan was to remove the primary incentive for the Botelli merger."

"Would it have worked?"

"No. If they'd hit Gina, Sanchez would have hit them so hard — to tell the truth, I think he probably will anyway. He's…partial to Gina."

"Partial?"

"Crazy about her. And I do mean crazy."

"Okay. I saw the report. Are you responsible for shooting Bobby Itchi and Ralph Cuomo?"

"I didn't have a choice. They ambushed us in the alley outside the club. Are Itchi and Cuomo going to make it?"

"Cuomo was DOA. Itchi will make it. He'll have to give up his ballet career, though."

"Sanchez' underboss, Miguel Ortega, saved my ass tonight. Can you get me some intel on him?"

"Ortega? Why isn't that name familiar to me?"

"I don't know. He's not one of the usual suspects, but he's well entrenched in Sanchez' organization. In fact, he seems to be the number two guy."

"Christ. How'd we miss him? Okay. I'll run him."

"Something else. Sanchez mentioned a first wife."

"Is that so?"

"Yeah. He told Botelli his first wife was Italian."

"Okay. We'll do some checking." There was satisfaction in O'Brien's voice. "So the Mexicans have landed."

"Yep."

"And you're sure you haven't been compromised?"

That gave him a start. "Yeah, I'm sure. Why?"

"It may be nothing. Then again…just watch your back. Something may be going down. One of your prize snitches ate it the night before last."

The chill Gabriel felt had nothing to do with the lack of heating in the dump he called Casa Contadino.

"Who?"

"Benny Barbosa."

Gabriel swallowed hard. "Benny? Fuck. We were supposed to meet night before last. He never showed. I guess that explains why."

"That would explain it. He was found face down behind Club Madrone on Mission Street. Shot mob style. Clean and quick."

Gabriel took a moment to absorb that. "Behind…Club Madrone?"

"That's right."

It was difficult to form the words. A mob hit at Club Madrone, and guess what mob guy had been on the premises. Granted, he'd been occupied part of the evening fucking the brains out of undercover police officer Gabriel Sandalini. Wasn't that going to sound terrific in court? Talk about stupid career moves.

"Any leads?" he got out.

"Barbosa was a snitch. Right there that means he wasn't a popular guy, and Club Madrone isn't exactly a church social. On the other hand, he was strictly small time. A straightforward beating would have settled him. Hard to imagine anyone bothering to waste the creep. And, like I said, this was a professional hit."

"Okay. Thanks for the heads-up."

What the hell had Benny wanted to tell him? Surely it had been more than the news that the Mexicans were in town. Surely Benny hadn't died trying to tell Gabriel something he already knew.

"We're getting close here. Don't get sloppy. Don't get cocky. You're in the home stretch, kid. We're all counting on you."

Kid. Gabriel's mouth curved in an acrid smile. "That's right. All my dreams are coming true," he said. And all his nightmares too,

O'Brien snorted. "Just watch your ass. Stay sharp. Stay focused. Trust no one. Not that I have to tell *you* that."

"No. You don't have to tell me that."

The line went dead. Gabriel tossed the phone back into the drawer and knocked it shut.

CHAPTER FOUR

If Botelli's house was a mansion, Sanchez' temporary home was a palace. Gabriel had never seen a residence this lavish and large. It could have served as a hotel.

Two days after the party at the Botelli's, Don Sanchez finally summoned Ricco for a business meeting at his Pacific Heights estate, ostensibly for a swim party for Gina. But it was clear from the buzz in the air that the long awaited drug summit was on. To Gabriel's intense frustration, his assignment for the day was to watch over Gina poolside with the other grunts rather than accompany Botelli at the meeting.

When he pointed out that Don Sanchez would have plenty of men on hand to keep an eye on Gina, Botelli chewed him out for the second time in less than a week.

"Where do you get off questioning my orders?" Botelli asked, smacking Gabriel on the back of the head.

"I'm not questioning, Ricco. I just thought —"

"Hey, I don't pay you to think! I got guys who think rings around you. Don Sanchez is right, *Giovanni*. You got a real attitude problem."

If there'd been any doubt he had made the wrong — or just too much — impression on Don Sanchez, Botelli's comment settled that. Giovanni Contadino's days in Botelli's organization — and probably on the planet — were numbered.

He ducked his head and said humbly, "Sorry, Ricco. I just…hoped maybe I could be of more use…."

"You keep Gina outta trouble. That'll be plenty useful," Botelli growled.

Which is why Gabriel was lounging poolside in a pair of black swim briefs that looked like they'd been swiped from some French Riviera gigolo while Botelli, Rizzi, and Bruno — Bruno "The Protector"! — met with Don Sanchez and his lieutenants in his inner sanctum. Adding insult to injury, he wasn't even wearing a gun. Sanchez' men had confiscated the

Botelli crew's arsenal the minute they arrived. Sanchez trusted no one — including soon-to-be family. Maybe *especially* soon-to-be family.

"What's the matter with you, G?" Gina had asked irritably. "If Ricco wanted you there you'd be inside with him. You're giving me a headache the way you're prowling around."

That had snapped Gabriel back to awareness. Gina wasn't totally oblivious, and he couldn't afford to show too much interest in what was happening indoors. He couldn't afford to bring more attention to himself, period. So, he stood as long as he could reasonably do so, by the full bar that had been set up beneath a breezeway by the pool — glasses winking and blinking in the sunlight — with uniformed serving staff hovering attentively. He fidgeted and snacked at the exotic buffet offering everything from truffled popcorn to duck confit quesadillas.

Finally, caught between crushing boredom and intense frustration, he retreated to one of the dozens of chaise lounges around the lake-size pool — to sulk, according to Gina. He ignored her taunting, half closing his eyes against the glare of sun on water while he watched her and her pals cavorting.

If he tuned out the splashing and shrieks of Gina and her pals in the pool, he could hear the swoosh of the waterfall behind him as it poured over the high, rock wall, the swish-shush as it showered down the face of the carefully arranged boulders, and the final wet slop as it hit the wide crystal-clear pool at the base. The waterfall-cooled breeze wafted across his skin, bringing with it the sharp, clean scent of aftershave with a hint of lime, and abruptly he remembered powerful muscles moving beneath supple bronzed skin, and large hands, brown, long-fingered, knowledgeable hands that had touched him, pleasured him...

His cock stirred under the tight black swim trunks, poking at the warm Lycra, finding no room to expand. Hell. Just what he needed — a sea serpent to scare the women and children. Casually, he shifted on to his side, trying not to overbalance the lounge chair, which rocked alarmingly.

"Enjoying yourself?" a familiar voice asked close to his ear.

"What?" Gabriel's eyes jerked open. As though Gabriel's unruly thoughts had conjured him, Ortega lounged gracefully on the lawn chair next to his own. One brown, muscular arm rested on an equally brown, bent knee. "Yeah. Sure," he answered shortly as Ortega's question registered.

Meeting his gaze, Ortega offered a slight tilt of his head — and the usual sardonic tug of his lips. "I thought so." He looked pointedly at the telltale bulge in Gabriel's briefs. That lickable twist to his lips deepened into a wicked grin. "Daydreaming on the job, Contadino?"

It was the first time they had spoken alone since the shootout at Ruby Blue, and Gabriel was dismayed at his body's reaction, at the way his heart sped up, the way his nerves jumped and his muscles tensed in a surge of excitement.

He drawled, "Yeah. Right up until I opened my eyes. Then it turned into a nightmare."

Ortega chuckled.

Gabriel sat up, reaching for the towel he'd dropped earlier, and pretending to wipe some of the suntan lotion off his oil-slick abdomen and chest. Holding the scrunched towel, he rested his hands in his lap, shielding his cock's inconvenient interest in its neighbor.

Ortega had settled back in the lounge chair, eyes closed, that irritating smile still on his mouth. Seemingly he had nothing on his mind but catching a few rays.

"So is the meeting over?" Gabriel asked.

"We're taking a break. Don Sanchez is phoning his papa."

"His papa!" Gabriel snorted.

"Don't you phone your papa?" Ortega had not moved, but there was a dark gleam beneath the half-closed eyelids.

"My old man is dead," Gabriel said shortly.

Ortega said nothing, but Gabriel could feel himself watched by hooded eyes. But then he suspected Ortega watched everyone and everything.

Blinking against the fierce sunshine, Gabriel looked for Gina amidst her friends in the glittering water. He heard her before he finally spotted her sitting at a table beneath an umbrella at the far end of the long pool. She was laughing in a way guaranteed to draw attention. Not that she wasn't getting plenty of attention already in that leopard-print bathing suit.

As he watched, Don Sanchez strolled up to the table and sat down beside her. Gina's friends cleared out like a flock of pigeons taking flight from a cat. Gina finished off her margarita and smiled widely and unfocused at her fiancé.

"Looks like papa wasn't home," Gabriel commented.

Ortega opened one eye. He studied Don Sanchez, and then he closed his eye again. "You seem very interested in my boss, Contadino," he said lazily.

"Well, you seem to think he's going to be my boss before much longer," Gabriel said.

Ortega didn't reply.

Gabriel watched Gina flirting with Don Sanchez, replenished cocktail in one hand, her other fastened possessively around his bicep. The obscene diamond ring shone from clear across the yard. Gabriel's mouth pulled into a cynical line. Every now and then he felt bad for Gina, but the truth was she knew what she was getting into, at least in principle, and she wanted it. Maybe as much as Sanchez wanted her. Not that she'd have to worry about it. Assuming this operation went down as planned, Gina would soon be looking for another bridegroom.

He glanced guiltily at Ortega, who rested supine in the sun, his smooth skin like bronze satin over his long strong bones and sleek muscles. Ortega's handsome face was relaxed — maybe he was asleep. The black, unruly hair fell across his forehead — shiny as silk. There were tiny laugh lines next to his eyes, and the faint smile lines ghosted next to his full mouth.

He just…did not look like a bad guy.

And what a stupid thought that was. Like bad guys looked any particular way.

Gabriel stretched, arching his back, trying to will his partial erection down so he could make it to the pool without attracting attention. The swimsuit was ludicrous. He hadn't brought one. But Gina had thrown a fit, and before Gabriel had even finished making his excuses, one of Sanchez' minions was handing him this scrap of Lycra. He'd never have chosen something this tight for himself. Not that he was self-conscious about his body. He wasn't buff, but he was lean and fit. He knew he looked good despite a couple of scars on his hide — the graze from a bullet back when he had still been a rookie, and the silver crescent from the stab wound he received when he "saved" Gina from her knife wielding assailant a year ago.

He glanced back at Ortega and was disconcerted to see the other man watching him gravely. Inexplicably, heat rose in his face.

Ortega's mouth curved into that irritating smile. He said softly, "Is the sun too much for you, Contadino? You look flushed."

Abruptly, Gabriel had had enough. He tossed the towel aside, strode the few feet to the edge of the pool and dove in. Even heated, the water was colder than the air and his problem shriveled away instantly. He broke surface, shook the hair out of his eyes. Striking out for the far side of the pool, he didn't look back — ignoring the throaty laughter behind him.

He really didn't get whatever game Ortega was playing. Was the dude flirting with him? Because however highly placed in Sanchez' organization he might be, Gabriel could guarantee Ortega his employer would turn him into dog meat if he ever suspected he was bisexual — let alone queer.

Gabriel reached the side of the pool and grabbed onto the black and blue tiled wall. He glanced back, under cover of scraping his chin length hair out of his eyes. Ortega's dark, half-closed eyes rested on him.

Heart thudding, he turned away and noticed Gina was also watching him — and, as a result, so was Sanchez.

Yeah. Because his life wasn't complicated enough.

Gina's eyes sparkled with mischief and desire and too many margaritas. She'd been pounding them down since ten o'clock that morning. The alcohol probably made it easier for her to smile and coo into Sanchez' battle-scarred face. But between the sun and the alcohol, Gabriel figured it wouldn't be long before she'd be passed out somewhere sleeping it off. He glanced at Sanchez. The Mexican was still staring at him. Those dark eyes held desire too, but of an entirely different nature.

Ducking under the water, he shoved off the edge of the pool, swimming in long, smooth strokes to the opposite side. Surfacing, he half pulled himself out of the pool, resting for a few moments on his folded arms, feeling the warmth of the sun on his bare skin. He kept his eyes closed, but after a time, he risked glancing over at Ortega.

Ortega's eyes were closed again, his face tilted up to the sun. Good. His attention was off Gabriel. But for a moment Gabriel continued to study him.

The fact that Ortega seemed to share Gabriel's awareness — well, that wasn't so surprising, was it? Ortega wouldn't have missed the humor or the irony in their situation, and after all, they had found each other attractive at the club. No reason for that to have changed — it was just a physical reaction. Lust. You didn't have to like or respect someone to lust after them.

Gabriel lowered himself back into the water and swam leisurely down the length of the pool, avoiding a couple of girls on neon-colored, animal-shaped rafts. He passed Botelli and Rizzi at the bar chatting up a couple of Sanchez' female guests. In a show of faith, Botelli had only brought a handful of his own men. They stood around the pool looking uncomfortable and out of place in jeans and Hawaiian shirts, checking their watches and patting their empty shoulder holsters. Only Gabriel had been forced into swim trunks.

Whatever Gina wanted, clearly went. In fact, while the purpose of this summit on the mount might be business, the social get-together arranged around it had been planned with Gina's comfort and pleasure uppermost, with Gina as the center of attention.

If Sanchez wasn't genuinely besotted, he sure gave a good impersonation of it. Once again Gabriel rested on the side of the pool watching as Sanchez' battle-scarred, black-clad troops milled in the background, moving around the guests in their colorful swimwear and tropically hued clothing like killer whales gliding through a lagoon.

There was movement to his right. Sanchez was helping Gina pour herself into a chaise lounge. Though her movements were slightly uncoordinated, she still exhibited a sensual grace as she tugged the grim-faced man down beside her. For a moment Sanchez set aside his usual stiff formality, accepting her brief, teasing caress with a self-conscious pleasure. It was clear when he moved away that he did it reluctantly. He kissed her hand, lingering over it while she smiled and murmured something Gabriel missed. Whatever it was, it made Sanchez' eyes go dark. Lust and yearning crossed his harsh face.

He straightened, speaking to one of the hovering bodyguards. "Jorge, move that umbrella to cover Señorita Botelli's beautiful face."

The man hastened to obey.

For a moment Sanchez stared down at the girl on the lounge. "Make sure no one disturbs her siesta until I return. I must make some calls." He nodded approvingly as the umbrella was positioned to shield Gina's limp form.

Sanchez strode away in the direction of the house, followed unobtrusively by one of his bodyguards.

Waiting until the men disappeared behind the wall of trees and hedges, Gabriel hauled himself up out of the pool. He spared a quick glance for Gina who, losing the struggle to raise her head, dropped back on the flowered cushions, slipping into a drunken slumber, her bikini-clad body lax, her long dark hair shadowing one side of her slack face.

Good. One less potential problem. She'd be out for hours by the look of things.

He glanced across to Ortega, but the lounge chair was empty. He cast a quick look at the pool and bar. No sign of the man. Well, maybe he had gone to take a leak. Maybe he had decided to stop torturing Gabriel and had gone to put some clothes on.

Either way, one less pair of observing eyes.

Gabriel strolled over to where he'd left his towel, conscious of the indifferent looks of Sanchez' and Botelli's men. No one was paying him any undue interest. He dried off briskly, draped the towel around his neck and wandered toward the back entrance of the house.

There was loud laughter behind him. One of Sanchez' guests dove into the water, making a huge splash and drawing the attention of poolside guests. Gabriel glanced down at Gina as he walked past her. She didn't stir.

Once he was on the other side of the wall of greenery, the noise level dropped considerably.

There was no sign of Sanchez or his bodyguard, but the sudden flash of sunlight on one of the French doors along the side of the house alerted Gabriel to the direction they had likely gone.

Sticking to the trees and statuary as much as possible he made his way quickly across the emerald lawn, reaching the outlying shadows of the house. He slipped through a back entrance.

It was a good twenty degrees cooler inside the house. Gabriel shivered in his damp swim trunks, padding softly across an elegant room with deep plush carpeting, silk-covered furniture, and a fortune in modern paintings.

He peeked through a doorway and saw a uniformed maid arranging fresh flowers in a long series of crystal vases.

Quietly crossing the doorway, he looked down a long, empty hallway richly paved with scarlet and navy mosaic tile so perfect it looked like an oriental carpet. There were a couple of closed doors that Gabriel guessed led onto poolside rooms, although the house was so well insulated he couldn't hear anything to indicate he was within a mile of the pool.

At the very end of the hallway were double doors of worm-eaten golden oak. Next to the ornate, antique doors was a security touch pad.

It might as well have had a sign tacked next to it: SANCHEZ' LAIR — KEEP OUT!

The tile was chill beneath his bare feet as Gabriel advanced. He was still a few feet away when one of the side doors he had just passed, opened. Sanchez himself stood framed in the entrance — and Gabriel realized that this must be the room with the French doors that Sanchez had disappeared through a few minutes earlier. Bird song and the gentle splash of the garden fountain drifted through the open windows behind the drug lord.

"Señor Contadino." Sanchez' voice was flat and unsurprised.

"Don Sanchez!" Gabriel ducked his head respectfully. "I seem to have taken a wrong turn."

"Yes, you have," the drug lord returned in that voice that gave away nothing.

A shiver of unease rippled down Gabriel's spine. Or perhaps it was just too much air conditioning and not enough clothing. "It's a big house," he said meekly. "I keep getting lost."

Sanchez said nothing, studying him with those light, impersonal eyes.

Gabriel wondered if he could take the other man if he had to. Sanchez was big and powerfully built. He held himself like a fighter. But Gabriel knew that Sanchez was unlikely to harm him even if he did wonder what the hell he was doing wandering around the house. After all, Gabriel wasn't the only guest lost in these palatial surroundings that afternoon. Besides, he was the property of Botelli, and if anyone was going to deliver corporal punishment that duty should rightly fall to him.

He said, still more humbly, "Sorry for disturbing you, Don Sanchez."

Sanchez' lip curled with something that might have been private amusement — or might have been something totally different. He questioned, "What were you looking for?"

"My clothes," Gabriel replied without missing a beat.

Don Sanchez didn't move, didn't speak. The hair at the back of Gabriel's head prickled.

Sanchez turned back into the room, spoke in Spanish too quietly for Gabriel to hear.

He continued to stand in the drafty hallway, wondering if he had been dismissed or what his next move should be. Then the door to the side room opened fully and Sanchez' bodyguard stepped into the hall, closing the door after him.

"Hey," Gabriel said.

"*Vamos a movernos!*" the bodyguard said, jerking his head down the hallway.

Gabriel nodded, heading back the way he had come. As he passed the bodyguard, the man reached out and shoved him hard. Gabriel stumbled forward, but kept his footing, turning warily.

The bodyguard jerked his head again for Gabriel to precede him.

"You do that again, asshole, and you'll be eating your teeth."

The bodyguard grinned widely displaying a front row of gold choppers.

Great.

The bodyguard started forward, and Gabriel pulled the towel from around his neck, bracing to meet him. Big arms, massive shoulders — the ape probably relied on power over speed — although he seemed to be moving pretty quickly —

"Hector!" Ortega stood at the end of the hallway. The familiar voice was sharper than usual, but as the two combatants halted, Ortega added in his usual honey-warm tone, "I will see to Mr. Contadino."

Hector had instantly frozen to statue stillness. "*Sí,* Señor Ortega," he said without inflection. His eyes rested malevolently on Gabriel's face, but he gave no other hint that he regretted the interruption.

Gabriel turned to Ortega. Not many men look authoritative wearing nothing but a pair of swim trunks, but somehow Ortega managed it. "Coming?" he asked crisply.

Gabriel nodded, walking down the hallway toward him. He draped the towel back over his shoulders. "Thanks, but that wasn't necessary," he said.

"No?" Ortega glanced pointedly at the towel around Gabriel's neck. "Were you planning to defend yourself by snapping a towel at Hector?"

"I can take care of myself. I was trying to find my clothes."

"In Don Sanchez' private quarters?" That even tone was as unreadable as Ortega's face.

"I got lost," Gabriel said irritably. "Is that a crime around here?"

"Ah."

"Ah what?"

Ortega said nothing.

An innocent person would push. Gabriel pushed. "What else?"

"What else indeed."

They crossed the pristine living room, the walls covered in expensive art, and Gabriel was suddenly reminded of those amazing paintings in the Club Madrone — right before Ortega had made his presence known.

Ortega said, "If I were you, I wouldn't wander around this house alone. Don Sanchez does not like you."

"I wasn't wandering. I was looking for my clothes."

"They would be at the cabana, would they not?"

"No, they wouldn't. I didn't bring swim trunks. Someone dug me a pair up and I changed here at the main house."

Ortega seemed to consider this seriously. "Why didn't you simply ask one of the servants?"

"I didn't see one."

Ortega's smile was frankly disbelieving. "Not that I object to seeing you without clothes," he remarked. "Your skin is just the color of honey, and I know you taste as sweet."

Gabriel's breath caught in his throat, his heart jumping hard against the walls of his ribcage.

"Yeah, well, forget about it," he got out roughly.

Ortega shrugged. Stopping to confer with one of the maids, he led Gabriel down another hallway, pushed open a door leading onto a bedroom that looked out over the other side of the house: brick terrace, rose gardens and fountains.

Gabriel walked into the bedroom, glancing warily around as Ortega followed him into the room.

Catching the suspicious look, Ortega said blandly, "I will wait to escort you back to the pool. I would not wish you to get lost again."

"Suit yourself," Gabriel replied. Turning, he found his trousers in a neat pile on the end of the bed, and shook them out.

He was used to dressing and undressing in a locker room, but the steady, silent way Ortega watched him made Gabriel self-conscious as he pulled his damp trunks off.

For something to say, he held the wet trunks out, saying, "What am I supposed to do with these?"

Ortega took the wet swim trunks, dropped them on the floor, and pulled Gabriel into his arms. His strong arms wrapped around Gabriel's back and his naked, warm body felt wonderful rubbing against Gabriel. His mouth came down on Gabriel's astonished one, and he tasted like pure, golden, distilled heat. Like sunshine and tequila — only better.

And for one crazy moment, Gabriel grabbed him back, kissed him back. And then he remembered where he was and what Ortega was. He tore free, planting his hands in the bigger man's furry chest and shoving him away.

"What the hell are you doing?"

"It hasn't been *that* long, surely?" Ortega murmured. His hands gripped Gabriel's waist and he slammed him back into the nearest wall, pinning him there with his body, chest to chest, one leg shoved between Gabriel's legs. His mouth found Gabriel's and closed it in the most effective way possible.

For a moment Gabriel didn't even struggle. Then he tore his mouth free.

"Are you crazy?" he hissed. "You're going to get us both killed."

"You seem to like taking risks."

"This isn't a risk, it's suicide." But oh God, it was difficult to ignore that body pressing against him, the moist mouth a few inches from his own, the soft, furry chest brushing his own sensitized skin, the erection jabbing into his belly — and his own answering poke. Half-heartedly, he attempted to free himself. As much as he enjoyed risky sex, this was madness.

One of Ortega's big, square hands cupped his jaw, stilling him. He rubbed insinuatingly against Gabriel, and the scent and taste of the older man was intoxicating and infuriating. Espresso-dark eyes held Gabriel's gaze for so long and so seriously that Gabriel began to forget why this was such a terrible idea.

But as Ortega's lips sought his own again in a kiss as soft and light as the fall of a shadow, he remembered, and shoved the other man back hard.

Ortega staggered a step and then straightened. His face was dangerous before it smoothed out into his normal amused expression.

"As I told you before, I have no wish to take what is not truly desired." He glanced pointedly to Gabriel's cock. "Though, admittedly, the message I'm getting is confused."

Gabriel's lip curled. He brushed past Ortega, snatching up his trousers. Back turned, he gave himself a couple of hard, unobtrusive flicks so that he was able to zip up quickly.

He said gruffly, "Hey, we all know sometimes the little head wants what the big head doesn't."

Neither spoke for a few seconds.

"How old are you, *gatito*? Not very old, I think. Not even thirty, are you?"

"What's that got to do with anything?" Gabriel yanked on his shirt, doing up the buttons swiftly.

Ortega didn't answer.

Gabriel tucked his shirt in. Did up his belt. He threw the other man a curious look. What did Ortega want? Why was he still watching him that way?

"Let me give you a word of advice," Ortega said finally.

Gabriel's mouth twisted cynically. "Go on."

"If you're hoping to get back into Botelli's good graces by bringing him some information about Don Sanchez, don't waste your time. Botelli wouldn't know what to do with any such information. He's Don Sanchez' man now. And if Don Sanchez tells him to get rid of you, he'll get rid of you."

Gabriel shifted nervously, bracing his hands on his hips. "Is that what Don Sanchez is going to tell him?"

Ortega said nothing, his black-velvet eyes holding Gabriel's.

"Not today, perhaps," Ortega said finally. "But if I were you, I'd start looking for a new job."

CHAPTER FIVE

Sanchez didn't see a place for Gabriel in his organization, and no way was Botelli going to argue with that. The obvious thing to do was to contact O'Brien and ask to be pulled out. Gabriel wasn't going to be of use to anyone dead, and that's what Ortega was talking about. The typical drug lord severance package was a bullet in the brain.

How long did he have? That was the question. Because if his instincts were right, things were liable to shake loose pretty quick. In which case it didn't matter whether Sanchez liked him or didn't like him or saw him as a candidate for promotion or merely fertilizer for the rose bushes. Sanchez himself would be wearing prison blue and trading favors for cigarettes and protection. And Botelli would be right there beside him, loyal lapdog tagging at his heels.

So he would wait awhile to call O'Brien. Not too long. He wasn't stupid. But he'd worked long and hard — devoted over a year of his life to this gig — and he didn't scare easily.

"Hey, *paisan*!" Botelli stood at the patio bar. He waved to Gabriel as the younger man walked onto the deck, followed by Ortega.

With a wordless nod of greeting, Gabriel walked over to stand at Botelli's side.

"You're supposed to be keeping an eye on Gina," Botelli said. His face was flushed with sun and alcohol, and there was a nasty glitter in his shoe-button eyes.

Gabriel glanced at Gina who was still sprawled unconscious on the lounge chair.

"I went inside to get dressed."

"Yeah, I see that." Botelli's mouth curled as he deliberately looked Gabriel up and down.

Something was in the wind. Ortega was right. Botelli's tone was dismissive and borderline insulting. Gabriel glanced at Ortega, who had joined their half-circle. Ortega's eyes met his, and Gabriel knew that his own recognition of his falling popularity was there for the other man to read.

"What are you drinking, Señor Botelli?" Ortega asked smoothly. He beckoned to the bartender to replace the older man's drink.

Botelli said — and there was the faintest slur in his voice. "Any idea when your boss is going to be ready to talk business again?"

"He will let us know." Ortega was courteous and deterring at the same time. He raised his eyebrows at Gabriel, who said, "I'm on duty."

"Christ, have a drink," Botelli said. "We're going to be here all goddamn day."

"Tequila," Gabriel told Ortega.

"*Blanco, Gold, Reposado*, or *Anejo*?"

"Uh….*Reposado* would be good. Thank you." He hoped that was right. How the hell was he supposed to know there were four different types of tequila? All he knew about tequila was you used the cheap stuff in margaritas and the good stuff doing shots.

Ortega flicked Gabriel a cool look and nodded in response to his confident request. "*Reposado*," he told the bartender.

"Uh!" mocked Botelli, who probably didn't know the difference. He took one of those heavy-handed swipes at Gabriel's head. Gabriel ducked. He kept smiling, but it wasn't easy.

"Ignore them," Ortega said. His tone was so easy and friendly it was impossible for Botelli or his men to take offense, but Gabriel had the oddest sensation that Ortega had just blocked a punch meant for him. The other man's fingers brushed Gabriel's as he handed him the caballito glass. He explained to Botelli. "This is traditional tequila that has rested in white oak casks called *pipones* for about a year. *Reposada*."

Gabriel was acutely aware of the feel of Ortega's fingers for the fleeting seconds they had touched his own. He kept his eyes on the pale liquid in the glass.

"You're wasting the good stuff on him," Michelangelo Rizzi, Botelli's own underboss, drawled. He downed half his own drink, setting the glass on the bar too hard.

Ortega ignored him. "You sip it," he said, and though his words were casual and spoken toward Rizzi, there was a note in his voice as though he and Gabriel were alone, speaking just to each other.

Gabriel sipped the tequila. It was mellow, warming, gentle on his palate. He imagined he could taste a hint of the blue agave. He glanced up, and Ortega was studying him, a hint of a smile playing around his mouth. There was a look in his eyes —

No.

The smile had to be mockery and the glint in Ortega's eyes was — it didn't matter what it was. Gabriel was not going to go there. He sipped his tequila and kept his eyes lowered while the other men talked and joked. He could feel Ortega watching him, and he ignored him. He concentrated on the job. The Botelli faction felt they were being dissed by Sanchez — and they were. Sanchez was making it very clear that it was a buyer's market, and he had reservations about what Botelli was selling.

But then Sanchez was being disingenuous there. Because he wasn't crawling into bed with Botelli merely because Gina was part of the deal. Botelli's distribution network was still — even after the feds and the competition had ravaged the ranks of his organization — the best on the West Coast. Compared to Botelli, Scarborough and his brand of punks were also-rans.

Hector appeared on the outskirts of the group. He spoke respectfully to Ortega.

"Don Sanchez is ready to resume the meeting."

Ortega nodded. "Gentlemen." He gestured to Botelli and Rizzi, and the men gathered their drinks and headed back inside the house, Hector trailing at a discreet distance.

Gabriel sipped his tequila.

Guests came and went. Gabriel ate some melon and white chocolate cookies and had another tequila. Gina woke up cranky from her siesta, and Gabriel spent some time catering to her, bringing her aspirin and iced water. He sat nervously smoking several cigarettes while Gina raced her friends up and down the pool — her friends allowing her to win four out of five laps.

All the while he tried to think if there was some way to find out what was being said at the meeting inside the house. He'd spent over a year worming his way into Botelli's confidence, and now at the last minute he was being shut out because…why? Because Gina was a little too fond of him? Or had that legendary sixth sense of Don Sanchez' kicked in and warned him something wasn't quite right about Giovanni Contadino?

There was no way to know for sure, but frustration was making him crazy.

The guests were filing into the pool house for a late buffet when Bruno appeared.

"Mr. Botelli wants you," he said to Gabriel.

"Well, that's lousy timing!" Gina protested.

Bruno spread his hands wide in a gesture of apology. Gabriel was already heading across the lawn back to the main house.

"I'll fix you a plate, G," Gina called after him.

Don Sanchez' study was thick with cigar smoke when Gabriel slipped inside. The double doors closed softly behind him.

"…Miguel will travel to Mexico to meet with these men," Don Sanchez was saying. "If you wish to send —"

Rizzi broke in, "But what do we need opium for? We traffic heroin. Why would we want to diversify in this economy?"

Botelli shot his underboss a warning look and then smiled at Sanchez. "You wanna branch out, Don Jesus? Is that it?" Botelli was always open to expanding the business, but from what Gabriel had observed, he was wary of straying too far from the familiar.

"Opium latex is the basis for making heroin." Though his tone was polite, Sanchez spoke as though pointing out the obvious.

And hearing that note, Rizzi said shortly, "Since when?"

Botelli frowned at him. "Opium to heroin is the process they do in South America, not Mexico."

Condensation had formed on the side of Sanchez' margarita glass. It made a ghostly squeak — like a tiny windshield wiper — as he stroked the smooth glass with his thumb, over and over. Nervous tic? No way. Sanchez had no nerves. He said easily, "Until now, yes. Our new supplier — potential supplier — is from the mountains of Mexico, the vast poppy fields of Sinaloa."

"Sinaloa?" Despite himself Botelli was impressed. "Sounds like a good excuse to vacation in Mazatlán."

Everyone laughed except Don Sanchez who said, "They are an old family, well entrenched in generations of opium production."

After two full minutes, Gabriel was finding that obsessive slide of flesh on glass both annoying and dirty. He looked away and found Ortega watching him through a veil of blue cigar smoke.

"Who are *they*?" Botelli asked.

"Old family friends. Carlos Piñero is the patriarch of that clan. His sons have been off in Colombia learning their trade. They have finally brought the latex process back with them and are now manufacturing some of the purest heroin available." Sanchez smiled and sipped from the salt encrusted glass. Gabriel suspected he did it deliberately, allowing suspense to build.

Botelli said, "And you believe they are open to sharing this process?"

"It is ours, yours and mine — if we move quickly. We must impress them with our strength and resources. Capture the channel while it is still open."

"You planning to buy in your old family friends or strong arm them into cooperating?" Rizzi asked.

Sanchez offered a hint of that crocodile smile. "We will be generous in our offer."

"What if they're not interested in our offer?" That was Botelli. He had a lot of experience with people not being interested in his offers.

"We have other methods of persuasion."

And dead men can't say no, Gabriel thought. No one had batted an eyelash at his entrance and they seemed to be ignoring him now. He wondered why he had been summoned, especially since he was not currently in Botelli's favor.

Rizzi asked, "What about the supplier we got? Gallvado has been very accommodating."

Sanchez looked at Ortega, who said, "This new avenue of opportunity offers a kilo at half of Gallvado's price, and it is ninety percent pure." He leaned back in his chair, his jacket loose and open, offering a glimpse of his shoulder holster. Yet his voice was the educated, confident voice of the head honcho of any Fortune 500 company. "Gallvado's product is one step up from black tar; twenty percent pure at best."

Ortega's big hands were unexpectedly graceful as he emphasized his words with quick, cutting motions. Gabriel bet if he closed his eyes he could have a conversation with Ortega without saying a word, letting those sure, knowing hands talk to him, release their passion, use his skin for a tablet to write on.

"And what if Gallvado isn't happy with our new supply channel?" There was an undercurrent of resentment in Rizzi's tone. Gabriel remembered the underboss was the one who had brought Gallvado's operation to the game eight months ago. Now he was at risk of losing that nice under-the-table cut Gallvado slipped him each month.

Ortega was smiling as he studied Rizzi's unhappy expression, and Gabriel was certain Sanchez and his people were perfectly aware of Rizzi's side deal with Gallvado.

"Competition. That's the American way, no?"

"No," Botelli said. "I don't like competition."

Sanchez chuckled. "Me neither, *amigo*." And his basilisk stare rested on Gabriel's face.

Gabriel tensed. There was a fraught moment, and then the stem of the margarita glass snapped in Sanchez' grip. One of his men scurried to remove the broken glass from his master's hand. Sanchez gave the glass over automatically as if it happened every day. And maybe it did.

He smiled that tiger's smile at Ortega. "If needed, Miguel will see to it that the connection is properly severed."

Rizzi mocked, "That your specialty, Ortega, severing connections?"

Ortega's gaze was untroubled as it met Rizzi's blue one. "When necessary."

"Unfortunately, sometimes it is necessary." That was Sanchez, and he was looking straight at Rizzi.

Rizzi met the look, but he seemed uncomfortable all at once.

Botelli said jovially, "What do you think of that, Mike? Why should Ortega get all the fun? What do you think of a vacation in Mexico, all the tequila you can drink and all the whores you can fuck — all expenses paid. You and Ortega should get to know each better, anyway."

Rizzi curled his lip. "I think I got better things to do. I think I need to stay local. I think you should send Contadino. If Gina can do without her…bodyguard for a week."

Gabriel's stared in disbelief at Rizzi. A sudden, sharp silence followed the underboss' words — and the chill that slithered down Gabriel's spine had nothing to do with the room's air-conditioning. It seemed to him that every man in the room was looking at him with some sinister knowledge. But, Gabriel risked a look at the Mexican drug lord, and it seemed ominous to him that Sanchez was not looking at him at all. Instead he was staring fixedly at the globe of the world on a stand in the corner. Ortega was looking, though. Ortega studied Gabriel in that level way, his face revealing nothing.

"Hey," Gabriel said thickly, "you can say what you want about me, but you better show more respect for the *signorina*."

Maybe it wasn't the snappiest comeback in the world, but it was along the right lines.

"That's right. You watch your goddamned mouth, Rizzi." Botelli's face was red.

Rizzi, equally flushed, shrugged. "No offense, boss. I'm just saying, if we can afford to spare anyone for a few days, it's Giovanni. I thought that's what we were discussing earlier."

"Send Contadino, by all means," Ortega said, surprisingly. "He's proven himself a good man in a fight." He managed to convey, without saying so, that he doubted the same was true of Rizzi.

Rizzi straightened abruptly, glaring at Ortega.

Gabriel didn't kid himself that Ortega was speaking in his defense so much as taking opportunity to insult and belittle the other underboss. This was a simple staking of territory. But it was good timing. Sanchez' amber gaze had swiveled from the globe to the two men. Botelli spared Rizzi a black look then fingered his lower lip in a gesture Gabriel recognized as a sign that he was weighing the pros and cons. He said, "Someone should look out for the Botelli interests in this. Think you could handle this, Gio?"

Gabriel's pulse skyrocketed. The chance to meet with suppliers, growers, to gather names, locations, delivery channels, routes — everything they would need to shut down this new supplier and distribution channel before it ever got up and running. It was almost too good to be true.

"Hell yeah," he said gruffly.

Botelli nodded approvingly — but thoughtfully too. There was something going on here that Gabriel didn't quite follow. Sanchez was gazing out the window at the fountains sparkling in the late afternoon sun.

Sanchez' gaze turned from the window to Ortega. "Yes," he said thoughtfully. "It is good for young men to learn how these things work. Take him with you, Miguel." And he smiled the smile that Gabriel distrusted. "Teach him."

There were probably several layers of meaning to that simple phrase, but Gabriel didn't care. He was going inside the Mexican pipeline. He couldn't wait to let O'Brien know. This was way beyond anyone's expectation.

Once again Ortega was studying him with that enigmatic gaze. And that was the downside of all this. Keeping at bay his own physical attraction to Ortega. He couldn't afford to get distracted — not that Ortega seemed like a guy who forgot his priorities or put pleasure before business — but judging by their earlier encounter in the guestroom, the interest was far from one-sided. In fact, Gabriel couldn't help wondering if that might have been a factor in Ortega's push to have him along.

If so, this trip was going to be a learning experience for everyone involved.

CHAPTER SIX

The airstrip was a tiny half-cleared field on a flat section of mountain plateau. Gabriel knew they were somewhere south of Sinaloa, but no one had mentioned the name of the village, and he was pretty sure it wasn't going to appear in any tour books. Even Ortega had referred to the final leg in the journey simply as their destination. Gabriel wasn't sure if that was because he wasn't trusted with the information or because it went without a name, this collection of ramshackle tin buildings, open sewers, and kids sleeping naked in the streets with stray dogs.

The sun had barely risen when a small private plane whisked them away from the tiny airport on the edge of Mexico City. Buckled into the sleek four-seater, Ortega spent the entire flight on his cell phone or making brief entries into a small laptop.

The phone conversations had been low voiced and terse. Gabriel hadn't been able to catch more than one word out of three, and he didn't dare try lip reading Ortega. The man was far too aware of him.

Well, that went both ways, because trying to listen unobtrusively to Ortega's conversation inevitably led to thoughts about Ortega's firm, full mouth and how it felt against Gabriel's skin, the way he had kissed Gabriel — demanding and yet gentle — and to the way he had tasted.

Gabriel tried to distract himself by watching the landscape change beneath him. But that wasn't entirely successful. He especially didn't like flying in a small plane where winds and air currents buffeted and tossed them like they were no larger or important than a sparrow on the breeze. It wasn't that he was afraid, exactly, or that he wasn't confident enough to relinquish control in the right set of circumstances, but speeding through the clouds and ceilingless sky was not the right set of circumstances. Nor did his restless nature take well to confinement — although Ortega's close proximity reminded him all too well how much he craved confinement in the context of sexual submission, being overpowered and controlled during intimacy. Or what passed for intimacy in his experience.

In fact, the only thing that kept him from disregarding the seatbelt sign and pacing the tiny aisle was the knowing, amused look Ortega gave him the moment he finished restlessly thumbing through a stack of firearms and high fashion magazines and started shifting in his seat. One look from those dark, warm eyes and Gabriel knew Ortega read his edginess perfectly.

That knowing look irritated the hell out of Gabriel and kept him in his seat — although by the time they landed in wherever this was, he was about ready to spontaneously combust.

Through the side window, Gabriel saw a long black limo and four jungle camouflage Jeeps waiting for them. The Jeeps were crowded with grim-faced men dressed in khakis and conspicuously armed with automatic weapons and submachine guns. Like old-fashioned bandits, wearing bandoliers, grenades and spare ammunition draped across beefy chests. And although Gabriel had expected something like this, its deadly reality churned his guts. All at once he felt a very long way from home. His only ally in this Godforsaken outpost was a drug lord's second in command. Automatically, he reached up to touch his holstered weapon. The weight of it against his side was reassuring.

Gabriel wasn't the kind of guy to sit around feeling lost and lonely. He unsnapped his seatbelt and stood, starting down the aisle. A hard hand fastened on his arm, stopping him in his tracks.

"Wait," Ortega said curtly. He was leaning across the seat, staring out the small window. His expression was hard and unreadable.

"For what?"

"I'm…not sure."

Gabriel made an impatient sound, pulling his arm free. "Well, let me know when you figure it out."

Ortega said nothing.

"I hope the welcoming committee doesn't think we missed our flight and leave."

"They aren't here to welcome us."

Gabriel's heart jerked with something very like alarm. "What's that supposed to mean?"

Ortega said evenly, "Those aren't Piñero's men."

"How can you tell?" Gabriel asked, peering out the window. He figured if you'd seen one death-dealing drug lord you'd probably seen them all. "I thought this was your first trip down here?"

The sound of a cartridge clip sliding home pulled his attention from the window. Ortega's Glock gleamed sleekly in his big hand. He held it with the confidence of a man very familiar with his weapon — and not from practice on a shooting range.

"My first trip, yes. And yours," Ortega said wryly. "Hopefully not our last."

Gabriel drew his own pistol. "What the hell does *that* mean?"

"None of these men are in uniform."

"Uniform? You mean like military?" Gabriel stared through his window onto the Third World. Other than the inevitable emaciated stray dog and the cadre of limo and Jeeps waiting to greet them, there was nothing to see but dirt and the shaggy vegetation of this mountain terrain.

"Police. Federales. Carlos Piñero is the local law. Chief of police to be exact."

Christ. Crooked cops for contacts. "Wow. Business entrepreneur and yet he still has time to serve and protect the people. The dude's a candidate for Man of the Year." He moved down the aisle to the next window, keeping low. No one was approaching the plane. So far no one had moved. "So these guys are...?"

"Perhaps our competition for the new supplier. Perhaps not."

Ortega pressed a button on the panel in the arm of his seat and the faint buzz of an intercom system sprang to life. "Raphael, keep the door closed, *por favor*. We seem to have a greeting committee — and not the one we expected. Best to keep the engines running. We may have to take off in a hurry."

Ortega, as usual, sounded calm — if crisper than usual.

Gabriel said, "So what happens next? What are they waiting for? Reinforcements? They have an arsenal out there now." He threw Ortega a mocking look. "Your reputation must precede you."

"Don Sanchez' reputation precedes us." Ortega's smile was wry — and fleeting — as they heard shouting from outside the plane.

They fell into defensive positions on either side of the bulletproofed oval window.

Pistol raised and ready, Gabriel watched Ortega. He was the expert here, and Gabriel wasn't too arrogant to admit it. He stole a look through the window. A horseshoe of rough, unshaven men crowded around the plane door — they seemed to be debating whether to shoot it open or not. But at the shout behind them, they turned to watch a dust cloud to the north come rolling down the runway. Gabriel couldn't make out what was creating it, but it was approaching very fast.

"I believe it may be the cavalry," Ortega remarked.

They were both silent as the men by the plane raced back to their vehicles. The limo shot off like a black streak, the jeeps roaring to life behind it.

Gabriel agreed, "They sure seem —"

He broke off as an explosion hit the ground where the vehicles had been parked, leaving nothing behind but a curtain of smoke and dirt. He swayed as the sonic blast hit the plane like an unseen ocean wave, making the metal creak. It was too far away to do more.

"Jesus!" Gabriel exclaimed. "What the fuck was *that*?"

"A mortar," Ortega answered quietly. "They are not aiming at us."

"Good to know!"

The limo and trailing Jeeps were already disappearing into the dusty distance. The two men stared at each other.

After a shocked instant, Gabriel found himself grinning — and Ortega was smiling too and shaking his head.

"Man, these are some *loco caballeros*!"

"*Sí*," Ortega said — which struck Gabriel as hysterically funny. Watching him, Ortega began to laugh as well.

He and Ortega were still chuckling with giddy relief as five huge black SUVs barreled up to replace the earlier entourage. Big, burly Mexicans in uniforms proclaiming them to be part of the local constabulary burst out of the SUVs' doors, firing at the retreating Jeeps. Bullets sang through the air, riddling the outlying tin buildings and empty oil drums. Another mortar blast landed in the wake of the fleeing vehicles, fired from a vantage point atop one of the SUVs.

And with that, the skirmish was over.

"Welcome to Mexico," Ortega said, and he lightly touched his gun barrel against Gabriel's raised weapon in a salute.

It was difficult not to like the man at moments like this.

"Let's do what we came here for." Gabriel shoved his pistol back into his holster as Ortega holstered his own weapon.

"One thing," Ortega said, and Gabriel gave him an inquiring look.

"Down here we have only each other to rely on. Whatever our feelings about the merger between our two organizations, here we must be a team."

"Sure," Gabriel said.

Ortega's mouth twitched. "That means we must work together. Trust each other — as we did at the club."

Without thinking, Gabriel responded, "Which club?"

"Both." There was an unexpected softening in Ortega's expression that caught Gabriel off guard. His gut tightened with unwilling emotion as Ortega added, "Though I think the first night took more trust. *Sí*, Contadino?"

"Jesus, you *are* a romantic," Gabriel said sarcastically. "Since when does sex equal trust?"

"The games you play, *gatito*, are dangerous indeed with a partner you don't trust."

"Uh, can we maybe not talk about this now?" Gabriel asked testily, color flooding his face at that godawful nickname. Ortega had the damnedest habit of saying out loud things most people wouldn't even dare think.

"Just remember what I've said." Ortega moved to the front of the cabin and popped the seal on the outer door. Once the thick door cleared the opening, the stairway descended with the touch of a button.

Waves of humidity hit Gabriel like a slap in the face, carrying the smell of cordite and rich soil with it. He joined Ortega at the top of the steps, following him wordlessly. It was his job to remember every possible detail of this trip. If he did his job right, when he returned stateside he would have one hell of a file for O'Brien. And a big part of that file would be Miguel Ortega.

He had to admit Ortega was a smooth customer. He looked like he'd strolled out of the pages of GQ — hard to believe a few minutes earlier he'd been positioned at the plane window, Glock in hand, ready for a firefight. Beside him, Gabriel felt young and scruffy and off balance as they faced the battery of eyes of Piñero's men.

Not that Piñero's crew seemed that interested in them — they seemed unable to tear their eyes away from the trim and beautiful private plane — and the briefcase in Ortega's hand. A dozen sets of hard eyes raked them over — and not everyone's weapon was aimed at the fleeing Jeeps.

A few feet from the nearest SUV, a portly man with miles of gold braid on his shoulders stepped forward, a toothy smile on his face and a cigar stuffed in one cheek. He spoke around the cigar as if it was a growth on his tongue instead of a removable object.

"Señor Ortega. Welcome. I am Lieutenant Tito Ferreño."

Ortega nodded, cool and collected as though he'd walked into his club.

"A pleasure. This is my associate, Señor Contadino."

In Gabriel's opinion there was something too…avid…in that cop's grin and the way his bright eyes sized up Ortega's finely tailored suit and titanium briefcase. Personally, he wouldn't trust the lieutenant as far as he could drop kick him. As those snapping black eyes turned their attention his way, Gabriel leveled a chill return look.

The man licked his lips nervously, his gaze lighting with something more than passing interest as he inspected Gabriel.

The ragged toothed smile did nothing to allay Gabriel's instant dislike. "Señor Contadino." Ferreño's voice was raspy from a lifetime spent drinking, smoking, and shouting orders.

Gabriel nodded curtly.

"My apologies for the earlier disturbance." Ferreño gestured vaguely in the direction in which the Jeeps had disappeared. "No doubt bandits or gunrunners looking to steal your money and your plane. These mountains are full of desperate men." Once again his look seemed to linger on Gabriel's face.

"So we have heard," Ortega replied. "Was that the reason for that show of force? An illustration of what might happen without Señor Piñero's protection?" Despite the challenge, Ortega still spoke in that honey-baked drawl, as though such crude tactics amused him.

Lieutenant. Ferreño spluttered, "No, no, señor! How could you think such a thing?" But something malevolent flickered across his coarse features. "Would Captain Piñero dare to show disrespect to the great Don Sanchez?"

Ortega smiled. "Don Sanchez and Captain Piñero have been friends for many years," he said cryptically.

"And you came to *us*."

The sun was hot, the mountain air thin and tainted with the distant smell of the primitive sewers. Gabriel could hear flies buzzing and the sound of the pilot moving inside the plane. Ferreño was silent, his men motionless.

"Yes," Ortega answered, and though his voice was still smooth there was an edge to the velvet that Gabriel had not heard before. "This time bearing gifts. Next time…" He raised his shoulders eloquently.

Gabriel stood easy, readying himself for whatever the next minute or two might bring. There was a hiss in the air — it sounded like a rattlesnake, but it was just some kind of insect.

Cicadas or something? He could feel Ortega's tension, though the other man stood relaxed and tall — jacket unbuttoned.

A trickle of sweat wove its way down Gabriel's spine. Pretty ironic if he died in a shootout protecting Ricco Botelli's illicit interests. Yet he felt strangely calm at the idea.

The lieutenant shrugged. "Maybe there wouldn't be a next time."

Ortega laughed and the hair prickled on Gabriel's scalp. "You know better than that, *amigo*. There would be a next time. Like there was in Nuevo Leon."

The words *Nuevo Leon* seemed to ripple through the ranks of Ferreño's thugs.

Eyes narrowed, Ferreño pulled a pair of sunglasses out of his pocket. He didn't put them on, instead twirling them, undecided, as he stared at Ortega, reevaluating the situation.

Suddenly he laughed. "But why are we standing here baking in the hot sun, gentlemen? Captain Piñero is most regretful that he was unable to meet your plane, but he sends his best regards. He is attending to official business at the moment." Ferreño made a snipping motion with his fingers. Gabriel was unclear whether that was supposed to indicate Piñero was opening a garden center or chopping someone's hands off.

Ortega's smile was a close-lipped tight line, polite but not completely mollified.

In reply, Ferreño's uneven smile widened insincerely. "Tomorrow he will contact you and Señor Contadino to arrange a time to meet. In the meantime, it is his wish that you will accept the hospitality of our humble village."

Ortega nodded curtly.

Ferreño gestured toward the open doors of the SUVs. "Rooms have been arranged for you at our finest hotel. I will take you there myself." His beady black eyes rested on Gabriel once more, and he actually licked his lips.

Do I know you, asshole? Gabriel wanted to ask, but he controlled himself. Ortega preferred a more subtle approach, and this was Ortega's show. But there was no point in wasting subtleties in apes like Ferreño. He ran a casual hand through his hair, letting the bastard get a good look at the Walther 99 under his arm.

Gabriel nearly started as Ortega's hand rested lightly, possessively on the small of his back. And annoying though it was, that subtle staking of claim did reassure Gabriel.

"Thank you," Ortega said courteously. "My associate and I look forward to meeting with Captain Piñero." His eyes met Gabriel's, and there was a flash of humor as though he read Gabriel's mind perfectly. Gabriel looked back at Ferreño.

The lieutenant was staring at Ortega and Gabriel. He laughed suddenly, a harsh bark of sound. Turning on heel, he waddled toward his SUV.

"After you," Ortega said to Gabriel, a teasing note in his voice.

Gabriel grimaced and turned to follow Ferreño.

"Great. What the hell are we going to do for a day in this dump?" he muttered to Ortega.

Ortega chuckled, shooting Gabriel a look that warmed his face. "I imagine we will find something to amuse us."

CHAPTER SEVEN

The hotel was located in the main plaza of a surprisingly, seemingly prosperous town. Prosperous by Third World standards. It was kind of like stepping back in time. Cheerful and busy plump women in colorful local dress went about their daily business, giggling children tagging at their heels. Casually dressed men stood on street corners smoking and having heated discussions. Gabriel noted many faces with those distinctive Indian features that tracked back to ancient civilizations. And speaking of ancients, he noted what seemed like a disproportionate number of toothless and walnut-wrinkled elderly people — along with stray dogs running everywhere.

He also couldn't help noticing that as the fleet of black SUVs barreled through the narrow streets, most townspeople stopped what they were doing and stepped into the shadows of doorways and alleys. The cops were definitely not the good guys in this corner of the world.

Lieutenant Ferreño deposited Ortega and Gabriel outside a two-story pink stucco building that boasted iron balconies dripping with flowering vines. At its breezy, white, painted, slate doors, men in drab street clothes guarded the entrance with machine guns held at the ready.

Ferreño's driver peeled out and disappeared down the narrow street, leaving Ortega and Gabriel with their luggage dumped at their feet.

"Aloha, assholes," Gabriel muttered, staring after the vehicle.

Ortega picked up his own small bag, slinging the strap over his shoulder. "Come. We should get out of the heat."

"Is that possible?" Gabriel wiped his forehead with his sleeve, and bent down to grab his bag. "We've been here about an hour, and I already hate this fucking country."

"Do you kiss your mother with that mouth, Contadino?" Ortega's hand fastened on his shoulder, drawing him toward the front entrance.

Gabriel said shortly, "My mother liked me just fine." He instantly regretted the childish response when Ortega threw him a quick look. But the truth was, the old grief still caught him off guard sometimes. His mom had been bursting with pride the day he'd graduated from the academy. Just as well she couldn't see him right now. Even in the name of justice, she wouldn't approve of some of the things he did in this undercover life.

"Sorry, *amigo*," Ortega said. "I didn't know." His voice was quiet, and there was no particular inflection, yet it closed Gabriel's throat for a moment. Clearly he was running low on sleep.

He said flatly, "At least she…understood me. She knew what I was didn't change who I was."

"No?"

"No." *What a strange conversation to be having in a dusty street in a town in the middle of nowhere.* "She was good with how I turned out." He shrugged. "The old man, not so much." The expression on Ortega's face bugged the hell out of him. Who was Ortega to give him that thoughtful, measuring — disapproving — look? He answered it with a brittle, insolent smile. "Lucky for me, nobody's left that gives a fuck what I do anymore, eh?"

"All alone, Contadino? That is sad, *sí?*" The unexpected understanding took Gabriel aback, even alarmed him in some undefined way. Christ, what was it about Ortega? And even more alarming was the realization that he'd told Ortega the unvarnished truth — not that it differed a lot from his cover story, but he hadn't been thinking of his cover at all. He had simply told the truth, spilled his guts to a crook, a killer.

"In this line of work we're all alone," he returned, setting off toward the inviting shadow of the hotel entrance.

"True," Ortega said, falling into step beside him. "Which makes the moments of togetherness all the sweeter, eh, gatito?"

He was definitely teasing Gabriel now, and Gabriel muttered, "I need a drink," pushing his hair off his face as he walked away. "And stop calling me that," he added automatically, knowing it was useless. For whatever reason, Ortega seemed to get a kick out of that stupid nickname. In fact, he was smiling that enigmatic smile as they walked through the courtyard to the huge archway into the hotel.

Two armed men stepped into their path, blocking the entrance into the hotel.

"Jesus," Gabriel said. "What *is* it with this hellhole?"

Ortega murmured something he didn't catch.

Casually cradling a submachine gun in his arms, one of the men, his stubbled face streaked in sweat, spoke to Ortega after a quick, dismissing glance in Gabriel's direction.

"Excuse me, *señor*, but there is a fee for parking your car. One you must pay before entering the hotel."

"But as you can see, my friend, we have no car," Ortega replied kindly, as though spelling things out for a child.

Gabriel sighed and put his hand out for Ortega's briefcase. Ortega handed the briefcase over and unbuttoned his suit jacket. He stood there perfectly poised, smiling faintly, vaguely reminding Gabriel of an old-fashioned gunslinger.

The men blocking their way stiffened, not missing the significance of Ortega's confident stance. Gabriel had to bite back misplaced amusement. It had only been a half-serious attempt anyway. These fools could have hardly failed to notice their marks had been dropped off by Lieutenant Ferreño. They were just trying it on in the hope that he and Ortega were soft targets, civilian businessmen. But they had caught a shark in their net when they accosted Ortega, and it tickled Gabriel to watch this go down.

The man blustered, "But you might need a car, *señor*. The fee lessens the time you might have to wait for one. You never know when you will need to leave quickly from a place, *si?*"

"*Si,*" Gabriel drawled. "I've wanted to leave this place ever since we arrived."

Ortega's mouth quirked. The men bristled, turning dark hostile gazes on Gabriel, who gazed stonily back.

"Perhaps that could be arranged, *gringo*," blustered the first man, with a look at his companion. "For no additional fee!"

That *no additional fee,* quoted here and now in that thick accent, struck Gabriel funny, and he laughed.

The man's face reddened, and he lunged forward. Gabriel moved to meet him, and was incensed to find Ortega between him and the thug. Ortega made some quick, vicious move Gabriel couldn't see and the other man staggered back, eyes wide in his face.

Ortega ignored Gabriel's furious look. "Listen, *amigo*. Your mistake is understandable, but we are guests of Chief Piñero. I would regret to tell him that all was not as promised. I think his disappointment would be…considerable."

The man's beady eyes blinked rapidly.

Pissed off to find himself still blocked my Ortega's broad shoulder, Gabriel said, "I think we should just shoot Señor Let's-Make-a-Deal and save Chief Piñero some room at *his* hotel."

"You see? My young friend is not used to local custom," Ortega said, and Gabriel realized he was trying not to laugh. It calmed his own anger.

"Maybe I was mistaken on the parking fee, *señor.*" The man gave a nervous, dry laugh. "Captain Piñero will no doubt have made all the arrangements for your stay."

"No doubt," Gabriel said — and the dark eyes flickered his way furiously.

"It is an easy mistake to make," Ortega assured the two men gravely.

Stepping out of their way, the man said to Gabriel, "I will remember you, *señor.*"

"Looking forward to it," Gabriel returned.

"You make enemies when you grind a man's pride in the dust," Ortega observed, opening his suitcase.

The hotel rooms were a pleasant surprise — large and lavishly appointed with heavy old furniture that would probably have fetched as much in some pricey Beverly Hills boutique as the heroin they were there to buy.

The adjoining rooms had balconies that looked out over the quaint town square with its stone fountain and flowering shrubs. Lush, green mountains could be seen just beyond the tiled roofs. The music from the fountains below soothed and lessened the heat of the late afternoon.

"Ego," Gabriel said dismissively. After a quick inspection of his own nearly identical room, he had joined Ortega to go over their plans for the evening.

Dropping down on the white chenille bedspread, he watched Ortega methodically unpack his few belongings and place them neatly into the large cupboard. He found himself mesmerized by the sight of Ortega's big hands smoothing the fabrics of his clothing as he hung shirts on hangers, fingering collars and cuffs.

"The two are linked, yes." Ortega's dark gaze held Gabriel's solemnly for a moment. "Just because a man is a fool and a bully doesn't mean he isn't dangerous."

Gabriel's lip curled. "Come on, Ortega. You don't think those two oafs are a significant threat." He deliberately stared at the full-length cheval mirror, taking in his own scowling reflection. Watching Ortega's hands was getting him hard. Just that.

He crossed his right ankle over his left knee, blocking Ortega's view of his crotch — not that Ortega seemed to be paying him any particular attention except to lecture him on bad guy etiquette.

"It is easier to make friends than deal with enemies," Ortega said.

"Oh yeah? Is that another Spanish saying?" It was the first time Gabriel had referred even obliquely to the night at Club Madrone. He wasn't sure why he brought it up now. It wasn't a good idea.

Ortega glanced at him once, an intense, long stare that made a shiver run up Gabriel's spine, and then Ortega was back to unpacking as if nothing had happened.

Gabriel watched him remove a shaving kit from his suitcase and place it on the bedside stand. The community bathroom was down the hall. They'd share it with anyone else staying on this level of the hotel.

"If I'm not worried, why should you be?"

"We are here to find contacts, establish connections."

"Make friends and influence people," Gabriel mocked.

Ortega threw open the flimsy doors to the balcony. The last of the day's sunshine was still startlingly bright after the cool gloom of the room. When the sun went down the balmy evening air would chase the remaining staleness from the room. And the stars at night would be seen clearly from the bed.

Gabriel watched Ortega in the long mirror. One large, well-shaped hand was unconsciously caressing the butt of the holstered Glock. "Ignorance is courageous," he said almost absently.

"Hey, it wouldn't do either Botelli's or Don Sanchez' rep much good if we'd rolled over and let them fuck us."

Ortega smiled faintly, and moved over to the bed. Gabriel had to tilt his head back to look the other man in the eye. The deep V of Ortega's dove gray shirt exposed that silky dark pelt. Gabriel could smell the scent of clean sweat and faded aftershave. Longing stirred within him.

"No," Ortega murmured. "That would not do at all." Slowly he reached out and ran a fingertip up Gabriel's throat, a light, caressing stroke that made the hair on Gabriel's body stand up — and his hair wasn't the only thing coming to life.

He swallowed hard. Of course he needed to say something quick and cutting and move out from under that delicate tracing touch. But the words seemed to have dried in his throat.

Then Ortega's hand dropped to his side. He gave Gabriel a playful wink. "I can think of much better ways to spend our time here."

Gabriel laughed, hoping it didn't sound ragged. He got off the bed. Distance. That's what he needed. Distance to help him sidetrack the want rushing through his veins. "Are we going to be here that long?"

"Long enough," Ortega said.

What the hell were they talking about? Gabriel wasn't sure anymore. He said lightly, "I wouldn't want to cheapen the memory. You know, once you've had perfection —" He was trying to make a joke, offering Ortega the line, hoping he took it and turned the moment into something else — anything else.

"Maybe you have not found the right person." That dark look was hypnotizing, and that black velvet voice was doing things to Gabriel's nerves.

He moved over to the doorway looking onto the balcony, staring determinedly out. "I'm not looking."

"Sometimes these things find us whether we are looking or not." Ortega slipped past him, gently brushing Gabriel's shoulder and arm as he stepped out onto the balcony.

Gabriel laughed, a short acid laugh.

Ortega faced him, leaning back against the iron railing. The setting sun behind him and the shadows of evening threw his profile into classic lines.

"You're very young to be so cynical, Contadino. But then the young are the most cynical."

"You know, you could probably make a fortune writing for the greeting card companies."

Untroubled, Ortega was smiling in that steady, maddening way. Something about the unspoken challenge there drew Gabriel forward. He moved to stand just in front of Ortega, trying to read the other man's expression in the dying light. The private amusement in Ortega's eyes was getting under his skin.

"What, are you telling me you're some big romantic?" he sneered. Except it came out more huskily than he intended.

Ortega shrugged, a tiny knowing gesture that said he understood only too well everything Gabriel was thinking and feeling. The midnight-dark eyes held his own for a long, long moment — and Gabriel realized he was holding his breath, expecting Ortega to kiss him.

He wondered if he would punch the bastard or let his mouth take Gabriel's.

Ortega gently brushed a stray lock of Gabriel's hair behind his ear.

"*Sì*," he said. "Attachments are not good for ones such as ourselves." And he pushed off the balcony railing, starting back inside.

As he passed Gabriel, Gabriel grabbed his hand, and even he wasn't sure what his intention was, but when Ortega's strong lean fingers laced with his own, he didn't fight it, staring at Ortega's strangely austere face. The heat in Ortega's eyes was also in his touch.

But once again it was Ortega who broke the spell.

Releasing Gabriel's fingers, he went through the doorway.

"Come on, Contadino. We need a drink. Possibly several."

Gabriel told himself that he was relieved, but strangely that flood of emotion felt more like disappointment.

The early evening was warm and heavy with moisture. They found a cantina next door to the hotel, with open-air tables under a tile roof. The support posts were rough-hewn tree trunks with baskets of vines and flowers hanging from them. The staff was friendly, and the food turned out to be excellent. Three old men sat at a table by the door, quietly drinking and watching them. Occasionally, a pair of children ran out from the kitchen area, peeking around the door at the new faces in town and then scurrying back.

The food was very good. Spicy pork wrapped in hot, freshly made tortillas. And, though Gabriel hated to admit it, the company was good as well. Ortega seemed to be making an effort to charm. He was warm, friendly, intelligent, and easy to talk with. He might be one of the bad guys, but he was sure as hell a different breed from Botelli and his thugs.

It was confusing, really. The file Gabriel's captain had read him before he'd left Frisco painted a picture of a much different man than the one he was getting to know.

Maybe Ortega had saved Gabriel's ass at the Ruby Blue club because it was the practical thing to do, or maybe he had a certain code, but that didn't explain why he'd intervened with

Sanchez' goon at the mansion, or that subtle display of possessiveness in front of that pig Ferreño. None of it jibed with the ruthless, vicious history O'Brien had recounted to Gabriel.

True, most street reputations were exaggerations and embellishments. Gabriel's own reputation as Giovanni Contadino was almost entirely lies with a few half truths tossed in for credibility. So what part of Ortega's rep was the real thing? There was no question he was a hard man, a cool customer in a fight — no question he didn't back down from confrontation. But there was no hint of the swaggering bully that typified the men around Botelli. Maybe he was just a better breed of villain.

Still puzzling it over, he tuned in to hear Ortega's recount, "Peryera points the Spanish bayonet in the bartender's face —"

Gabriel nearly choked on his tequila. "Spanish bayonet? You mean like the cactus?"

Ortega nodded, dark eyes glinting with laughter. "Exactly like the cactus."

"Those things are *sharp*, man."

"Unlike Peryera," agreed Ortega, and Gabriel struggled not to laugh again.

"So what happened? He demanded all the money in the register?"

Ortega shook his head. "No. He demands a bottle of Dogfish Head beer." He was grinning at Gabriel.

"What the hell is *that*?" Gabriel asked. He was chuckling at the image of this desperate, alcoholic, vegetation-wielding bandit.

"Dogfish Head is a specialty brewery."

It seemed a funny thing for a Mexican gangster to know, but along with the other contradictions, Ortega seemed pretty well educated. Or just well informed. "So what happened?"

"One of the other patrons knocked him out with a barstool."

Gabriel burst out laughing, attracting the gleaming gaze of the elderly men on the patio. Ortega watched him, smiling, and Gabriel realized two things: he'd had too much to drink — and

Ortega still wanted him. It made him giggle. And it made him feel pleasantly warm.

Still holding Ortega's sultry gaze, Gabriel downed his third shot of tequila and bit into the wedge of lime. The tang of the juice chased the bite of the tequila down his throat. Bringing his hand to his mouth, he deliberately, slowly licked the web between thumb and forefinger, then sucked on it to savor the last of the salt he had sprinkled there with the first shot.

Ortega never blinked, taking in every move Gabriel made, and somehow the simple act of drinking was turning into foreplay. The heat flooding Gabriel's body and tingling in his cock had nothing to do with the alcohol.

Ortega, too, shifted in his chair, seeking a more comfortable position.

"How long have you been part of Don Jesus' family?" Gabriel asked.

"About two years."

Two years. Why hadn't that shown up on any of the FBI intelligence Gabriel had read?

"And before that?"

"You've heard of Don Pedro Castellano?"

Gabriel hesitated. Would foot soldier Gio Contadino be aware of one of the patriarchs of the Mexican Mafia — even one who had ended his long career in a spectacular hail of bullets in a rare joint effort of Mexican and American law enforcement? "Sure," he said, and shrugged. "One of the old-timers, right?"

"I was with Don Pedro for three years. I worked my way up through the ranks." He raised his brows as though daring Gabriel to make some comment. "After Don Pedro's death, I offered my services to Don Jesus."

"Yeah, he seems to think the world of you," Gabriel drawled.

"Don Jesus trusts no one," Ortega said flatly. "I've proven my worth, and he treats me accordingly."

"Well, you've got a lot in common," Gabriel said. "You're both men of the world, educated, cultured." He was deliberately laying it on thick, but it was true. Still, Sanchez' sophistication seemed more like a veneer, while Ortega had that certain air, that confidence that Gabriel had often noticed in people born to money and position. He wondered what would turn a man like Ortega to a life of crime — because in his case the usual explanation of stupidity, ignorance, laziness, or lack of opportunity just didn't seem to fit.

Gabriel's own background was blue collar and hard scrabble. He'd worked his ass off to overcome it, faking his way through most social situations by reading men's magazines and watching TV. But he wouldn't fool anyone who really came from a privileged background. But then, he didn't want to. Gio Contadino wasn't supposed to be anything but a street-smart punk.

Ortega's dark eyes held his for a long moment. He gave a slight shrug. "Yes," he said. "We have things in common." He raised his glass. "Here's to having things in common." He tossed back the last of his tequila. He was drinking much more slowly than Gabriel, but that last move had something defiant in it.

Gabriel studied the older man curiously, surprised when Ortega rose suddenly.

"We should move inside before it is dark," Ortega said, putting a generous handful of bills on the table. Gabriel grabbed the open bottle of tequila they had been drinking from, gathering up the salt shaker and uncut limes from the bowl on the table. The sun would be setting soon. Ortega was right. It would be best to be indoors in strange territory once night descended, but he teased him anyway. "Are you afraid of the dark?"

"We've not made many friends here," Ortega remarked. He took in Gabriel's armload with resignation. "You like to drink, Contadino."

"So what? Don't you?"

"Oh, yes."

"What else are we going to do here?" He asked it challengingly as they went inside, and was irked when Ortega didn't pick up on it. The other man had paused to sample a grape from the platter of fruit on the bar. He looked thoughtful.

"Not ripe yet?" Gabriel asked.

He expected some sexy double entendre, but Ortega didn't answer, and Gabriel couldn't read his expression as they left the cantina and walked toward the hotel.

He asked abruptly, "You have family?"

"*Sí.*" Ortega glanced at Gabriel. "I do not see them, but Spanish families are very close-knit no matter how far outside the circle you choose to live your life."

"Is their problem with you being gay or you being connected?"

Ortega said, "I choose to live the life I desire. It is not the one my family would have me live."

"No kidding."

Ortega shot him a curious look. "You said your mother understood you. Do you mean she knew you were gay or you were…connected?"

"She knew everything she needed to know," Gabriel answered.

"And you have no other family?"

Gabriel couldn't see why Ortega was so interested in his family life or lack thereof, but he said, "Keeps it nice and simple. It's just me and the job. That's all I have to worry about. Making my employer happy. When this job is done, I'll move on to the next one." He added wryly, "Assuming *your* employer lets me live that long."

Ortega didn't comment on that. "It is a young man's dream. No one to question or bemoan his choice of lifestyle." He spoke in that gently teasing tone he occasionally used.

Gabriel's laugh was short. "Yeah. I guess the closest thing I have to family now is an old knee-breaker by the name of Micky Collins. Strictly small time." He smiled faintly at the memories. "He was always nagging me to stick to the straight and narrow. But I haven't seen him in years. He's probably living in the bottom of a bottle by now."

"Ah." Ortega asked, "What of your own father?"

Gabriel made a disgusted sound. "Ran out on my mom when she found out she was going to have a baby. And my

stepfather — I used to *wish* he'd run out too. What an A-hole."
He clamped his mouth shut. He wasn't about to share those
memories. He'd already talked too much, his tongue loosened
not by the drink and tiredness so much as this man's
unexpectedly easy companionship.

Any answer Ortega might have made was forestalled as down
the street a black SUV turned the corner and glided silently
toward them — followed by two more vehicles.

"Just when it looked like I might finally get to turn in early
with a good book," Gabriel drawled.

Ortega said quietly, "Let me handle this. *¿Comprender?*"

"Don't I always?"

Ortega did not respond as the lead car stopped a few feet
from him. Doors flew open and several armed men jumped
down from the vehicles, but no one made a threatening move.

Lieutenant Ferreño squeezed himself out of the backseat.
His face mirrored their own lack of pleasure. Not that Gabriel
or Ortega wasted much time studying him, as a small, trim man
with skin as dusky as walnuts, black sunglasses, and an old
fashioned handlebar mustache that reminded Gabriel vaguely of
cartoons he'd seen as a kid, climbed out of the front passenger
seat of the SUV. Even in his casual dress uniform with its open
neck and short sleeves, the man looked crisp and formal, the
image of control and discipline — an impression reinforced by
the fact that he wore glossy black boots and carried one of
those silver-tipped equestrian whips.

Definitely eccentric, although something about him reminded
Gabriel a bit of Don Jesus. It was hard to pinpoint what it was
exactly. A certain energy? Restrained tension? Or just good old-
fashioned psycho vibe?

Ortega's demeanor subtly changed, became…deferential.
"Chief Piñero, it is an honor to meet at last. I am Miguel
Ortega, the lieutenant of Don Jesus Sanchez."

Piñero studied him. It should have been comical — the black
sunglasses were a ridiculous affectation in the failing light —
but instead there was something ominous in the still, sightless
gaze. The shades turned to Gabriel.

Ortega said, "My associate, Giovanni Contadino. He represents Ricco Botelli's interests."

"Who is this Botelli?" Ferreño asked insolently. Clearly they were not forgiven for the afternoon's confrontation.

"Botelli controls our West Coast distribution network," Ortega said matter-of-factly, and then he smiled. "And he is the brother of Don Jesus' lovely fiancée."

"*Ah.*" Piñero said. "*La Familia.*"

Ortega, still oozing charm and affability, said, "*Sí.* Your reputation demanded that both houses honor you with their presence, Captain."

Piñero smiled, his teeth small and white and perfect beneath the perfectly trimmed mustache. "So?" Slowly, he removed his glasses and held out his hand.

Ortega shook hands, still smiling, still relaxed, confident, and yet respectful. Even Gabriel had to admit it was well done. He began to see how Ortega had climbed so swiftly through the ranks: competence, ruthlessness, and charm. It was an unbeatable combination.

Piñero's eyes were small and black, like shoe-button eyes or the eyes on a stuffed toy. They studied Ortega with keen attention and then moved on to Gabriel. Piñero nodded once, and let one corner of his mouth twist into something Gabriel thought might be a condescending smile.

Whatever. Gabriel resisted the urge to roll his eyes. This macho shit was bad enough at home. Here in the old country every action and phrase seemed weighted. Personally, he thought he'd go nuts if he had to spend his professional life in macho posturing — never mind all the class war bullshit.

"That was quite a welcome party you threw for us, Captain Piñero," he remarked. "Fireworks and lead party favors all around."

Ortega shot him a warning look, eyes narrowed, mouth straight-lipped. Gabriel raised one shoulder. Okay, he could keep his trap shut, but it seemed nuts not to call this runt's bluff.

But Piñero laughed. "First impressions, *sí*? They can be most misleading. This is what I tell Tito."

Ferreño glowered at them. Piñero laughed again. "*Señors!* Let us conduct our business indoors like gentlemen." He beckoned with his little whip toward the cantina, and his uniformed men darted past, securing the premises.

Ortega and Gabriel followed Piñero back across the dusty road, Ferreño at their heels wheezing like a fat, asthmatic dog.

They went inside the cantina and found the patio abruptly, conspicuously, empty. Piñero's men arranged themselves along the raw wood posts. Piñero took a chair at a small table, Ferreño positioned himself behind his captain's chair. Gabriel wondered if he was supposed to stand at attention behind Ortega. If so, there was about to be a breach of protocol.

Ortega pulled a chair out, wood scraping the stone floor as Piñero lit a cigarette and blew out a stream of blue smoke. Gabriel sat down and followed suit, reaching into his pocket and fishing out a pack of cigarettes. He selected one, and cupped his hands around it as he lit up. He glanced at Ortega who was looking at him disapprovingly, and he nearly laughed. Ortega certainly had some weird hang-ups for a crook.

The woman who had served them earlier appeared on the patio with a tray of local hors d'oeuvres and a bottle of wine. Her hands were not quite steady as she set down a platter laden with white fish seviche with habañero chilies, potatoes with chorizo, and achiote-marinated pork wrapped in banana leaves.

She poured the wine, which Piñero sampled. Languidly, he waved her off, and she went gladly, avoiding meeting the bold gazes of the uniformed men ranged around her patio.

Piñero handed the wine glasses around, smiling affably.

"I admit I was…dismayed to hear talk of Nuevo Leon," he remarked. "This is most unnecessary between family."

What the hell was Nuevo Leon? Gabriel wondered. Ortega had mentioned it earlier in the standoff with Ferreño. It sounded vaguely familiar, but he couldn't quite place the reference. He glanced at Ferreño, who was bristling at the reminder.

"Threats!" Ferreño spat.

Piñero made another of those languid gestures. "One assumes not."

Ortega smiled that easy, meaningless smile and helped himself to the white fish seviche. Suddenly Piñero chuckled, a deep, unexpected sound.

"Well, then let us get down to business."

Gabriel sipped his vine. He didn't care much for wine, but this wasn't too bad. He watched Ortega sampling the wine. The older man raised his eyebrows in surprise, so perhaps it was actually a good vintage.

Ortega and Piñero talked and drank. Gabriel drank and smoked and listened. He might have been invisible for all the attention the other two men paid to him, but that was exactly as he would have wished.

"You may tell Don Sanchez and Señor Botelli we are in business," Piñero said graciously after the hors d'oeuvres had been eaten and another bottle of wine drunk. "Terms accepted as discussed."

"Forty thousand per kilo," Ortega agreed. "Ninety percent pure cocaine?"

"*Sí.* Fifty kilos to start, as Don Jesus requested."

That caught Gabriel's attention. *Ninety percent pure?* Even uncut that would be a street value of thirty-five million. Cut…wars could be fought and won on a budget of that size. He asked curiously, "You don't want a bigger cut of the profits?"

Piñero and Ortega both laughed. Even Ferreño seemed to find that funny.

"Whose side are you on?" Ortega inquired, clearly amused, and Gabriel flushed hotly.

It was Piñero who explained, "In Mexico, forty dollars is like four hundred, Señor Contadino. Cut it as much as your customers will tolerate. The more you profit, the more merchandise you will want from me. It's a good cycle, yes?"

"*Sí.* A very good cycle, Chief Piñero," Ortega said.

Piñero added blandly, "And, after all, it is Don Sanchez and Señor Botelli with the distribution network and channels. The finest product in the world does me no good if I cannot move it safely and securely."

"Very true," Ortega said. "I will let Don Sanchez know of your cooperation and" — he glanced briefly at Gabriel — "hospitality."

Gabriel rose, smiling politely at Piñero and Ferreño, who was still eying him like he should have come wrapped in banana leaves.

The leave-taking rituals dealt with, he scooped up his bottle of tequila and bowl of limes once more, ignoring the amused smirks as he preceded Ortega off the patio and into the street.

They returned to the hotel, not speaking, but Gabriel could tell Ortega was pleased.

Behind them the sound of car doors and low engines broke the quiet. He went through the hotel archway, Ortega's footsteps slow and deliberate behind him.

"So that's it, huh?" He threw over his shoulder.

"That's it," Ortega said.

In the hotel lobby one of the old men from the cantina approached them with a bucket and several empty glass jars in his hand. He stopped in front of them, scooped a pint jar of thick whitish liquid from the bucket, put an old rusty lid on the jar and handed it to Ortega.

In response to Ortega's elegantly raised eyebrow, the old man said, "*Pulque.*"

Was that Spanish for puke? Gabriel wrinkled his nose, but Ortega smiled.

"Ah, the drink of the Aztec kings. Very potent stuff." He accepted the jar graciously, inspecting the contents and nodding his approval until the old man smiled widely. "*Apasionadamente, sí?*"

The old man nodded. "*Algo que quita la sed. Calor Mexicano.*" He winked and limped back to the table to join his companions, who laughed and gestured, obviously pleased with their generosity — or enjoying having pulled another joke on a gullible tourist. They raised a jar and each took a gulp of the same thick liquid.

"Something that clears the thirst? What did that mean? You're not seriously considering drinking that?" Gabriel inquired, studying the jar. "It looks like glue." Or worse.

"Mexican heat, Contadino. The drink of the Aztec kings and priests."

"Yeah, well you notice what happened to the Aztecs. Are you supposed to eat it with a spoon?"

"You can mix it with nuts or fruit if you like. They used to give it to pregnant and nursing mothers. It is very nutritious."

"Whatever. I think I'll stick to cornflakes," Gabriel said.

"Depending on the fermentation process, its alcoholic content is anywhere from three to eight percent. And it has a flavor you will remember for the rest of your life."

"Now *that* I don't doubt," Gabriel said. "Three to eight percent, huh?"

Ortega's smile was indulgent. "Come, we will enjoy what is left of our last evening in Mexico. Tomorrow will arrive soon enough."

That sounded promising — for all the wrong reasons. Warily, Gabriel followed Ortega up the winding staircase to the hotel's guestrooms on the second floor. The hallway was wide and open, paved in tile.

Gabriel's heart was beating fast. Were they going to —? Was he going to —? As much as he wanted to, this was *such* a bad idea. Even for him. Such a reckless and foolish idea. But, Christ, he wanted it. Wanted Ortega. Just one last time.

Gabriel stopped at the door of his room. He took a deep breath. Ortega went on down the hall.

"I think maybe I'll just have an early night," Gabriel forced himself to say.

Ortega stopped and studied him. A funny smile touched his sensual mouth. He held up the jar of *pulque*.

A reluctant smile tugged at Gabriel's own mouth. "Something tells me that would be a really bad idea," he said.

"Afraid, *gatito*?"

He *was* actually, though probably not the way Ortega thought. "I'll see you in the morning," Gabriel told the older man.

He shifted the bottle and bowl, feeling around for his key, trying not to watch Ortega as the other man unlocked his own door. Vaguely, he was aware that Ortega had opened his door an inch and then paused — he expected to hear another joke as he slipped his key into the lock.

Two things happened. Ortega hit him full on with a flying body tackle that sent both men tumbling down the slick tiled floor — seconds before an explosion ripped through Gabriel's door, the force of denotation throwing both men down the stairs.

CHAPTER EIGHT

Gabriel landed on his back, upside down, head and shoulders supported awkwardly on a wooden step several stairs from the top. He opened his eyes, blinked. Splinters of what had been his hotel room door dusted his face and clothes. He wiped them away cautiously. A broken plank rested on his hips.

His eardrums throbbed painfully. Sounds reached him, muffled and distant as though heard underwater. He twisted his head to see what new danger approached, reaching with difficulty for his shoulder holster with numb fingers.

Dust and powdered plaster drifted around them thickly. Ortega's grime-streaked face popped into view, upside down and blurry. Blood trickled from a cut beside his eye.

"Are you hurt, Contadino? Can you answer me?" His voice had that dull, beneath-the-waves sound to it. "Are you injured?" Sure, strong hands fumbled over his body checking ribs, feeling limbs.

Mostly he felt stunned. Gabriel shoved the big, intrusive hands off. "Oh, never better! What the fuck just happened?"

"Good, still cursing and bitching. You're fine." Ortega expelled a long breath and, to Gabriel's astonishment, leaned forward, pressing his forehead to Gabriel's. "Thank God for that."

"You okay?" Gabriel asked gruffly.

Ortega nodded, drawing back. His brown eyes studied Gabriel's face.

"You're…uh…bleeding," Gabriel said, and pointed beside his own eye.

"So are you," Ortega said. He reached out to brush the corner of Gabriel's mouth with the edge of his thumb. Gabriel's mouth tingled beneath that gentle touch. He raised his brows at the bright red dripping down Ortega's thumb, and reached to the cut beside his mouth.

Gabriel sagged against the stairs, shaken.

"*Señors! Señors!*" The hotel staff was rushing across the lobby below.

Ortega loomed over him again, his upside down mouth tantalizingly close to Gabriel's. Gabriel blinked at him, then tried not to go cross-eyed as Ortega closed the gap. Full lips pressed to Gabriel's forehead, marking the spot where their heads had touched.

For a moment, the memory of that first night with Ortega overwhelmed him — his restrained power, the masculine scent of musk and lime, the warmth of his breath…

Gabriel sucked in a sharp breath and closed his eyes. Those soft lips brushed his left eyelid then his right. Then, Ortega's mouth sealed his in a kiss, and instantly Gabriel ached with need.

Upside down the kiss should have been awkward, instead it was electric. He couldn't help it. He reached out as Ortega's arms closed around him, locking them into this crazy kiss tasting of sweat and the tang of blood and something exotic and distinctly Ortega.

Gabriel wrapped fists in Ortega's shirt, yanking him closer, matching Ortega's hungry passion. The world seemed to spin and tilt, and, gasping for air, Gabriel tore his mouth away.

"Fuck. I don't care," he whispered shakily. "I want you."

Ortega whispered back in a low, unsteady tone that shot straight down Gabriel's spine to his cock, "Tonight is ours, *gatito*. Tonight you are mine."

The tequila hadn't survived the blast, but the thick mason jar of pulque had. Alarmed and suspicious hotel staff rescued it, some limes — and Ortega and Gabriel — from the hallway debris.

Confirmed as neither dead nor seriously harmed, Gabriel and Ortega were presented the keys to two private suites on the other side of the hotel, with assurances — that felt more like warnings — that the police would soon arrive. Gabriel had doubts. He thought the police were responsible for this attempt on their lives. Ortega seemed convinced otherwise, theorizing that the crude device in Gabriel's doorway was the result of Gabriel's earlier efforts in the hotel courtyard to win friends and influence thugs.

They thanked the shaken hotel staff for their concern, pocketing both sets of keys. They accepted the rescued pulque and scattered limes. Shocked murmurs followed them up the opposite staircase.

The first room came with double bed, balcony terrace and private bath. Gabriel switched on the lamp as Ortega closed the door behind them, locked it, and threw both sets of keys onto a nearby dresser.

His eyes met Gabriel's and he grinned a wolfish grin. "There's no aphrodisiac like a near miss with violent death," he said. Gabriel tilted his chin in challenge — barely having time to set the heavy jar of pulque on the nearest table before Ortega grabbed and threw him against the wall. The crucifix hanging over the bed swung silently with the force.

Ortega's lean, hard body pinned Gabriel flat, his left leg wedged between Gabriel's, his muscular thigh hard against Gabriel's swelling cock.

"Your eyes look golden in this light," Ortega muttered, and bent his head to Gabriel's. Ortega's teeth clicked against his. His lips parted to that hard, hot, forceful kiss. Gabriel's lips tingled, gooseflesh breaking out over his scratched, bruised skin. But, despite the way Ortega dominated and controlled the embrace, his lips were silken and sweet, coaxing Gabriel to accept — even welcome — their plundering. Gabriel murmured — he wasn't sure what — as his nostrils filled with the scent of gunpowder and dust mixed with sweat and male arousal. Oh God, he loved that smell. There was nothing else like it.

He arched into the large hands roaming his body, wincing when Ortega yanked his hair, angling his head so Ortega could deepen the kiss. Gabriel thrust his hips against the powerful body imprisoning his own and, in response, Ortega pressed back, tussling pleasurably for control.

Gabriel's heart thudded happily, loving — needing — every minute.

"What if the cops show up to question us?" he gasped.

"We will not answer the door." Ortega heaved Gabriel higher up the wall.

Gabriel stared down at him through narrowed eyes. "What if they break the door down?"

"We will shoot them dead for disturbing us."

As Gabriel laughed, Ortega recaptured his lips for another blistering kiss. As Ortega's tongue touched his, the sizzle of passion rippled down Gabriel's spine to explode somewhere behind his balls.

He whimpered, limbs weak, cock painfully hard. He gripped Ortega's torn, dirty shirt, twisting and yanking until the battered fabric tore even more. The sound filled the room, uncontrolled and illicit, loud over the hum of the ceiling fan and the crickets outside their window.

The room spun and dimmed, as the weight of Ortega's half-naked chest pressed Gabriel mercilessly to the coarse plaster wall. The hold on his shoulders was fierce; he'd have bruises tomorrow.

That started him laughing. They'd nearly been blown to bits, and he was thinking about the bruises Ortega might leave? He tittered into Ortega's mouth, and the other man drew back.

"You find something funny, Contadino?"

"You're damn right," Gabriel responded. "Don't tell me you don't see the joke is on both of us?"

Ortega's eyes narrowed. "Will you still be laughing when I bend you over the dresser and fuck you until they hear you screaming your pleasure in the streets below?"

Gabriel shivered with horrified delight at the thought. He said gravely, "Well, no, in that case I guess I'd be too busy screaming, right?"

Just for an instant Ortega looked astonished, then his firm mouth curved into a reluctant smile. "You are truly loco, little one. And I am going to take you again and again tonight."

Gabriel swallowed hard. Abruptly he tried to twist away. Ortega slammed his shoulders back against the rough plaster. Gabriel doubted he could break free from Ortega if he needed to escape for real. The thought was exciting — and terrifying.

"Let me go," he ordered shakily.

Ortega shook his head with finality, and Gabriel gazed helplessly into those smoldering eyes, that gaze that knew far too much about him and his secret desires.

"Damn you," he whispered. He pounded the back of his head on the wall in a frustrated wish to clear it, but a large hand and a firm grip on his jaw stilled the action.

"No," Ortega ordered.

His cock rubbed against Ortega's hip, and the sudden, added stimulation sent a jolt of electricity straight to his asshole. Another one of those helpless mewling sounds tore out of his throat.

"Oh, *God…*"

Ortega stared at him, his gaze searching Gabriel's face, traveling unhurriedly from the disordered hair, his eyes, his nose, then the quivering curve of his mouth. Gabriel felt that dark stare cut straight to his soul. Expose him layer by layer. See right to the heart of him.

"What the hell do you *want?*" The desperation leaching his voice surprised him.

The light of lust in Ortega's eye went from sultry to serious. "Not so much. One night. Now. This moment."

Gabriel raised his eyes to meet Ortega's and whispered, "That's it?"

"That's all." There was something bleak in those black-velvet eyes. "Neither of us can afford complications in our lives."

"You stop now, I'll shoot you myself," Gabriel warned. His hand still gripping Ortega's torn shirt, he wrenched the other man toward him. The shirt tore further, revealing a bronze and muscular chest before Ortega fell against him.

Ortega snorted, pulling back. They wrestled for a moment before Ortega pinned Gabriel, leaning in to murmur. "Shower first, eh? You smell like…cordite. Or is that brimstone, *pequeño diablo?*" His fingertip swiped a sooty streak from Gabriel's jaw, offered in illustration. "Granted, on you, hellfire is sexy."

"You're awfully fussy for a quick fuck," Gabriel retorted.

"I want to taste *you*, not plaster dust and wooden splinters." Ortega raised an elegant eyebrow. "Besides, this will not be a quick fuck. I intend to make this night last."

Gabriel nipped the smudged finger wagging teasingly before him. Ortega chuckled, examining his fingertip. "My kitten feels his fangs."

"I feel *something*," Gabriel said. "And I want to feel something *more* before I'm an old man."

"We will try not to rob you of too many minutes," Ortega said. He pulled Gabriel in for another quick kiss then turned him toward the bathroom. "I will not even insist that you wash behind your ears." He leaned in, his hot, wet tongue licking roughly behind Gabriel's ear.

Gabriel moaned, and Ortega laughed, giving him a push toward the bath.

Gabriel leaned into the tile wall, feeling the gritty face of the mortar on his chest, under his palms, against his forehead. A tepid drizzle gave way to a hot blast of rain. Eyes closed, neck arched, head falling back, he let rivulets of water carry the dust and grime and bits of plaster from his skin and hair.

"You have a cut…just…here." Ortega's mouth pressed against Gabriel's shoulder.

Gabriel flinched, straightened, fumbled for the bar of cheap soap, briskly rubbed it across his chest and shoulder, dislodging Ortega's lapping mouth.

Ortega made him nervous and edgy in ways explosions and death threats couldn't. Not because he was a ruthless, murderous dope dealer, but because he was also a genteel, educated man, an experienced lover — who was courting Gabriel, courting him in a way no one ever had. It was alarming. And seductive.

Gently powerful hands massaged Gabriel's neck, easing cruel knots of tension from tight muscles. Gabriel sucked in a sharp breath. It hurt and it felt like heaven. The massaging grip traveled into his wet hair, steely fingers working magic, soothing away banked tension.

Gabriel couldn't wrap his mind around it. Ortega didn't need to court Gabriel. They were going to fuck. He had to know that.

"You're tensing up again," Ortega commented, fingers digging into Gabriel's muscles.

The scent of soap filled Gabriel's lungs and a cascade of silky suds flowed down his shoulders and back. Slick lather and strong hands, *large hands*, rubbing, kneading, working warm water and suds into chilled flesh. So mesmerized by the feel of those hands, it took a moment to realize what the sexy bastard was doing — *washing Gabriel's hair*!

Gabriel had occasionally showered with a lover, but no one had ever tried this. Cherishing didn't have a place in Gabriel's sexual encounters. He'd never missed it, never wanted it — until now. Instead…instead he was moaning and pushing into Ortega's grip. And Ortega was murmuring sweet Spanish nothings into his ear — no mockery, no teasing, just unbearable loving as he guided Gabriel under the showerhead, rinsing soap from his hair, scrupulously keeping it from spilling into Gabriel's eyes.

"Fuck. We're wasting time." He pushed his ass into Ortega's groin, the thick hard length of the man's cock sliding over his cheeks in a teasing pass before withdrawing.

"Time with you is never a waste, *gatito*," Ortega assured him, and Gabriel could hear that now, Ortega *was* teasing him.

He was tired of being laughed at. Maybe Ortega wouldn't think it funny sitting in a federal prison. But, Gabriel didn't want to think about Ortega with those animals.

Ortega's soapy hands explored Gabriel's chest, suds running in bubbly streams down his torso. Ortega's hands followed the cloudy paths, hot, heavy, and exciting, leaving a physical trail of heat so intense it created gooseflesh on Gabriel's skin. One big hand played with the suds caught at his groin, washing, rubbing, part cleansing ritual, part foreplay. Gabriel concentrated on the pull and tug, the delicious rhythm up and down his jutting cock. Ortega's grip grew firm, almost rough

Surrendering to the pleasure, Gabriel's hips started a frantic, jerking dance, in contrast to Ortega's controlled, measured stroking.

One muscular arm confined him around the shoulders and chest while the other gripped his hip hard enough to leave fingerprints. Fingers stroking his skin, teasing over the vulnerable hollow of his low back, shimming the crack of his ass and sliding under the curve of his cheeks. It was slow, determined exploration that left Gabriel squirming with anticipation.

Water splashed and sputtered, tickling, teasing, like Ortega's questing fingers. Ortega's one-armed embrace tightened. Gabriel leaned into it with relief, his last resistance draining away with the water. Something uncoiled in Gabriel's chest. Something heavy and strangling slipped loose and fell away. Gabriel realized that he felt...safe. It had been so long, he almost didn't recognize the feeling, almost couldn't put a name to it. *Safe.*

Piñero had tried to kill him. Sanchez wanted him dead. Hell, Botelli wanted to kill him half the time. Even this man would eventually want him dead. But here, tonight, in Miguel Ortega's arms, he was...safe.

A long, thick finger rubbed over the clenched ring of his asshole and slid into him far enough to touch his prostate. Stars burst behind his closed eyelids. He whimpered helplessly, pushing down, trying to drag more of Ortega inside.

"More. Please..." Gabriel wriggled frantically, trying to work his hips in rhythm with Ortega's finger, shamelessly humping into the fist working his cock, trying to get off as quickly as possible.

"You are begging, *gatito*?"

"*Sí*!" Gabriel hissed.

The hand on his cock moved down to cup his balls, knowledgably tugging and kneading, a finger occasionally reaching back to rub over the sensitive strip of flesh behind his sac. The sensation melted Gabriel at the knees, only Ortega's hold keeping him upright. The finger in his opening swirled and tapped over his prostate one last time then moved deeper, rotating in a wide circle that stretched and filled Gabriel as if he was speared on a cock and not a man's single digit.

A second finger joined the first on the next upward thrust. Gabriel couldn't stop the mewling that vibrated from deep within.

Those fingers moving with luscious expertise in his body…he wanted to jam both digits to the hilt, feel them deeper, harder. He wanted to buck and ride Ortega's hand to completion but suddenly Ortega had stopped thrusting, holding his exploring hand still while his other fully grasped Gabriel's leaking prick.

Gabriel groaned and writhed, but Ortega merely tightened his hold, molding Gabriel to his body, immobilizing the smaller man by forcing his groin back into Ortega's exploring hand and powerful thighs.

A coaxing, amused voice spoke into Gabriel's wet hair.

"What?" Gabriel asked fretfully. "What are you saying now?"

"I said you are beautiful and wild and more than a bit crazy." Ortega's breath was hot down Gabriel's wet neck. Ortega nibbled on the edge of his ear and moved down Gabriel's throat and shoulders, licking and nipping in a random pattern of love words and sharp caresses. "Always in such a rush, Contadino. Like the way you drink tequila. Doing shots instead of sipping and savoring. You must learn the pleasure that comes from lingering over fine things, relishing, instead of being satisfied with the buzz of a quick fuck."

"Oh, and I suppose you're going to teach me?"

"I *am* teaching you," Ortega said inarguably.

"Right now I'll take the fuck, thanks." Gabriel squirmed harder, trying to direct the enormous erection pulsing against his ass cheek.

A warm chuckle vibrated seductively against his neck. "Right now, kitten, you'll take what I give you."

Gabriel's retort was lost as Ortega claimed his mouth to kiss him hard and long. The instant Gabriel relaxed into the kiss, Ortega began thrusting his fingers again, a fast hard rhythm that pushed Gabriel to a new high in the first few strokes. It felt so good to be full, to be touched, consumed, filled and possessed.

Gabriel's cock slid through the tight-fisted grip, streaming water lathering the soap in Ortega's palm while friction warmed it until it surpassed the shower's temperature. Steam and the scent of arousal filled his lungs. Anticipation sizzled down his spine, gathering in his balls. The tug and stroke on his cock battled for primacy in his mind against the deep thrust of fingers up his ass.

Moaning, Gabriel bucked, sensations rocketing deep into his groin where they exploded in a rippling climax that made his heart skip a beat and his lungs falter.

He stared down woozily, watching his cream spill over Ortega's big, tanned hand, washed away in the lather, trickling away in milky foam. Dazed, Gabriel imagined it leaving behind his own invisible scent, covertly marking Ortega. It was just a notch on the bedpost thing. He was not claiming Ortega. He wasn't. Really. He couldn't have him. Didn't want him. Except for right now.

"Oh God. Oh God. Oh *Christ…!*"

Gabriel rode his orgasm, waiting for it to crest, strung tight with frenzied tension as it continued racing higher and higher with each of Ortega's deep thrusts as the big man pounded into him. Finally a flick of the fingers inside his palsied channel touched the hard nub of his gland and sparked a firestorm whipping through Gabriel's nervous system.

He cried out, withering in Ortega's restraining arms like a snapped flower. The room swam, his vision dimmed, and his knees buckled — the cold tile rushed up at him. But he found himself held upright, securely cradled in Ortega's comforting embrace, one arm wrapped across his chest, the other wrapped around his waist, his back molded to Ortega's torso. The firm shaft of Ortega's still rigid cock was hot against the small of Gabriel's back.

And he felt it again, that intense feeling of being safe. Physically and emotionally safe.

"Let go," Gabriel muttered. "That was too much. I need some…room." He pushed against the restraining arm, letting Ortega know he was ready to stand on his own two feet again, and the man released him.

"As you wish, *gatito.*" That phrase, the same one Ortega used that first night when they had parted at Club Madrone, made Gabriel tingle — with what, he didn't know. Pleasure? Aggravation?

He couldn't help staring at Ortega's huge, jutting cock. Instinctively he reached out, fascinated by the contrast between his own slighter body and the darker skin and dense curly hair that trailed down Ortega's chest and abdomen. His fingers twitched, anxious to touch the red-brown satiny flesh, to feel the pulsing ropes of veins he could see entwined around that thick, eager shaft.

Ortega captured his wrist, stopping him. Startled, Gabriel finally gazed up into Ortega's handsome, chiseled face, seeing desire and need in the man's eyes. And yet, Ortega's passion, unlike Gabriel's, was tempered with patience.

"Not yet. I prefer to wait." Ortega gave him that knowing, worldly smile that both enticed and irritated Gabriel. "Anticipation has its own rewards."

"If you say so." Gabriel could still feel what it was like impaled on that wide rod of smooth steel wrapped in molten satin. Even after having come, Gabriel was ready for more, his body and sexual appetite never satisfied until he'd been properly, completely claimed and fucked. His asshole clenched at the delectable thought of more from Ortega.

He grinned cheekily, pushing Ortega's hand aside and wrapping his fingers around his dick. "Then let's find a drier spot. I'll see if I can't think of a nice *reward* for you." And he drew Ortega out of the shower and into the bedroom by his ever so patient cock.

CHAPTER NINE

"We will play a game." Sitting crossed legged and naked on the bed beside Gabriel, Ortega tossed a coin in the air and deftly caught it. "It will teach you some much needed patience."

"I thought we were already playing games," Gabriel drawled. Lying on his back, he reached out to stroke a teasing finger down Ortega's cock. "Hey, batter batter."

Tall, Dark and Superior ignored this. Lifting his shielding hand away, Ortega showed Gabriel the backside of the coin. It faced up, glinting in the muted lamplight. "Tails it is. Turn over."

"Why?" Gabriel asked suspiciously. "What did I win?"

"Nothing — yet." Ortega knelt, and before Gabriel had time to react, the bigger man had him in a wrestler's hold. He was planted face down on the mattress. The old bed springs protested loudly — as did Gabriel.

"Hey! What are you…what the fuck —?" He tried to wriggle away, but Ortega held him in place.

He pulled the pillow out from under Gabriel's head and stuffed it under Gabriel's abdomen.

"Watch it!" Gabriel shifted and Ortega seized the advantage, pulling Gabriel's hips higher over the pillow.

His smooth cheek brushed Gabriel's jaw. "Do you trust me, Contadino?"

A light hand ran down his back to a gentle caress at the crease between his cheeks. The teasing touch sent a thrill of alarmed delight scudding down his spine. He forced himself to relax, easing clenched fists in the sheets. "I trust you to fuck me."

Ortega leaned hard, resting his body heavily on Gabriel. Ortega nuzzled Gabriel's neck, languidly lipping the fine sheen of sweat. Gabriel shivered as tiny gusts of breath warmed each freshly tongued patch of skin.

Rising, Ortega packed more pillows beneath Gabriel's hips, raising his ass. It felt vulnerable and slightly embarrassing, and — predictably — it excited Gabriel.

Turning his head, Gabriel watched Ortega fill all three shot glasses to the rim with the milky liquid the old man had dubbed Mexican heat. It was odorless, but Ortega assured him it packed a serious punch.

"It's considered the drink of crude peasants now, but long ago only priests and nobility were permitted to drink *octli*. And the penalty for drunkenness was death."

Gabriel mused that Ortega knew a lot about about alcohol.

Ortega sliced a lime with his boot knife, the fruit's juicy pulp glistening and strangely erotic. Ortega settled on the bed beside Gabriel, his thigh casually pressing into Gabriel's side.

Gabriel twisted his fists tighter into the fabric. Only his desire to prove Ortega wrong about his lack of patience kept him in check.

"Tsk-tsk." A finger tapped the end of his nose.

"Yeah, yeah. Cut the crap and get on with it."

Ortega sighed. "You are always in such a hurry. You will miss your life's important moments."

"I'll take a picture."

Shaking his head, but clearly amused, Ortega lifted one of the three shot glasses. "This is a drinking game called *Espera*."

"*Espera*? It's called Wait? Did you just make this up?"

"Do you care?" Ortega set one full glass, cold and heavy, on Gabriel's back just below his neck, in the hollow between his shoulder blades. Ortega steadied him with a touch.

"These are the rules, Contadino. Listen closely." He placed a second glass in the middle of Gabriel's back, in the lowest hollow of his spine. "The object of the game is to balance three full shot glasses." Ortega ran a teasing finger above the curve of Gabriel's nearer butt cheek — not quite touching, but so close that Gabriel could feel the static electricity of the illusory contact.

He placed the last full glass at the start of Gabriel's ass crease, perched precariously against the swell of his butt. It felt like a blunt finger teasing sensitive skin, the weight of all three objects exaggerated, perversely erotic.

Gabriel fought off a shiver, fearful of dislodging it all, of having Ortega win this damn game. His nipples tightened, and every slight shift of the mattress rubbed the coarse weave of the sheets over their swollen tips. As Ortega moved, disturbing the bed, each zing of sensation hummed in the erect nubs.

"Next, the one lying down is rubbed with lime and sprinkled with salt. We will have to do without the salt tonight."

"You are totally making this up!" Gabriel had a hard time not laughing.

"*Silencio*," Ortega warned. "You nearly tipped the lot over just then."

Gabriel huffed out an exasperated breath, but lay still as Ortega squeezed sliced lime and drizzled the juice down the leanly muscled planes of Gabriel's back.

The juice was warm but the sensation was still startling. "Warn a guy first, bastard!" Gabriel gasped, just managing not to jump.

"If you spill the drinks you lose your turn," Ortega informed him smugly, lightly palming Gabriel's ribs and flanks, polishing him with the tingling juice. It tickled and stung his scratches, and yet felt good.

"Fuck!"

"Not unless you win the game."

"What happens if *you* knock the glasses over?"

"I won't."

"Your skin shines like polished gold," Ortega murmured, smoothing the sticky juice into Gabriel's skin in long sweeping strokes, pressure firm and calming, scent intoxicatingly. His low, accented coaxing sent shivers down Gabriel's spine, but Gabriel stayed motionless.

Ortega chuckled. "Starting at the top, the other player, I in this case, drinks the shots one at a time, but I cannot use my hands until all the shots are gone." He flexed his fingers like a pianist before a tricky recital.

"If you have to drink that slop, either way I win."

Ortega ignored him and laid a hand on his back, holding him motionless.

Gabriel snorted. "Here's an idea. Why don't we skip the hangover and just fuck?" His movement sent a few warm drops of liquid into the crack of his ass. He started, but Ortega's hand on his back held him motionless.

"*Espera!* The only way you win your prize is if you lie very still until the last shot is taken."

"You still haven't told me what that prize is." Face resting against the sheet, Gabriel glared sideways up at Ortega. "If it's a plastic whistle, I'm telling you now —"

Ortega leaned in close, his breath light on Gabriel's skin. Tucking a strand of hair that had fallen across Gabriel's face, he said softly, "If you win, my tongue will follow the trail of glasses like…Cortez exploring his brave new world…" His fingers drew a line down Gabriel's back that ended in a light, teasing exploration of his opening. "Marching across the planes, braving the…humid…tangled…jungles, rappelling down into the…hot…slick…trembling…canyons…hmmm? Where do you think the expedition will lead?"

Gabriel almost lost it. Sweet fucking Jesus. The thought of Ortega's elegant mouth kissing him that way — that tongue —

He moaned.

Ortega chuckled. "*If* you win," he said pointedly. "I do not think you will. You are starting to quiver just with the thought of it. Lie *still*. If you spill another drop, you lose your turn."

"Let's go, Cortez, turn on the *heat*."

Ortega bent over him, but he still nearly gave the game away with a nervous jump as the other man's tongue touched down to lick the sticky juice that had run down the angles of the shoulder blades. He bit his lip, regulated his breathing. Ortega's tongue paused, delicately lapped at a small pool at the base of the first glass.

Holding his breath in anticipation, Gabriel nearly sighed when the weight of the glass disappeared. Angling his head, he watched Ortega down the pulque in one swallow, the shot glass held by only his lips. When he was done, Ortega spit the glass into his hand and set it on the bedside stand.

"One down."

"How was it?"

"Very fine indeed." He licked the last of it from his lips, then winked at Gabriel. "How are you holding up, Contadino? Restless?"

"Nah. Never been in such a comfortable bed. I can really use the rest."

"You can," Ortega agreed gravely. "I have never seen you so still. Always you are restless, in motion, a ball of nervous energy."

"Speaking of balls," Gabriel retorted. It made him uneasy that Ortega watched him so closely — and read him so well. Already the muscles in his legs were tensed, needing to move. Three minutes of lying motionless had him desperate to be up and moving.

The broad, rough tongue returned to his skin, tracing his spine's dips and hollows, tracking from the site of the first glass to the wobbling second. The tongue drew a wet circle around the base of the glass and then…disappeared.

Legs nearly vibrating with the effort to keep the glasses from spilling, Gabriel stiffened when the bed dipped slightly. Ortega's body felt scorching. The tang of his clean sweat and soap smell made Gabriel's head swim. His cock jerked, begging for more attention than the chafe of bleached sheets. He felt the wetness beneath his abdomen from his own precum.

A tremor rippled through him when the weight of Ortega's stiff erection thumped suddenly against his thigh. The remaining glasses trembled but didn't spill.

"Careful, Contadino." The cautioning was more amused than threatening.

"*You* be careful," Gabriel retorted hoarsely.

Protracted, agonizingly pleasurable licks bathed the curve of his rib cage, the pressure firm and hot. Gabriel groaned and reached blindly for the bars of the wooden headboard, willing twitching muscles to relax. He'd just managed to lessen the tension in his shoulders as Ortega began a new assault on his skin, licking dried juice from the underside of Gabriel's butt cheeks.

Every long wet lick left a trail of heated flesh, the sticky sweet dissolving against Ortega's tongue. The mattress dipped beneath Ortega's hands and his tongue darted into the deep crease between the taut mounds.

Gabriel inhaled sharply, but Ortega didn't relent, delving deeper into the warm valley. Gabriel's breathing turned ragged.

"Christ, *wait*." The cry was urgent, strained. He *had* to move, either to pull away or to move backward onto the stiff, questing probe. His nipples throbbed and his cock pulsed with need that was increasingly painful. He trembled with the effort to stay still, somehow restraining himself. "Wait!"

Ortega chuckled softly. One more slick, teasing swipe of his tongue…so close, so maddeningly close to Gabriel's hot eager little hole — then Ortega relented.

"Very good, Contadino. Your will is stronger than I thought." Abruptly the weight of the second glass disappeared.

Gabriel stole a glance as Ortega downed the milky liquid, holding the glass with only his lips, their full lines pulled taut around the mouth of the small vessel. This would be what Ortega looked like sucking cock. Ortega's tongue darted out, licking the last of the white liquid from the bottom of the glass. Gabriel had to close his eyes, imagining only too well what it would feel like to have that slick, pink muscle probing, tasting, tormenting his body.

Suddenly that seductive sun-satin voice was murmuring against his ear, offering a litany of blush-inducing compliments. Gabriel wanted to believe them, but he was convinced that Ortega was mocking him to win this crazy game.

"From the moment I saw you, I knew how it would be between us. The moment your eyes met mine, I felt it, and you felt it too. Once could never be enough with one such as you…" On and on the absurdly seductive words went.

He was rock hard, his cock painful and leaking, and inside his brain he was begging Ortega for more — more sweet words, more caresses.

"Yeah, yeah. That's what they all say," Gabriel choked out. "Come on, Ortega. Get on with it."

There was sharp, astonished silence, and Ortega chuckled drily, withdrawing. "So young and so jaded."

He repositioned himself on his knees behind Gabriel, and the thick weight of his long cock nudged the exposed strip of flesh just above Gabriel's balls. Gabriel's ass seized in a kind of panicked lust.

He felt Ortega's breath on his nakedness then the third glass lifted off his back. There was a moment of silence while Ortega drank, and then the glass clattered onto the nightstand, nearly sending Gabriel out of his skin. The glass spun to a standstill, coming to rest against Ortega's pistol.

"You win, Contadino."

Gabriel turned to look and Ortega captured his mouth in a rough kiss. Hot and primal, it stole breath from his lungs. His prick jumped and his sac pulled up as a big hand locked in his hair, dragging his head back. Then abruptly the kiss was over.

"Time to reward your patience."

A grunt escaped Gabriel as Ortega covered his body with the long, muscular length of his own. The big man's satiny hard cock rested tantalizingly in the valley of Gabriel's ass.

Ortega shifted, moving down Gabriel's body, and Gabriel stilled as Ortega tasted him, licking and biting every square inch of Gabriel's skin between neck and ass. He shivered beneath the skillful assault.

When Ortega's big hands finally spread his cheeks, the headboard creaked beneath Gabriel's white-knuckled grip.

The warm, wet touch at his opening zapped him with a delighted sensory overload ending somewhere at the base of his skull. He groaned, clenching his ass tight, afraid anything more than this precise and subtle touch would set off his climax, ending the pleasure prematurely, wasting all of Gabriel's efforts to remain still.

"Wait. Jesus, wait." It came out as a soft, embarrassed plea. To his relief, the skillful, slippery exploration halted. Gabriel took a couple of deep breaths, struggling to regain control. A feather light kiss grazed the small of his back.

"All right, *gatito?*" And the indulgent tenderness of that was nearly Gabriel's undoing.

Gabriel moaned. No lover had ever spent this kind of time on him learning his body, testing his limits, finding new ways to make him shudder with desire. A lover who brought passion as well as lust to bed, turning sex into almost unbearable intimacy.

But then he had never had a real lover before — only sex partners.

Ortega's big hands rubbed and kneaded Gabriel's ass cheeks, slowly, deliberately. Then Ortega spread them wide like an oyster shell, and Gabriel's pearl was the vulnerable pink core of his body cooled by the air wafting from the ceiling fan overhead. He started to shake…waiting for what he craved…and then the press of wet heat pushed against the ring of muscle guarding his opening. Invasion of the sweetest kind.

"Oh Christ. Oh yes, *please*. Yes…"

Slick and stiff, Ortega's tongue slid into his channel then darted out. In and out, stiff and slick, hot and wet, again and again Ortega fucked him with his tongue.

Gabriel squirmed in the tangled bedding, whimpering, but that wonderful, terrible kiss followed him remorselessly. Gabriel heard the soft animal noises he made and they excited him more, the loss of his control — the surrender to this bigger, stronger man — making him wild.

"Touch your nipples," Ortega ordered throatily. "Pinch them."

Heat flooded Gabriel's face. He shoved his hands beneath his chest, plucking at his nipples, already swollen and tingling. It was embarrassing and exciting to touch himself like that. He twisted and tugged the tiny nubs, horrified and titillated that he wished it was Ortega's hands on him.

He pinched himself in time to Ortega's tongued mini-thrusts, catching the sensitive nubs between his finger and thumbnail and pressing down hard. It hurt, and it felt wonderful.

Ortega ran his tongue around the tender opening of Gabriel's anus, his mouth trailing down, moistening the rosebud wrinkles, teasing lower still to work the fleshy strip between Gabriel's hole and his sac.

Gabriel stilled his hands, closed his eyes at the scrape of light beard, like fine-gauge sandpaper, against his sensitive flesh.

"Beautiful…so very beautiful. Delicious. *Amante muy joven.*" Ortega's fingers smoothed his cheeks, laying him wide.

Gabriel buried his face in the linens, trying to block the endearments —then straining to hear Ortega's husky, accented words.

The urgent buzz at the base of his cock warning that orgasm was approaching fast was almost a relief. He needed physical release, but even more he needed this alarming assault on his mind and emotions to cease.

He pushed back, urging Ortega to go still deeper, hoarsely pleading in half coherent sentences.

There was a sudden shift in Ortega's rhythm, the firm strokes inside and delicious pressure abruptly turning into broad swipes over the outside ring of muscle. Gabriel grunted and cried out, the buildup of tension easing off, his orgasm dialed back from boiling over to simmering again. He pounded his fist on the bed and swore in every language he knew.

Suddenly the world shifted and he was lying on his back. Ortega loomed over him, smug and amused. Gabriel would have knocked the expression off his face if Ortega hadn't pinned his fists over his head.

"Uh-uh, Contadino. Your prize was a rimming, not a climax. For that you have to...*espera.*" Ortega leaned in and captured Gabriel's mouth, swallowing the string of filthy curses.

The kiss demanded submission. Gabriel fought — averting his face, arching his back, pushing against Ortega's weight and greater strength — even though he knew it was useless.

Ortega controlled the moment until Gabriel's anger subsided along with a portion of his frustrated anatomy. Ortega grinned, his smile very white in his handsome face. "And now it is your turn to try out the local Mexican heat, *si*?"

"How about I just pour it over your head and strike a match, you Spanish prick."

Ortega laughed, moving to allow Gabriel up. Once Gabriel shifted, Ortega stretched out in the newly vacated spot on the bed.

"The goal is for you to set me on fire without the use of actual flame, Contadino. Or are you not up to the challenge?" One eyebrow rose, baiting — and Gabriel's temper went with it.

He said sweetly, "Careful what you wish for, Señor Ortega," and had the satisfaction of seeing Ortega's eyes narrow. He reached for the coin on the nightstand, tossed it, checked and said, "Heads. Your lucky night, hombre."

If possible, Ortega looked even more unbearably self-satisfied.

Pouring the pulque from the jar into the three glasses, Gabriel planted each one with care down Ortega's broad, well-muscled torso, starting with the high point of Ortega's breastbone between two hard, brown pecs. The second glass balanced in the dip of Ortega's flat belly button, and the final glass rested a bit above the patch of dense black hair that surround the big man's majestic cock. His erection threatened its precarious perch.

"Maybe we should just sing happy birthday, blow out your candle, and call it a night?" he suggested.

"Most amusing," Ortega said thickly.

"You ain't seen nothing yet," Gabriel informed him. Gabriel grabbed the unused portion of lime and streaked it lightly over Ortega's skin, grazing his nipples, his mouth curling as the brown tips hardened.

Ortega bit his lip but remained stoic, only his breathing betraying his struggle for control.

Straddling Ortega's body, Gabriel lowered himself to the Spaniard's muscular thighs, his own still hard and unsatisfied cock poking Ortega's. With a tight smile for Ortega's watchful stare, he squeezed the last of the lime, letting the juice run down Ortega's twitching cock. He tossed the spent fruit rind over his shoulder to land in the deep shadows of the room. The shiver running through Ortega vibrated Gabriel's entire body. Although the glasses rippled and a few drops spilled, the glasses did not fall. It seemed even gravity bent to Ortega's will.

Ortega's thick shaft curved gracefully toward his guarded face. Against his will, Gabriel admired that raw masculine beauty. The large head of Ortega's cock was a dusky pink-brown, darker than the hefty length. His slit was long — a secret smile beaded with a single liquid pearl. The hood of the uncircumcised foreskin pulled back beneath the glistening head. Beautiful. Bastard.

Gabriel's empty ass tightened in frustrated memory. Sweat broke out over his skin. The fan whispering overhead barely stirred humid air.

"Look at you," he murmured, mocking Ortega's teasing and sweet talk. "*Usted pavo regordete magnífico!* All plump and basted like a Thanksgiving turkey. Unbe-fucking-lievable! We could title this picture 'What We Did on Our Summer Vacation' and tack it up in the employee lounge. Does Don Sanchez *have* an employee lounge?"

Ortega spluttered. Glasses wobbled and nearly spilled.

Gabriel cooed, "Easy, *mi amigo grande del amor.* You must slow down and smell the pulque. Always in such a hurry! You're going to miss the best moments of life. Of course you'd miss them lying here imitating a drinks tray too, wouldn't you?"

Ortega bit his lip, steadying himself by monumental effort. "You are cheating, Contadino," he scolded.

"*Me?*" Gabriel leaned forward, avoiding the small glass wobbling on Ortega's breastbone, and taking one of Ortega's teats into his mouth, teeth grazing, lips working the puckered flesh.

Ortega groaned from deep within.

Gabriel bit back a sour smile. He let feathery soft ends of his hair tickle the Spaniard's chest. His tongue flicked, teasing the imprisoned nipple. He slid out from under the strong hands laced through his hair attempting to hold him in position against the bronzed, muscular chest.

Moving to Ortega's other nipple, he licked the tip with darts of his tongue, wetting the dusky nub, enjoying the way it blossomed beneath his ministrations. Ortega released a long, low sigh, arching just enough to rub the head of his cock into Gabriel's stomach without disturbing the shots.

"You like that?" Gabriel whispered.

"I do," Ortega said huskily.

Gabriel pulled back and their heavy cocks swung against each other, thumping weight against weight. A shock of lust burned through him. His balls ached. His entire body ached with indescribable need.

Enough's enough. He straightened, picked up the first glass resting on Ortega's breastbone, and tossed the liquid back. Ortega's eyes widened.

"What…?"

Gabriel picked up the next glass, swallowed its contents as well. It could have been milk or glue for all he tasted. He raised his eyebrows in answer to Ortega's wordless astonishment. Ortega didn't say anything else, but Gabriel could see the disappointment lurking in those eyes. He hardened his heart against guilt as he grabbed the last glass and downed the pulque.

Too bad. Gabriel didn't like being played, manipulated, maneuvered. He wanted to be fucked, that's all. He didn't want to play mind games or drinking games or any games at all. He wanted a quick, hard fuck — okay, maybe not a quick fuck — but he sure didn't want to spend the night on foreplay, talking and caressing each other.

He licked his lips. That Aztec brew had a weird flavor — like you'd expect a magical potion to taste. "Game, set, and match," he said crisply. "You win. Congratulations. I lose. So fuck me."

For a moment Ortega lay motionless, studying him. "Were you perhaps starting to enjoy yourself?" he asked softly. "Is that why you threw the game?"

"Yeah, it was a blast," Gabriel replied flatly. "We've wasted enough time tonight. Let's get down to it." He shifted, positioned Ortega's cock at his opening and sank down, taking half the long, thick shaft in one move. "Save the pillow talk. Fuck me."

He meant to speak curtly, but the words squeezed out strained, choked — part pain and part relief as Ortega filled his hollowness at last.

Uncharacteristically silent, Ortega pulled his knees up, altering the angle of his cock, allowing Gabriel more leverage, enabling his slow, concentrated slide down the bigger man's thick rigidity. Gabriel hissed at the blisteringly hot sensation of flesh gripping flesh.

Painful. Very.

But this was what he wanted — needed — right now.

Eyes narrowed, watching Gabriel's expression, Ortega bucked up, a hard, efficient move. Gabriel slammed his ass down to meet it, shoving all of Ortega's length inside, momentarily consuming him with bright, burning pain. But he welcomed it, welcomed that sensation of fullness, of being stuffed, the feeling that he'd longed for since that night at Club Madrone. The painful possession chased away emptiness, filled him instead with overwhelming physical sensation, magnifying his senses.

Ortega began to thrust into him in a steady rocking motion, and Gabriel paced himself to match that smooth, powerful rhythm.

The room dimmed then grew more intense, every piece of furniture, every article becoming more distinct. The soft whirring beat of the ceiling fan, the creak of the headboard and springs, the low, paced rhythm of both his and Ortega's labored breathing. Gabriel heard the sweat trickling off his body splashing on Ortega's sculpted chest.

Coarse black hair dusting Ortega's groin tickled Gabriel's balls, crinkled beneath his sensitive perineum.

Rocking into Ortega's thrusts, Gabriel controlled the action, timing it to take longer and longer strokes, drawing Ortega's cock head out to the tight ring of muscle then pushing back down to spear himself on the wide shaft. His long-denied climax sparked to life again, expanding with lightning speed. Ortega gave his ass the pounding he wanted, banging into him with steady, fierce rhythm.

"Yes. Christ, yes!" Gabriel closed his eyes to shut out Ortega's dark, far too knowing gaze.

Strong hands grabbed his grinding hips in a bruising hold, throwing off his rhythm and breaking his momentum. Shuddering, Gabriel lost balance and pitched forward. He struggled to brace himself, placing hands on the bed.

The position shifted the thick cock inside of him and Gabriel gasped at the nudge against his prostate. A hand gripped his ass — a bruising touch in tender flesh. Ortega's other hand locked in Gabriel's hair, and the snap of pain in his scalp made him furious — anger colliding with lust and desperation. He slammed back into Ortega, and Ortega's breath caught raggedly.

Pushing back, Gabriel's jerky movements provided counterpoint to the other man's beat. He yelped as Ortega again hit the sensitive nub buried inside his channel.

Gabriel's climax washed over him with a deeply satisfying burn at his opening, the ring of nerves stretched and packed to their limit by Ortega's thick, long cock…sensation skittering up as Ortega's cock nudged his gland and lush feeling swept over his balls. His sac tightened and drew up, the root of his own cock…aching, swollen…

His climax crashed over him like lightning hitting an antenna. Sensation raced up his spine to explode in the base of his skull while the other prong of reaction shot down through his cock like a bullet, forcing spurts of cum out — the creamy escape like a release valve to the pressure pounding inside his chest.

Somewhere in the distance he was conscious of Ortega arching up, going rigid as a statue, uttering a desperate cry echoing his own. Wet warmth spread through his ass, flooding him with slickness that eased the passage of Ortega's still pounding cock.

Spent and exhausted, Gabriel didn't object when he was pulled down to settle against Ortega's sweaty chest, his nose buried in the musky curve of Ortega's armpit. He had a thousand complaints but they were too brittle to make the journey from brain to tongue.

Dimly, he heard Ortega murmur, "This round goes to you, Contadino."

CHAPTER TEN

The low whirr of the ceiling fan was the first thing to edge into Gabriel's awareness. Drowsy with the vestiges of too little rest and too much alcohol, he drifted. Usually his waking was like a curtain yanked to one side, the need to be alert and on guard dragging him to instant attention. But tonight he lay quiet, enjoying the play of shadows and moonlight, the rare sense of warmth and safety.

Through his lashes he saw the gun on the nightstand, outlined in moon glow. It lay next to an overturned shot glass and half a crushed lime. The shot glass and lime he could understand. It wouldn't be the first time he woke to the remnants of a night spent blocking out the loneliness of his undercover life, but the gun...the gun wasn't his.

Memory flooded him. Ortega. Ortega and his Aztec magic potion. The local brew they called Mexican Heat. Not a misnomer. He couldn't remember the last time he'd had such hot, raw, satisfying sex. He wasn't sure he ever had.

He turned his head on the pillow. The silver light from the open balcony showed a pillow indented where a head had rested — and empty sheets.

He was alone.

The disappointment was overwhelming for a moment. Too powerful to analyze. Then reason asserted itself. Ortega wouldn't leave his weapon. Gabriel smoothed his hand across the other side of the mattress, feeling the warmth of the sheets. A body had lain there recently, the coarse cotton still carried body heat.

He lifted his head, wincing at the reminder of how much he'd had to drink a few hours before, and sure enough there was Ortega's tall form standing at the doorway leading onto the balcony. The slats of the wooden shutters threw tiger stripes across his shadowed form.

Gabriel studied him curiously. There seemed something melancholy in the other man's still pose. Ortega seemed so…distant. So alone. It troubled Gabriel — and how stupid was that?

All the same, he'd like Ortega one last time. Despite his body's aches and pains, he already wanted him again. Nothing to do with emotions. Just practicality. Once they left this place, that would have to be the end of it.

Without turning, Ortega said softly, "Awake?" His voice sounded strangely intimate in the darkness of the room.

"Yeah."

When Gabriel didn't say more, Ortega glanced over his shoulder.

Gabriel slid to the edge of the bed and stood. Ignoring Ortega's silent gaze, he walked to the bathroom, leaving its door open as he relieved himself. Absently he ran his hand over his abdomen, fingers grazing sticky patches of dried liquids.

Over the waterfall of sound, he heard Ortega say something. He ignored it. Finishing, he grabbed one of the towels used after their earlier shower. It hung neatly on the rod. Either the maids here cleaned rooms in the middle of the night, or Ortega had a neat streak in him. Gabriel soaked the towel and used it to wash off. The lukewarm water felt good on scratched and tender skin.

He tossed the towel on the floor and stepped out of the bathroom, pausing at the sight of Ortega stretched out on the bed.

Gabriel swallowed hard. In the pure silver light, Ortega looked like a living breathing sculpture. His wavy black hair combed straight back off his forehead, his chiseled jaw propped on one large strong hand, his chest and abdomen sculpted in toned flesh and sinewy muscles. His cock was hard, curving up to lay against one hip, dusky purple and dark brown shades of flesh, the uncircumcised hood up, showing the smooth tip of his cock and the dark slash of the long slit.

"So what month are you supposed to be?" Gabriel finally managed huskily. Lust nearly closed his throat. He felt an emotion unnervingly close to yearning.

Ortega chuckled. His dark, knowing eyes held Gabriel's. "Are you asking me my sign, Contadino? Not very original."

Once again Gabriel had that funny inkling that he *had* somehow let Ortega down last night. He brushed the thought aside.

"I meant you look like you're posing for one of those sexy men's calendars," he said bluntly. He couldn't have explained why, but he wanted to break that easy confident intimate bridge that Ortega had forged between them. "Mr. August, maybe."

Ortega chuckled lazily. "Try November. Scorpio. When were you born?"

Gabriel hesitated, but there was nothing in Giovanni Contadino's false history to contradict this much truth. "May."

"May what?"

Gabriel said shortly, "Why? Planning on buying me a birthday gift?"

"Maybe. What would you like for your birthday?"

Unexpectedly, emotion swamped Gabriel. When was the last time anyone had asked him that? When was the last time anyone had given a damn what he wanted for his birthday — let alone given him a present?

He said, stretching out on the bed, "A night off. A good meal. A good fuck."

"We'll see what can be done about that," Ortega remarked, running a light, possessive hand down his flank. Thoughtfully, he asked, "How old are you again?"

"Old enough for whatever you have in mind." Already Ortega's unique fragrance — that hint of lime and bay tinged with other warm masculine scents — had become familiar and arousing to him.

Ortega stroked him absently, his mind evidently elsewhere — although his body was responding to Gabriel's proximity; that was plain enough even by moonlight. "If you could do anything you wanted, what would it be?"

"What do you mean?"

Ortega said slowly, "If you could do anything…drive racing cars…teach…"

Gabriel spluttered into laughter. "*Teach?* Me?"

Ortega raised one muscular shoulder. "Anything. Run your own restaurant. Paint."

Gabriel grinned, ready to mock, but he stopped, thinking it over. "I like what I do," he said. And it was the truth. He liked being a cop. He liked working undercover — nerve wracking and exhausting though it was. He liked believing that he was making a difference, being one of the good guys.

Although he could hardly tell that to one of the bad guys.

"What about you?" he asked.

Ortega said coolly, "Like you, I am content with the path I've chosen."

"You never have regrets for the lives destroyed —" Gabriel bit off the rest of it, but he could tell from the quality of silence that followed his hasty words that Ortega was astonished.

After a pause, Ortega said, "We do what we have to do, *sí?*"

"Sure." Gabriel lay flat and stared up at the ceiling — into the darkness of the shadows where the fan whirred creakily above them.

Ortega suddenly pulled him close, finding Gabriel's mouth with unexpectedly fierce hunger. Gabriel responded automatically, wrapping his arms around Ortega's broad back. It felt good to be held, to hold — to share this man's bed, mouth, breath…

Gabriel didn't know a lot about kissing. It wasn't something he went in for with sex partners — too personal, too emotional. But he opened to Ortega's tongue, accepted that sweet invasion, the slick probe of this velvet kiss.

At last Ortega drew back. His breath was light against Gabriel's face as he said, "I was on the balcony while you slept. I watched the fireflies. Millions of them — from the jungle that surrounds this place. I watched them flickering in the night like white petals, like neon petals."

"Poetry?" Gabriel said. Although he wanted to, he couldn't infuse his voice with the necessary jeering. The darkness, the silence, had removed too many barriers, and for this time their emotions were as naked as their bodies.

"Maybe. Maybe there is poetry in such things." Ortega still followed his own thoughts. "These were not the eerie green of the Spanish firefly, but blinding white flashes of lightning bugs. Beautiful to see. They weave in and out through the trees until they make you dizzy. Beautiful. Restless. Confusing." He leaned over Gabriel, his thumb tracing the line of Gabriel's lower lip, his gaze impossible to read in the gloom. "That's how you make me feel. Wanting more but knowing —"

Gabriel's throat tightened unbearably. "Don't," he said. He was shocked to realize tears were close. Why? What did he care what Ortega felt or thought or said — Ortega was nothing to him. A fuck. His enemy. His fucking enemy. Something close to hysterical laughter welled in his throat. Ortega was talking about *bugs*, for chrissake!

"As you wish, *gatito*." Ortega's lips found Gabriel's once more, sealing their mouths together in an exquisitely tender kiss. "Always as you wish." Gabriel's eyelids dropped shut, to stop the stupid moisture from leaking out.

Time seemed to slow, their movements languid and deliberate. Half-pinned beneath Ortega's weight, Gabriel had little choice but to submit to the other man's gentle seduction. The mouth moving insistently upon his own deepened, the kiss growing more possessive, leaving him breathless and bemused yet again.

Morning was painful.

Gabriel's bruised and battered body felt more sleep-deprived than usual — but then it was more bruised and battered than usual. He pried one eye open, wincing against the yellow sunshine and birdsong streaming in through the balcony. From the open doorway he could hear the sounds of the plaza below — and from next to him, the soft sleep sounds of Ortega.

He turned his head. He was not used to waking up with his sex partners. In fact, he was not used to falling asleep with them, and if he hadn't been so drunk and exhausted the night before, and if someone hadn't tried to blow him to kingdom come last night, he'd have left after he and Ortega had fucked the final time. There was something…dangerously intimate about falling asleep with someone you didn't know. Especially when what you did know made that other person your enemy.

Ortega's face was relaxed in sleep. He seemed much younger, and for the first time Gabriel wondered how old he actually was. Anywhere from thirty-five to forty, he guessed. No longer a young gun, but a long way from being an old man.

Gabriel studied the unlined face. Ortega's eyelashes were short and thick, like those of a bull. His mouth was soft and sensual in sleep, his jaw heavily shadowed with beard. He had a strong — very strong — chin, and a nice straight nose. Yes, he was a very handsome man. He felt a sort of softness as he stared at the lean, tanned, sleeping face — some emotion he couldn't quite put a name to. Affection? Tenderness?

No way.

No damn way.

He could not afford to feel anything other than admiration for Ortega's ability to fuck like a champion. Because anything else was…fatal. And pointless.

Gabriel could not afford to care. Ortega was going down with the rest of the scum. Sure he had nice table manners, and he talked about fireflies, and he had sweetly mopped Gabriel's spent body with a warm wet cloth after their last fuck — and he had kissed Gabriel's mouth in that melting, almost loving way —

It meant nothing. *Nada.* It couldn't mean anything because they were on opposite sides of the law, and Gabriel had read Ortega's file. They didn't come more evil than Ortega. Poetic shit about fireflies notwithstanding.

Ortega's eyelids lifted and his dark eyes were awake and alert. "What's wrong?" he asked, and his voice was sleep husky. His mouth curled into a half smile and he touched the frown between Gabriel's eyebrows. "What's troubling you, *gatito*?"

That light touch on his face…Gabriel closed his eyes, savoring it. Then he opened them. "Nothing. We have a plane to catch."

"It's a private plane. There is no hurry," Ortega said. His hand stroked Gabriel's cheek, brushing his rough jaw. His thumb brushed Gabriel's lower lip, tracing the line of his mouth. "There is time —"

Gabriel turned his head away and sat up. "I need to get home."

He could feel Ortega's silence.

"I do not think Botelli is in any hurry for your return," Ortega said at last.

Gabriel glanced around. "What's that mean?"

Ortega said slowly, "I believe Don Jesus will have suggested by now to Señor Botelli that he would prefer him not to…retain your services."

Gabriel didn't move for a moment. He had known that Sanchez didn't like him, wanted him gone — permanently. But this was different. "Are you telling me Sanchez told you to take me out?" He managed to keep his voice steady, but it wasn't easy.

"No," Ortega said levelly. "But he told me not to interfere if someone else tried."

It seemed a long time before Gabriel was able to gather his thoughts enough to listen to what Ortega was saying.

"…it would be an affront to Señor Botelli. Nor does Don Jesus wish to upset the señorita by appearing to be in any way involved in harm that might befall you."

Harm. Like blowing him up with a homemade bomb wired to a hotel room door? Nice. No wonder the local cops hadn't made any push to question them last night. Piñero and his gang were almost certainly behind that attempt, not the two hapless guards at the hotel entrance.

Gabriel rose from the bed. "Then the sooner we get out of here the better, right?" He was moving blindly, his mind racing while he tried to think what his next move needed to be. He would have to tell O'Brien, and O'Brien would pull him out immediately — and, goddamn it, he'd worked too long, given up too much for that to happen.

But if Sanchez wanted him gone, it didn't matter — he was done either way. And what point was there in dying for nothing?

He jumped as Ortega rested a hand on his shoulder. He hadn't noticed the other man rising and following him as he pulled on his torn trousers from the previous evening.

"What will you do?" Ortega asked.

Gabriel stared at him. It took his brain a moment to translate. "Talk to Ricco."

"Botelli won't know or care about this." Ortega hesitated. "It's possible I might be able to…help you."

"Help me how?"

Ortega eyes shifted. "I could talk to some people perhaps. It would depend on certain things."

"What things?"

"I can't say more at this time." The dark eyes studied Gabriel.

Gabriel shook his head. "Thanks, but I solve my own problems."

"This is not something you can solve on your own — not unless you run. Now."

"I'm not running."

Ortega sighed. "I was afraid you would say that. But you realize you have no choice? Botelli will not take your part against Don Jesus."

"Yeah. I got that."

Ortega seemed on the verge of speech, but he appeared to think better of whatever he was going to say. He gave another sigh, the weight of the world on his shoulders.

Gabriel moved away, picking his gun up from the bedstand and sliding it into his shoulder holster. Neither he nor Ortega spoke.

Ortega went into the bathroom to shower. Gabriel went out to the balcony and stared down at the plaza with its fountain. The water sparkled in the sun. Pigeons walked their funny crooked walk across the sunlit tiles. Children played, calling out to each other, laughing.

All at once he was very tired. His body hurt with myriad aches and pains. He was covered in cuts and scrapes. Bruises, too, but he wasn't sure which of those were from the explosion and which were the result of his night with Ortega. His head pounded from not enough sleep and an excess of alcohol — and too much worry.

He needed to get back to San Francisco right away and call his captain. But if he did that, O'Brien would yank him out faster than he could say the words *mob hit.*

There had to be some way around this. He just needed to get through the next couple of days. Then the first of Piñero's shipments would arrive — and all Gabriel's blood, sweat, and tears would culminate in bringing down the Botelli and Sanchez empires.

If he could just keep a low profile after he got back — avoid Gina like the plague, avoid catching Don Sanchez' eye — he could still be there at the finish.

He wanted that — wanted it bad enough to taste. He'd worked for it. Earned it.

And then he thought of Ortega — thought of him under arrest, led off in handcuffs — tried to picture the look on Ortega's face when Ortega knew the truth about Gabriel. His stomach knotted. It should make him feel good thinking of that smug bastard knowing Gabriel had played him, but he felt sick thinking about it.

It would be less painful if he were absent when Ortega and the rest of Don Sanchez' crew were taken down. He'd done his part. All he needed to do was report back to O'Brien everything he'd learned on this trip, and let O'Brien pull him out. Leave it to the uniforms to mop up.

But somehow not being there was almost worse.

What if something went wrong? Shit happened in big operations like this. What if Ortega got away? What if he was…killed?

Gabriel's heart seemed to pause for moment.

So…what if he just…didn't tell O'Brien about this latest development? It was only for a day or two. Forty-eight hours tops.

The shower stopped.

Ortega stepped out of the bathroom, a white towel discreetly wrapped around his waist. Gabriel bit back a grin at the towel.

Ortega had a funny streak. Ortega, too, was covered in bruises and cuts. He watched him dress in the battered tailored clothes of the day before. Ortega would look poised and elegant in rags.

Gabriel bit his lip. Ortega had saved Gabriel's life last night — and nearly lost his own doing it.

Seeming to feel Gabriel's gaze, the older man looked up, long brown fingers doing up the buttons on his shirt.

"What is it?"

"Nothing," Gabriel said.

Ortega observed him for a moment and then nodded once — accepting Gabriel's word or maybe just not caring enough to bother pressing for the truth.

And that was that.

After they dressed, they returned to their former rooms and found the police already sifting through the debris. A crude homemade bomb wired to Gabriel's hotel room door — that was the verdict. Curious looks were thrown Gabriel's way. No one seemed to have much to say.

These were low-level flunkies. There was no sign of Piñero or his second in command, Lieutenant Ferreño.

Ortega's room was largely undamaged except for the smoke and fire. Gabriel's room was a mess of broken furniture and fallen plaster. His belongings were scattered through the wreckage.

Someone had wanted him dead. Had taken steps to make it happen.

Ortega spoke to the cops, and then the officer in charge led them down to the manager's office where Ortega and Gabriel answered questions while the officer filled out his report.

At last the man seemed satisfied with their answers — or their lack of answers — and said he would escort them to the airfield. While Gabriel waited in the lobby, Ortega collected his belongings from upstairs. They left the hotel with their police escort.

The trip to the airstrip was made in silence.

The plane waited, gleaming in the hot sun. The pilot stood at the edge of the airfield smoking a cigarette.

The police officer bade them a safe journey, backed his vehicle up and sped away into the afternoon heat.

The pilot opened the aircraft door for them and they boarded. Ortega immediately occupied himself with his briefcase — checking to see that his laptop was unaffected by the blast the night before.

Gabriel sat across from him and stared out the window.

Soon the plane engines rumbled into life, the aircraft began to move down the tiny runway, and, at last, they were in the air.

The tin shacks and runway grew smaller, and the jungle, too, seemed to shrink below them to miniature size — like mold creeping across the surface of the planet.

Gabriel glanced at his companion. Ortega's face was preoccupied, his attention focused on his work. Gabriel felt oddly shut out. He should be glad Ortega was busy and not focused on him. Since when had he needed or wanted attention from a sex partner after the deed was done?

Nothing he was feeling made sense. He'd done his job well and the end was in sight. The new pipeline was open and the first delivery set for two days hence. Don Sanchez would be happy, Ricco would be happy. Shit, even Gina would be happy — hopefully not so happy she'd get him killed before he could wrap up this job.

Gabriel looked out the plane window. The mountains were tiny points far below, and as he watched, they vanished beneath the shredded cotton of the clouds.

Yeah, everyone was happy. Happy, happy, fucking wonderfully happy.

Part II

CHAPTER ELEVEN

Dropping his hold-all into the trunk of his car, and slamming it shut, Antonio Lorenzo watched the little red sports car carrying Giovanni Contadino screech out of the gates of the small private airport and roar away. He shook his head. Gina Botelli had been waiting when the plane touched down on this out of the way airstrip — and that was bad news.

Not that Antonio didn't see Contadino's dilemma. Pissing off the pretty Gina was just going to add to his problems, and he had plenty of those already.

Climbing into his Porsche, Antonio started the engine, then paused as his cell phone rang. He checked the display window, and recognized the discreetly anonymous number flashing. Turning off the engine, he got out of the car and went to find a payphone. It was getting harder and harder to do these days.

At last he located a working phone by the airport terminal. He dialed the memorized number and waited for the exchange to click him over.

"Hall." The voice was crisp and cold as a winter day. Instantly Antonio pictured his boss at the bureau, pasty skin that never saw the sun, snowy, prematurely white hair, and eyes as blue as Arctic water. That was Assistant Director Fred Hall. The field agents called him Snowman. Antonio suspected Hall liked that.

"It's me."

"You're forty-five minutes late."

"We were delayed leaving Mexico City. Nothing important." Antonio's eyes absently watched cars flashing by on the distant line of highway. His thoughts strayed to Contadino's tired, grim face as he had climbed into the sports car with the charmingly ruthless Senorita Botelli. Contadino had to be scared shitless, but he'd concealed it well behind that cocky, smart-mouthed mask on the long flight. Not that it was entirely a mask.

Contadino was a cool and sarcastic little bastard — and that appeared to go bone deep.

"You sure it was nothing important?"

"I am sure."

"What have you got for us?"

"It went like clockwork. You will have my full report before the end of the day." Antonio couldn't help the satisfaction that crept into his tone. Playing the role of Miguel Ortega for the last few years had been rough, but Antonio had always believed in his heart it would be worth the sacrifices he had made — and now he had the proof. This was the drug enforcement coup of the decade.

"It's definite," he added. "Carlos Piñero is Sanchez' newest drug supplier in Sinaloa. Competition was fierce, but in the end we managed the acquisition."

"You missed your calling, Lorenzo," Hall said acidly. "You've got a real gift for business."

Antonio checked his first response. He and Hall had never got along. Hall had a dismissive attitude toward all his undercover agents. He had particular problems with Antonio, who came from the kind of background that apparently bugged the shit out of a guy like Hall who'd had to scrabble every step of the way. There was nothing Antonio could do about that. It didn't help that Hall was rather a racist and a homophobe.

Instead, Antonio said, "The best news is the first buy will be very soon — within forty-eight hours."

Even Hall was impressed by that. "You have the details?"

"Not yet. You will know as soon as I do. Or shortly after." Antonio hesitated. "Hall, I wish to arrange a deal for one of Botelli's soldiers. Immunity and protection in exchange for information on Botelli's organization."

"Are you talking about the kid you asked for the file on? Contadino?"

"Yes. Young Giovanni's number is coming up fast, and he knows it. I think he might be willing to…negotiate."

Antonio had no idea whether that was true. Contadino was a contradictory mix. He was a punk — aggressive, arrogant, more than a little rough around the edges — but he wasn't cruel and he wasn't vicious. Antonio thought of that strange, moody question the night before. *You never have regrets for the lives destroyed?* Sometimes he even seemed to display a certain integrity. He'd shown courage and cool at Ruby Blue, clearly willing to sacrifice his life for Gina Botelli, but he'd taken pains to avoid involving innocents in the violence.

Still, Antonio did not examine why it was important to him to protect Contadino. It wasn't like there was a future for them either way.

He was startled when Hall gave one of those harsh laughs. "You think he might negotiate, do you? I've got news for you. Contadino is a *cop.*"

Antonio nearly dropped the phone. "*What?*"

"That's right." There was frosty satisfaction in Hall's voice. "He's SFPD." Hall's pleasure at catching Antonio in not instantly making Contadino was marred by his displeasure to find a lowly undercover cop on FBI turf. "Gabriel Sandalini. San Francisco PD Narcotics Division."

"There's no mistake? Contadino is an undercover *cop?*" Antonio nearly laughed.

"There's no mistake. Our informant in SFPD got the confirmation today. Sandalini has been deep undercover for eighteen months."

"*Madre dios.*"

"I know. He's a problem."

Focused on the possible detrimental affect Gabriel would have to the FBI's operation, Hall took Antonio's exclamation at face value. The truth was, Antonio was caught between chagrin and relief. On one hand, everything he knew about Conta— Sandalini was a lie. On the other, he was not falling for a young villain.

Antonio froze as he heard the echo of his own thoughts. *Falling for?*

Surely not. Surely what he felt — and Antonio could not deny that he did feel something powerful — was simply...but better not to think of this now.

"It solves one problem," he said to Hall. "SFPD must pull him out now. Sanchez wants him topped. There was an attempt in Sinaloa. Gina Botelli is a little too fond of Con— Sandalini. Sanchez does not tolerate competition."

"That's not going to be as easy as you think. We have a request in the channel right now to supersede SFPD in this operation, but these things aren't instantaneous. It could take twenty-four hours or more."

"Then contact Sandalini's superior and tell him he must yank him. The young man is on borrowed time."

"I can't do that."

"What do you mean, you can't do that?"

Hall said flatly, "We were able to infiltrate SFPD with an informant. You think Ricco Botelli hasn't managed to do the same thing? You believe Sanchez wants Sandalini out of the way because of the Botelli broad, but maybe he wants him out of the way because Sandalini has been made."

"I would know that," Antonio stated. "Don Jesus trusts me."

"We can't take a risk — we've all worked too long and too hard on this thing. You, if anybody, should know what's at stake here. If we try to contact SFPD directly — warn them to pull their operative out — our own interest in this sting is no longer covert."

"I tell you, Sanchez is going to have him hit. And it might be sooner rather than later." Antonio thought of Gina arranging to pick up Conta— Sandalini at the airport. Stupid bitch. She was going to get his head blown off.

So many things made sense now. Antonio chided himself for his blindness.

"Does Sandalini know Sanchez wants him dead? Did you warn him?"

"*Sí.*"

"Okay." Hall sounded calm. "Our responsibility ends there. Now it's his job to get himself out of there. You warned him, he'll tell his captain, and that'll be that. I just hope to hell his sudden disappearance doesn't put the wind up with Botelli and Sanchez."

Yes, that could be dangerous for Antonio, but for some reason all he could think about was the stubborn, set expression on Sandalini's face when he had said he wasn't running. He said, "I think Sandalini may try to ride it out. He's…young."

"I read his file," Hall said dryly. "Young, headstrong. There are a couple of documented clashes with superiors. And he's a risk taker. An adrenaline junkie."

Wonderful. Not that Antonio didn't already know this, he just hoped perhaps it was part of Sandalini's cover…no. The Club Madrone popped into his mind. Sandalini was reckless, a little wild. And…beautiful. For an instant he closed his eyes, recalling that exotic, fine-boned face with the wide, hazel eyes. The hard jaw so at odds with the sensitive, almost pretty mouth.

"We have to get him out," he said quietly.

"You've done what you could," Hall said. "You do anything more and you're liable to compromise your own position. Anyway, you just said the new pipeline test flight will be any day now."

"He may not have a couple of days. He may not have a couple of hours." Antonio considered the sparkle in Gina Botelli's eyes when she looked at Gio Contadino. How she couldn't keep her grabby little hands off him.

Hall said, "That would be unfortunate, but Sandalini's being there has the potential to throw a wrench into the whole thing. You know that. You know what's at stake here."

"Jesus Christ, Hall! He's a cop. You wish to stand by and see a cop killed?"

Hall's reply was like having ice water dumped over his head. "*Exactly*, Lorenzo. Sandalini is a cop. He knows the risks of the job, just like you do. Just like we all do. And if it'll make you feel better, he's supposed to be very good at what he does. If he's tough and savvy enough to have wormed his way into Botelli's family and survived for nearly two years, he can probably ride out another two or three days."

There was logic in what Hall said. The problem was, Hall didn't know the manic light in Sanchez' eyes when he felt he had been insulted. And his wayward betrothed's interest in a pretty young *cugine* was a serious affront.

Into Antonio's silence, Hall placated, "I've got no wish to see a good cop caught in the line of fire, but we're playing for major stakes here. This operation's been building over five years. You've invested a big chunk of your life in Miguel Ortega, made sacrifices and done things I don't want to know about to get there and stay there. No one will lose more than you will if this sours. And if you're right, and Sandalini knows the risk but chooses to stay in the game, then it's because he understands what's at stake too, right?

Stay in the game. FBI vs. Bad Guys. But to Sandalini…well, Antonio knew only too well what Sandalini had gone through to work his way into Botelli's organization, and he could understand why the young officer might imagine it was worth risking limb and maybe life to stay in a few days longer.

"Right?" Hall prodded.

Living on the edge, undercover, lurking on the fringes of society and moral corruption had instilled a certain autonomy in Antonio's decision making that field agents didn't typically enjoy. Antonio was as likely to follow Hall's directive as he was to ignore it. Antonio was torn. He could throw a wrench in the works himself. He could get Sandalini out of there, and to hell with how it compromised the rest of the operation.

But Antonio was not a reckless or impulsive man, nor was he foolhardy — and *he* rarely had clashes with his superiors. He silently weighed what Hall said — and all that he had not.

Hall didn't have a lot of interest in running undercover operations, but he was good at his job, good at overseeing operations like this, partly because he didn't look at his operatives as people. He saw them as pieces on a game board, and he maneuvered them accordingly. Hall was a bastard, but he was an efficient bastard. He usually won.

And the worst part of — the part that made Antonio's heart ache — was that no one life was more valuable when weighed against all the lives that would be saved by putting Don Jesus and Ricco Botelli out of business.

And, tragically, Sandalini — like any good cop — believed that just as surely as Antonio did.

Hall repeated his prompt. "Right?"

"Right," Antonio grunted. "Don't talk it to death."

There was a surprised, affronted silence from Hall. Then he said, "Okay. Then we're good."

Dead air hung between them.

Antonio said, "Yes. You will have my full report in a few hours." He replaced the phone into its hook a little harder than necessary.

Heart pounding with unfamiliar anger, he strode back to his car and started the engine.

A cop.

Christ.

He met his own dark frown in his rearview mirror, and a reluctant smile pulled at his mouth.

Antonio pulled onto the highway, pressing the gas and absently enjoying the way the Porsche responded to his handling. He needed to lay his hands on that police file. He wanted to know all there was to know about Gabriel Sandalini. And when this was over…well, it would be most amusing — satisfying — to surprise Officer Sandalini with the truth about Miguel Ortega. Assuming they both made it through the next forty-eight hours alive.

"How much longer are we going to wait, Ricco? They're late!" Michelangelo Rizzi straightened his tie yet again, his dry, sarcastic voice unusually small in the wide, empty space of the cavernous warehouse.

"As long as it takes," Botelli snarled back, although his voice also sounded diminished in the gloomy setting.

The building smelled of oil and rodent droppings, the air hazy with dust the cars had stirred up driving into the unkempt space. A trio of long, very wide porcelain sinks hugged the wall between a surprisingly clean bathroom and a twisted row of metal lockers. One of the tall, gooseneck faucets dripped a steady trickle of water, uncommonly loud in the enormous room.

Botelli looked out of place — sweating like a pig in his designer suit, dust coating his expensive shoes. Antonio's mouth curled. His gaze traveled, placing the position of each of Botelli's men in his mind. Rizzi — bitching as usual — stood next to his boss near the safety of their limo. Botelli's bodyguard, Bruno, stood at three o'clock from Botelli, watching Ortega and his crew with that sullen, stupid stare. Contadino — no, Sandalini — was as usual in motion, ranging uneasily along the perimeter of the building, eyes scanning the catwalks overhead. A couple of lesser grunts guarded the over-size doors.

Antonio did not need to look to see where Sandalini was. He'd been aware of him continuously since he'd arrived with his own handful of men. He could feel the undercover cop's eyes on him now, although he did not glance his way.

His first sight of Sandalini since parting at the private airstrip two days ago had confirmed his concern. The young man had a fist-size bruise on his cheekbone, and despite the easy stride, Antonio could see that he hurt when he moved. Someone had worked him over since their return from Mexico. And from the irritable looks Botelli every so often threw his subordinate's way, Antonio had a good idea who.

Well, he planned to hear all about it this evening. Once this operation was over, once he and Sandalini had been debriefed, he planned on getting very drunk together and then taking Sandalini to bed — for a week. When he wasn't thinking about the job, it was all Antonio thought about.

Rizzi threw Antonio one of his bitter smiles — which Antonio returned equably — then turned back to Botelli. "Ten past the hour. How much disrespect are you willing to stand for, Ricco?"

Antonio turned a mildly inquiring gaze on the West Coast crime boss, and Botelli flushed beneath it.

"Hey." Ricco shot Antonio an uneasy look. "No one is disrespecting anyone here. There's a million reasons they might get held up."

"Very true," Antonio said gravely. What Rizzi was really angry about was that Don Sanchez had sent Miguel Ortega in his place instead of coming himself. Sanchez had decreed that Botelli must appear in person for this first important meet, but he himself had declined to show. He claimed pressing and unavoidable business, but of course they all knew exactly why Don Sanchez had declined to show. It was the same reason he had blown off other meetings with Botelli, why he was late to meetings, why he canceled meetings, why he dismissed meetings early. Don Sanchez despised Botelli, and familiarity had only increased his contempt.

Sanchez thought Botelli ran a slack operation — professionally and personally.

The only concern here for Antonio was that Sanchez would not be present for the sting. However, they would have more than enough to arrest him, and FBI agents were watching Sanchez' mansion to make sure he did not escape their net.

Botelli gave Rizzi a poke in the chest. "Don Jesus is a man of his word. His supplier will be here."

With unusual testiness, Rizzi turned away.

Under pretence of double checking the positioning of his men at key points around the building perimeter, Ortega risked a look at Sandalini. Something moved hungrily inside his chest as he watched that slim, lithe figure moving with catlike grace back towards the men grouped around the cars. He could feel Sandalini's excitement and tension — it was like a magnetic field crackling around him. And Antonio knew why.

Antonio himself felt strangely calm. Focused and even a little detached. He always felt like this before going into battle — like the bullfighters in the stories his papa told him when he was a child.

As he stared, Sandalini's gaze met his and Antonio saw a flash of something. The attraction between them burned brightly always, but it wasn't that. No, there was a darkness in those honey-colored eyes. Regret. Guilt. Antonio's heart lifted. Sandalini believed Miguel Ortega was going down along with the rest of this rotten crew — *and he was sorry*.

Antonio's heart lifted. He smiled at Sandalini, and Sandalini colored. He looked away, moving over to the wall and propping one lean, jeans-clad hip on a workbench there. Antonio could see him deliberately tuning him out, concentrating on the scene before him — but the younger man's face remained slightly flushed, his jaw hard, his mouth held tight against emotion. One hand nervously tapped the wooden bench.

His tension went unnoticed by the others. But then everyone in the warehouse was strung tight, restless, anxious.

Ortega knew exactly how Sandalini felt. He felt the same. Today's meeting among Botelli, Sanchez and the Mexican connection — the connection that ironically Sandalini and Ortega had helped set up — was about to culminate in long prison terms for all involved. This was the first face-to-face meeting with the Mexican connection's stateside front man — and it would be the last. When the buy was complete, Antonio's team would move in and take down the two big cheeses, Botelli and Sanchez — and then scoop up all the rats.

As of that morning SFPD had been warned off, but Sandalini didn't know that. He would be expecting his own people to move in. Antonio intended to keep a close watch on the young man just in case not everyone on the FBI team had got the word there was an undercover cop in Botelli's crew.

Long and lonely months of intense and solitary work were ending, and Antonio could imagine what the younger man felt. That mix of relief and triumph — and letdown. Sandalini would have no experience with that rush and spiraling fall. Antonio planned to be there to help him come down any way he liked: drink, sex, talk. Maybe all three. It would be good to talk openly and honestly with Sandalini.

"I don't know why the hell we even have to be here," Rizzi continued to bitch. "What do we care where Sanchez gets the shit? So long as he gets it — and we know he does because we helped set up the deal!"

Sandalini's gaze automatically slid to Antonio's, and Antonio permitted his own mouth to curl. He liked seeing Sandalini's eyes light up that way — with secret, malicious laughter.

Botelli threw another of those uncomfortable looks in Antonio's direction before snapping out, "*Basta!* If Don Jesus wants us to make nice with his new suppliers, we make nice. If Don Jesus wants —"

The sound of a car horn pierced the night air and the low hum of an expensive engine purred at the garage door. One of

Botelli's foot soldiers sauntered to the wall and tripped the electrical switch to open the door.

A long, low, dark blue sedan with heavily tinted windows glided through the opening, stopping just inside the entrance. The driver expertly angled the car to block the entire opening as the closing door passed only inches behind the rear bumper.

Ortega glanced over, catching Gabriel covertly checking that his gun moved freely in his shoulder holster. He looked back at the heavily armored car.

The car doors popped open and four big ugly men — bodyguards — got out. Eeny, Meeny, Miny and Cujo. Their faces reflected ancient Indian heritage, although the grim expressions were contemporary enough and the dark, casual clothing, jeans, T-shirts, and guns.

With the bodyguards' appraisal of the men stationed in the warehouse, the biggest one — squat, tattooed, blocking the back seat of the heavy limousine — stepped aside and a new man slid out.

The Mexican was very tall, very lean — his ascetic, bearded face reminded Antonio of a painting he had once seen of Don Quixote, though the briefcase he carried was hardly stuffed with dreams or ideals. With an arrogant sway to his walk, he approached Botelli and Antonio.

Antonio sensed movement to his side, felt rather than saw Sandalini position himself. He'd read Sandalini's file, and he trusted him to know his job.

Everyone else waited, silently, warily.

One of the Mexican's henchmen, Meeny, a squat foot soldier with a pockmarked face, leaned over and whispered something in the ear of Miny, the chunky, tattooed man. The man did a double take and then murmured low and urgently to the first man.

Something about Meeny's pockmarked face was familiar to Antonio — and familiar in this context was not good. Then both men stared in Sandalini's direction. From the corner of his eye, Antonio saw Sandalini stand very straight and go very still.

Not good. In fact…very bad.

Sandalini had been made. Antonio knew it as surely as he was standing there. And Sandalini knew it too. Antonio looked at him. Sandalini's eyes were flinty and level, but he swallowed once, hard, and Antonio felt a wave of fierce protectiveness that shocked the hell out of him.

Miny, the tattooed man joined Don Quixote. Meeny maintained his bold stare, challenging Sandalini. Sandalini looked casually away, feigning disinterest — unawareness, even — of the scrutiny. But he shifted his feet, just a fraction, bracing for trouble — and even that much gave his game away.

Stopping a few feet from Botelli, the lean Mexican and his posse formed a straight line, the bearded stranger in the middle, a pair of guns on either side.

The silence stretched out as the groups took each other's measure. Botelli broke first, a fine line of perspiration tracing the top of his lip.

"I'm Ricco Botelli. Don Sanchez regrets he couldn't be here himself but he sends his regards — and his first lieutenant, Señor Miguel Ortega—" he glanced at Ortega, who merely nodded politely "—to pay his respects." He took one step forward and clasped his hands in front of his body, showing he was willing to make the first move in greeting, but unwilling to leave his own circle of men to extend his hand.

The bearded man didn't bat an eye nor did he answer.

Vaguely, Botelli gestured at his men stationed around the room, guns at the ready, all attention riveted on the newcomers. "Don Sanchez has honored the Botelli family with his trust and partnership. The Botelli organization controls the largest distribution network on the West Coast. We got the best people, the most police influence, and the cleanest cash available."

Nothing from the Mexicans.

"As a show of good faith, I'm here personally with my own first lieutenant." He clapped Rizzi on the shoulder. Then, to Bruno, he jerked his head in the direction of Botelli's own limousine.

Bruno retrieved a soft-sided brown leather case from the limo and brought it to Botelli, handing it over wordlessly. He took up his usual position at Botelli's back.

Botelli said with heavy jollity, "Let's conduct our business, shall we gentlemen, and we can adjourn to find somewhere more to our liking to spend the rest of our evening." He carried the case to the table, opened the flap and showed the stuffed packets of thousand dollar bills: the two million dollars previously negotiated for the first fifty kilos. "It's the cleanest cash you'll ever find."

Depending on how one defined *clean*, Antonio reflected.

The Mexican's men remained still as statues, only their eyes tracking activity.

"Will you stake your life on that, Señor Botelli?" The gentlemanly Don Quixote look-alike spoke harshly, and unease rippled through the space.

Botelli bristled, then seemed to relax as he studied the other's aristocratic features. The man's eyes were cold, the cast of cataracts beginning to form. The artificial light in the warehouse gave them an unearthly white glow. "To whom am I talking here?" he asked bluntly. "I don't like this anonymous stuff."

The weird eyes studied Botelli. "I am Victor. Only…Victor."

Botelli blinked once and then nodded. "It's a guarantee, Only Victor. You got the Botelli name on it." He held the man's harsh stare without flinching, although the sheen of perspiration had spread to coat his puffy face.

"Paulo." Victor gestured to the tattooed man, the one whose whispers probably gave Sandalini away. Paulo walked the distance between the groups to accept the briefcase. Retrieving it, he handed it off to another one of the grim toughs at Victor's side.

Accepting the second briefcase from Victor. Paulo snapped it open, facing it out so Botelli could view the contents. Two clear plastic bags of white powder lay displayed in the case as though they were the Crown Jewels of England.

Paulo extended the case slightly while Victor spoke. "A sample of the quality product we supply. It is uncut and four times the purity you have been used to from your previous supplier. Take it and test it. See for yourself."

Botelli turned to Sandalini, tipping his head in Paulo's direction. "You helped craft the deal, Contadino. Get the case from him."

Sandalini nodded curtly, and walked across the twenty feet or so separating the two groups of men. He met Paulo's stony stare coolly.

Paulo turned and spoke in guttural Spanish to the pockmarked man standing by the car. "Is this him?"

"*Si.*"

To Sandalini, Paulo said, "My friend thinks he knows you, *gringo.*"

"Move in," Ortega said under-voiced, for the benefit of the wire he was wearing. The deal was not quite complete, but it was all going to hell in a matter of seconds, regardless. They had what they needed. And even if they didn't —

Sandalini, ever the charm school dropout, said flatly to the staring man, "I don't think so. I'd remember a beauty like you."

Hefting the bags from the case, he returned Victor's slow appraising once-over with a direct look of his own. Then he turned on his heel, striding back to the invisible line of separation between the groups of men. Halfway there, Paulo's harsh accusing voice stopped him.

"I think my friend *does* know you." Paulo's hard-edged voice rose, the effect booming off the metal walls and echoing menacingly. "I think he is right. I think you are a cop."

It was as though someone had pulled a switch. Everyone froze.

Sandalini said aggressively, "I don't know what the fuck you're talking about."

His tone was…not quite right. Almost, but almost was not good enough now, and Antonio could have told him it was too late in any case. He could see it on the faces of the Mexicans. They knew. There was no question. Sandalini was blown.

The pockmarked man said, "You were in on that sting three years ago that pulled down Manno's numbers racket at his strip club. I was one of his runners."

"You've got me confused with someone else," Sandalini stated.

The pockmarked man smiled unpleasantly. "And you were at Club Madrone the night we took care of Benny Barbosa."

And this, Antonio thought regretfully with a detached part of his mind while he reached for his weapon, was the problem with inexperience. In that brief moment before he got control, Sandalini's face told the story. Shock, anger — and fear. It added up to guilt. Paulo pulled his gun and spoke to his boss without looking away from Sandalini. "He's a cop, *padrone*. I'm sure of it."

Seeing Antonio pull his pistol, Sanchez' men and Botelli's drew their own weapons. Sandalini, holding the two bags of heroin, stood motionless, caught between two walls of guns.

His eyes met Antonio's and there was emotion there that Antonio couldn't read.

Botelli began screaming and swearing a blue streak. "Is this true, you goddamned punk? You fucking little punk? You're a *cop*? I should drop you myself, you little fuck!"

Sandalini said nothing, eyes locked on Antonio's face, and Antonio said calmly, "Get down."

Sandalini's tawny eyes widened.

"FBI! Don't move!" The warehouse doors banged open and blue-clad agents in bulletproof vests and jackets marked FBI swarmed into the warehouse, weapons aimed at the men grouped in the center of the long room. A voice on a bullhorn was directing, "Throw down your weapons! This is the FBI! You are surrounded!"

Perhaps if the men in the warehouse had not already had their weapons drawn, had already not braced for violence, it might have played out differently. Perhaps it was simply the confusion of the moment. Whatever it was, instead of throwing down their weapons, Sanchez, Botelli and Victor's crews began firing.

Bullets whined, cutting the thick, dusty air, piercing or pinging off metal walls in ricochet. Rizzi broke and ran for the rear exit, and one of Victor's men popped him — an automatic reflex. Instantly, Sanchez' men turned their attention from the FBI and opened fire on the Mexicans.

Lost in his own world, Botelli, manic with rage, ranted, "You've think you can play Botelli for a fool? For a year you been taking my money, eating at my table, accepting my —" He aimed his pistol at Sandalini, who responded with the weapon most readily to hand. He hurled one of the plump bags of heroin at Botelli's head.

Bruno's bullet struck the bag as it left Sandalini's hand, and the bag exploded in a white cloud, showering Sandalini in powder. Bruno fired again, this time hitting Sandalini in the right shoulder. His knees gave. Another shot, this one fired from Victor's men, plowed into his back.

Coldly, almost indifferent to the hail of bullets around him, Antonio took aim, fired, and drilled Bruno between his eyes. Botelli's bodyguard went down firing, hitting his employer squarely in his plump chest. Botelli screamed, blood spurting from his breast as he sagged to the ground, too.

Antonio moved forward, firing steadily, making each shot count, working his way to where Gabriel lay sprawled, moving feebly in the dust. Kneeling beside the younger man, he pulled him over onto his back. Sandalini's face was coated in fine white powder, eyelids, nose crusted, lips caked with it. It looked comical — and ghastly. His lashes flickered, his dazed eyes opened and he stared at Antonio. His powdery lips moved but no words came out, and Antonio didn't know if Sandalini even really saw him. Blood soaked his chest and shoulder, mingling with the white dusting him like snow.

"I told you to get down," Antonio murmured. "Why did you not listen for once? Why didn't you wear a vest at least? You little fool. Why…?"

Already the fighting around them was ending, the men who had not immediately fallen to bullets throwing their guns down and putting their hands up in the air as more FBI agents teemed in.

"I need a medic. Pronto!" shouted Antonio, gently brushing the heroin from Sandalini's face. The bruise on the young man's cheekbone stood out starkly. "You must hold on," he urged. Sandalini's eyes were black and huge, his face as white as the powder coating it. Red dotted his lips, garish against the stark white. "*Madre mios*…you cannot do this now. *Fuck*…I need help here!" Antonio cried again as Sandalini's breathing changed, began to wheeze.

The younger man's body stiffened, and he began to jerk in a violent seizure.

"Lorenzo, are you crazy? Are you out of your goddamned mind?" That was Hall, running up, almost incoherent with outrage. "Since when are you bulletproof? Since when do you —?"

He broke off as Antonio scooped up Sandalini in a fireman's carry, running for the bank of sinks against the far wall.

"Lorenzo? What the hell are you doing? Is that Sandalini? Is he alive? Is he —?"

Antonio didn't hear him, his attention on the man he bore swiftly across the blood drenched, body-strewn floor. Beneath the shouts of Hall and the voices of his fellow agents barking out commands to the captured gunmen, he could hear the wet, desperate sounds of Sandalini's struggle for breath, feel his blood soaking into Antonio's clothes as the helpless body threshed and jerked. It was all he could do to hang onto him.

Don't die, Antonio prayed, fighting a wave of despair as he listened to the agonized grunts from the body he held. *Hold on, gatito.*

The smell of blood mingled with dust and gunsmoke — and heroin. He held his own breath as best as possible to avoid inhaling the deadly uncut drug into his own lungs.

Sandalini was limp as they reached the long bank of industrial sinks. Antonio lowered him carefully, turning the taps on full, unaware of the soft, pleading words that fell from his lips as he urged Sandalini to hold on, to stay with him, to fight.

Rusty water spat, choked, and then gushed out in a clean spate. Lorenzo held the unconscious man beneath the flow, washing away the poison powder. Sandalini's head lolled brokenly. He was so still…Antonio feared he was already dead.

In which case, Antonio had just blown his own cover for nothing. The handful of soldiers left alive from the Botelli, Sanchez and Mexican faction were witnessing the end of five years of painstaking undercover work as "Miguel Ortega" struggled desperately to save the undercover cop who had betrayed them all. All his work — his sacrifice — was disappearing, swirling down the drain of a rusty old sink in a milky, blood-streaked tide.

And it didn't matter.

Nothing mattered but the struggling life burning out under his frantic grip as Sandalini began to seize again. Terrible seizures. Bone snapping, ligament tearing, breath stealing seizures. Antonio struggled to hold the slighter man, to keep him from slamming his head into the sink fixtures or the sides of the basin. A terrible sound rose from the back of Sandalini's throat. Tears stung Antonio's eyes.

And then suddenly Sandalini went completely rigid, frighteningly still, heart pounding against his rib cage so hard and fast Antonio imagined it would tear out of his chest.

Just like that it was over. Sandalini went limp, boneless. Lifeless? To Antonio's horror, he could hear nothing in the chest beneath his ear — a complete and dead silence.

Panic and fear, emotions Antonio rarely experienced, flashed through him. He hauled Gabriel out of the huge porcelain sink with a strength he didn't know he possessed. He settled Gabriel on the concrete floor, ripping his bloodied and bullet-riddled shirt open and beginning CPR, roared for a medic.

CHAPTER TWELVE

Twenty-one days and counting.

Twenty-one days Antonio Lorenzo patiently kept vigil at Gabriel Sandalini's hospital bedside.

That didn't count the nightmare eternity while Antonio had fought to save Gabriel's life in a South San Francisco warehouse. Fellow officers told Antonio his battle had lasted roughly eight minutes, but Antonio was convinced he had aged a decade before paramedics finally arrived to take over.

Antonio still couldn't think of those worst minutes of his life without his stomach roiling in nausea. But, against all odds, it appeared Gabriel would live.

But in what condition? That remained a question.

Just a week ago, one of the doctors said that Sandalini must have an incredible will to live to have survived even this long after all that he had suffered.

It took ten hours of surgery to remove bullets and repair damaged organs, tissue, and bones of a man not yet thirty. Gabriel's punctured, collapsed lung slowly re-inflated, and the chest tube was finally removed. Fourteen days later, doctors removed Gabriel from the ventilator — although it wasn't taken from Gabriel's bedside for another anxious twenty-four hours. The lack of machinery made it look as if Gabriel was improving, but Antonio missed the illusion of security the equipment had brought to the situation.

And the situation was grim. Twenty-one days after being shot, Gabriel remained in a coma. But, being shot was the least of his problems. It had taken weeks for his blood and respiratory systems to rid themselves of the heroin and other drugs with which the heroin had been cut.

Antonio shifted in a hard plastic chair, studying the man lying so still in the hospital bed. It never failed to strike him, that unnatural stillness. Gabriel had always been restless, active, in motion. A bundle of physical and nervous energy.

Long black lashes curved disarmingly against ivory cheeks. Those eyes. The rare, almost amber color and the wide, exotic shape, exotic in the sharp, young face.

That smart mouth — Antonio's own mouth tugged in a grim smile. Gabriel's lips were soft and pink from the ice chips Antonio had brushed against them a few minutes earlier.

Maybe we should just sing happy birthday, blow out your candle, and call it a night?

Little wiseass.

He felt he knew Gabriel pretty well now. He read his file several times — what was there on the page, and what was between the lines. He had talked to Gabriel's captain and some of the cops who worked with him. And everything he heard, he liked. Gabriel Sandalini was tough and smart. He'd had almost no advantages growing up, but he'd resisted the temptations of the street, worked hard and become a cop. A good cop. Nobody argued that. Even the superiors with whom he'd clashed agreed he had integrity, courage, and a lot of promise.

Gabriel was good at his job, but the job was all he seemed to have. He was liked well enough, but he had no close friends, no family. Contadino's story about the father who'd run out on his mother, the stepfather who a young boy had wished would disappear — this jibed with his personnel file, and Antonio was touched that Gabriel had told him the truth about this during their time in Mexico. He could have fed Antonio Gio Contadino's cover story, but he hadn't. Antonio hoped it was a sign that Gabriel had felt something for him, that perhaps he had trusted Antonio more than he realized. Hope was all he had.

Antonio's world had shrunk to this chair, this room, this hospital. He slept on a cot in a commandeered doctor's lounge and ate from vending machines or the hospital cafeteria. He drank gallons of bitter, cold coffee and spent hours watching the motionless figure in the bed of this pale green, glass enclosed, sterile-looking cubicle of the bustling intensive care unit.

This was his choice, but, in truth, he wasn't needed anywhere. His cover was blown — and, according to his superiors, for too little effect. The good news coming out of Operation Tequila Sunset was that Botelli's West Coast distribution network was broken, not the least because Ricco Botelli had died in the warehouse shootout. The bad news, Jesus Sanchez was still in business, virtually untouched despite five years of Antonio's relentless effort. Don Jesus had been tipped off before the feds could move in and he'd slipped back into Mexico with Gina Botelli.

There was other bad news, too. Word on the street was that someone had placed a contract on Gabriel Sandalini's life.

It seemed a cruel joke. If Sanchez wanted revenge on anyone it should be Antonio Lorenzo, who had earned and then betrayed his trust — and who, after a year in Sanchez' operation as his right hand man, had collected enough information to make life — and business — difficult for the next few months. But the only threat was against Gabriel, who, barely clinging to life, was no threat to anyone. Blind, crippled, and brain damaged wasn't enough. Someone wanted Gabriel dead. O'Brien, Gabriel's captain, believed that the contract was supposed to serve as a lesson and a warning to SFPD.

But anyone coming for Gabriel would have to go through Antonio. He left Gabriel's bedside rarely — to attend to his personal needs or to check in with his superiors.

Day in, day out Antonio sat at Gabriel's bedside, keeping watch on every person — be it doctor, nurse or orderly — allowed past the guard posted outside the room. Antonio was on a first name basis with all the staff, from housekeeping to the main pulmonary specialist and the thoracic surgeon.

"Gabriel?" Antonio said softly.

Not so much as an eyelash twitched to acknowledge that the patient heard, but the nurses said it was good to keep talking, to hang on to that connection.

Acid words and soulful eyes, elegant bones and a street fighter attitude. So many contradictions.

"You going to spend the rest of your life sleeping, Gabriel?"

Gabriel. The name alone made Antonio's chest tighten. Like the archangel of the same name, Gabriel had fallen from grace for twenty-one days, waiting for the angel of death to collect him or give him back his life. *Hero of God*, that was what the name *Gabriel* meant, and this reckless, sharp-tongued, defiant young man *was* a hero — regardless of what the fools at the FBI thought.

He reached out, tracing thin motionless fingers with a gentle touch.

"Any change?"

He managed not to jump, but it wasn't easy. Gabriel's boss, Captain David O'Brien, stood at the foot of the bed, studying its motionless occupant. He looked tired and worried.

"No change," admitted Antonio. Unhurriedly, he moved his hand, resting it on the sidebars of the bed.

O'Brien sighed. "I just thought I'd drop by for a minute. See how he's doing."

Watching Gabriel's sleeping face, Antonio said softly, "He is fighting his way back."

"I hope you're right." O'Brien turned his faded gaze to Antonio's face. "What do the docs say? Don't they have any ideas?"

Not many ideas that Antonio liked. He said calmly, "His body is healing, but they are not sure about his mind. The latest CAT scan shows none of the residual brain damage they expected from the heroin and his seizures but..." Antonio shrugged, his own eyes returning to the bed. Gabriel looked like a fallen angel, his hair black and silky against the carved pallor of his gaunt face. "There's no doubt the chloroquine mixed with the heroin has caused permanent damage. Only time will tell how much."

"Why the hell was a malaria drug used to cut the heroin?"

"We think one of the rival factions for Sanchez' business paid off someone inside the Mexican pipeline. The lab reported levels of cholorquine so high it would have killed anyone who used the heroin, even after it was cut for sale. Bad junk would have destroyed Botelli's reputation on the streets."

"It's a hell of a shame." O'Brien never entered this room without making this comment; Antonio had to swallow his exasperation.

He kept his feelings out of his voice, "He's young, strong. He has the will to live. He will live."

"He won't be strong after this. Even if he's…well, all there. That lung that collapsed — it's not going to take any strain. And his eyes —"

"He will adjust."

O'Brien gave him a funny look. "You don't know Gabriel. He's not big on adjustments. Head-on collisions are more his style."

True enough. But Gabriel had no choice this time.

Into his silence, O'Brien said regretfully, "He's too young for this. I saw the doctor's final report on the retinal testing. Early retirement, disability. Washed up way before his time. Hell of a shame."

Antonio's anger — or perhaps it was fear — flared. "There are things in life besides being a cop." He caught the look O'Brien shot him. Antonio made his voice smooth again. "He just doesn't know it yet."

Gabriel's captain meant no harm by his thoughtless comments. And unfortunately there was truth to the things O'Brien kept himself from speaking. The weeks sitting beside Gabriel's bedside were proof of that. There was nothing in Gabriel Sandalini's life but being a cop.

Captain O'Brien studied Antonio thoughtfully. He said at last, "You don't owe him anything. I read the report, and I sat through the hearing. I got the official explanation of what went down. And I got the unofficial explanation. You weren't to blame."

His tone implied others were, and that was no secret to Antonio. O'Brien had filed formal complaints against the FBI's handling of the case — and against Assistant Director Hall. But they all knew it wasn't going anywhere. If there was a scapegoat in this fiasco, it wouldn't be Hall.

Antonio said nothing. He had read the reports — hell, he had written some of them — and he had testified at the hearing. Logically, he knew that he wasn't to blame, but he blamed himself all the same. It was nearly unbearable that he had been unable to protect Gabriel. Antonio did not like feeling helpless — or a failure.

O'Brien sighed, hands in his pants pockets, absently jingling the coins, the musical sounds joining the muted hospital sounds. Antonio felt O'Brien's curious stare. "Well, you've sure as hell been a good friend to him. I hope he appreciates it when…if…"

"When," Antonio said with certainty. He met O'Brien's tired blue eyes, and saw that O'Brien did indeed understand. In fact, something close to a smile crossed O'Brien's lined face.

"He's going to need a friend."

"He will have everything he needs," Antonio said calmly, and understanding or not, O'Brien blinked at the sweeping assumptions there.

Movement on the bed pulled Antonio from his thoughts. He leaned over, slipping his hand through the side rails. Gabriel's limp hand lay on the well-washed blanket, but Antonio swore he'd spied an infinitesimal twitch.

Very lightly, he traced the length of one thin finger.

There. The tiniest flex.

Antonio stroked the underside of Gabriel's hand, a feathering touch. Fingers quivered and closed around his. For a moment Antonio was too choked with emotion to speak. There was something almost trusting…childlike in that curl of thin fingers around his own index finger.

"That's it, Gabriel. Come on, *gatito*, you must wake up now."

Antonio rose cautiously, bending over the railing. With his free hand, he gently combed long strands of silken black hair back from Gabriel's face. He brushed his knuckles against the chalky, smooth skin stretched taut over high cheekbones — the same skin he helped shave everyday. He felt a tiny muscular contraction.

Wrapping his big hand around the fingers clutching his own, resting his hand against the side of that gaunt face, he pitched his voice low, keeping the tone teasing and persuasive. "*Gatito*, are you in there? Time to wake up. I want to hear the sweet sound of your belligerent voice swearing gutter oaths at me again."

The long, inky eyelashes flickered. Glistening moisture gathered beneath Gabriel's eyelashes.

Antonio bent closer. "Gabriel? Can you hear me?"

Antonio released his hand. Dropping the side rail, he sat gingerly on the edge of the bed. He took Gabriel's hand again, chafing it gently. Thin fingers felt fragile as bird bones.

"Yes, you're coming back, aren't you? Retracing your steps, *sí?*" He stroked Gabriel's cheek. Instinctively Gabriel turned his face into that touch, seeking the caress like a magnet drawn to steel.

Antonio leaned lower still to stroke a colorless cheek. Tears slid slowly from Gabriel's eyes. Antonio brushed them away. "You're all right, *mi gatito parvulo*. You're safe now. It is confusing, *sí?* But it will all make sense soon…"

Gabriel blinked. His lips parted, and the tip of his tongue ran over them trying unsuccessfully to wet the surface.

Antonio awaited any sign that Gabriel was still himself, that intellect and personality had survived all terrible trauma. Deaf to muffled sounds of hospital activity beyond the glass partition walls, all Antonio's attention stayed focused on the man in the bed.

Gabriel's Adam's apple bobbed as he swallowed hard and licked his lips again. Antonio's eyes followed each little move; he warmed his voice, hoping to anchor Gabriel to the conscious world.

"Where…" Gabriel coughed and licked his lips again. He blinked several times. "Where am I?" His voice was raspy, weak from disuse.

Antonio spoke calmly, gently. "General Hospital. Intensive care. You've been here for three weeks."

Gabriel's irises were black with only the thinnest band of hazel around them, permanently dilated to their maximum diameter to let light reach optic nerves that no longer functioned. The dilated and fixed stare was expected, but still painful to witness. Antonio made sure none of that pain showed in his voice. "You've been in a coma."

Turning his face toward Antonio's voice, Gabriel frowned and blinked harder, the hand not clamped tightly in Antonio's grip moving to rub his eyes. "Who are you?"

Antonio reached for the call bell tied to the railing and buzzed for a nurse.

Capturing Gabriel's hand and gently pulling it away from his face, Antonio took a firm grip of it as well. "You know me, *gatito.*"

Gabriel released a shallow, shaky breath. "Ortega?"

"Si. Although Miguel Ortega is not my real name — any more than Giovanni Contadino was yours."

"What are you talk…?" Gabriel's voice died way. "I don't understand."

"Give yourself a minute." Antonio's abject relief that Gabriel seemed merely confused nearly closed his voice off again.

"What are you doing here?" Gabriel wriggled his fingers, but didn't work very hard at pulling away. "What happened?"

"I'm an FBI agent on loan to the Drug Task Force. I was undercover with Sanchez' cartel. My name is Antonio Lorenzo."

He watched uneasily as the other man tried to focus. Antonio was relieved when a nurse who had been in the room earlier started toward the cubicle.

"Okay." A noticeable tremor rippled through Gabriel. "So you're an FBI agent sitting at my bedside in the intensive care unit of the hospital, holding my hands in the dark because… *why?*"

Antonio could hear panic creeping into Gabriel's words — read it in his body language as suspicion dawned. He said steadily, "Because I wish to be here with you. Because I care for you."

Gabriel's heart rate jumped. The monitor on the wall emitted an insistent, annoying beep. Gabriel said breathlessly, "What the fuck are you talking about? I don't… Why are we in *the dark?*"

Antonio had tried to imagine this scene often. "We are not in darkness, *gatito*. It is the afternoon."

The strained whimper tore at Antonio's heart. He tried to find words of comfort, tried to hold to the hands fighting him, but he was terrified of hurting Gabriel more than he just had. The nurse arrived as Gabriel began to scream.

Gabriel was calm, still feeling the effects of sedatives. He lay quiet in the hospital bed, curled on his side, face buried in the curve of his elbow. Beneath the coarse hospital blanket, his knees were almost to his chest. The restraints had come off after sedation kicked in, though there were still red shadows on his wrists. The sight of those chafe marks angered Antonio, although he knew the staff had acted to protect Gabriel from his own hysteria.

When Antonio tried to intervene, the harassed hospital staff had nearly thrown him out of the cubicle. But, unexpectedly, Gabriel had responded to his voice — reaching out. Antonio had folded him into his arms, holding him tight, soothing him with murmured reassurance and endearments as the sedative was administered. At Antonio's insistence, the foam-padded Velcro bands were removed

Once Gabriel had calmed, he'd grown distant and quiet, pulling away from Antonio, sleeping or staring at the pictures in his memory. He had said nothing until now.

"What did you say your name was?"

"Lorenzo. Antonio Lorenzo."

"And you're FBI?"

"Yes."

Silence while Gabriel seemed to consider this. "What happened?" he asked finally.

"Do you remember the warehouse?"

Gabriel was silent, processing. He swallowed and said, "I remember…" and he didn't finish.

His last vision must have been a scene from a nightmare.

Antonio said, "It does not matter. Botelli was killed in the crossfire. Michelangelo Rizzi died as well."

"What about Sanchez?" Gabriel asked.

"He escaped," Antonio admitted. "Somehow he received word of what happened. Before we could move in, he managed to leave on his private plane — he took Gina Botelli with him."

"She go willingly?"

Antonio said cautiously, "There is no reason to think otherwise."

"Except that she hated him!" There was tight anger in Gabriel's voice; Antonio knew it stemmed from many things.

"Our contacts in Mexico say that Sanchez and Gina married the day after they arrived."

Gabriel was shaking his head. "She couldn't stand him. No way did she willingly marry him."

His insistence seemed strange to Antonio, but perhaps it was easier to focus on Gina's plight than his own. He changed the subject. "What happened when you returned from Mexico?"

"What?"

"There was a bruise on your face that night at the warehouse." He touched Gabriel's averted face with gentle fingertips. A tiny shiver rippled through Gabriel's body. "You moved as though you hurt."

Gabriel was silent for so long Lorenzo thought he might have dozed off again. "Botelli. He found Gina coming onto me when we got back — after she picked me up at the airport. She didn't want Sanchez. She was crying…"

Antonio pushed gently, "And?"

"Botelli walked in and caught her. His face was…" His breath caught unsteadily. *"Fuck."*

"Take your time." Antonio wanted Gabriel to talk. Talking was good. It kept him connected to the here and now.

"I thought he was going to kill us both. She was hanging onto me, crying and trying to kiss me. I was trying to push her away without hurting her — without pissing her off too much. Botelli grabbed her and threw her out of the room. He backhanded me…"

Antonio gently brushed his cheek again, and Gabriel wiped his eyes impatiently, as though something obstructed his view.

"He knocked me around a little." He shrugged. "Could have been a lot worse."

And not much later it had been.

Gabriel lapsed back into apathetic silence. Antonio was unsure if he should let him rest or if more talking would be good for him. Eventually Gabriel would have to be officially debriefed, but he was far from well enough now.

Antonio watched him cocooned in a fortress of coarse blankets and flat pillows. Every so often the thin fingers made cautious exploration…identifying the pull of the monitor wires on his chest, the pinch of tape at the IV in his arm, the dry swoosh of oxygen from the tube under his nose.

After a time, Gabriel uncurled and rolled onto his back. He turned sightless eyes to the ceiling. "Are you still here?" His tone was short.

"I am still here."

"Why?"

Now there was a question.

And the answer was one that Gabriel Sandalini was clearly not ready to hear. Antonio himself still struggled occasionally with it. After all, at nearly forty, he had been comfortable with being a lifelong bachelor, a gallant and worldly lover, taking his pleasure and returning it with all his considerable skill — no strings attached. But from the moment an insolent young punk with blazing eyes and the unexpectedly sweet smile of a Madonna had caught his eye, his life — and heart — hadn't been the same.

He asked neutrally, "Do you not want me to stay?"

"I don't care what the fuck you do." The tone held a shaky bravado that made Antonio's heart ache.

"Then I will please myself and stay."

Was it Antonio's imagination or did Gabriel relax a little? They were silent, only occasional muffled announcements from the hospital loudspeaker interrupted the rhythmic sounds of the machines and monitors.

"Why does my side hurt?" Gabriel touched a tender spot on the midsection of his right ribcage.

"You were shot in the chest. Your lung collapsed. They took out the chest tube about a week after surgery." Antonio didn't say that the injured lung would likely prove a chronic problem.

"And here?" Gabriel rubbed at the strip of cartilage that ran down the center of his rib cage. The movement pulled the IV line and made him grimace at the sudden stabbing pinch of the tiny plastic catheter and unyielding tape on his arm.

"CPR." Antonio added reluctantly, "I'm sorry. I had never actually done it before on a real person. I may have been too...*enthusiastic* in my efforts to revive you."

"You —?" Gabriel's face twisted, fingers moving nervously over the mattress in quest of something to cling to. They closed on a fold of blanket. "Didn't know your own strength, you fucking conquistador?"

It was a weak attempt at humor and the old attitude, but it was still something. Antonio said, "I did *not* break any ribs. Not one. The paramedics said I did well considering the circumstances."

"And the circumstances were...my heart stopped?" The thin blanket was bunched and knotted in Gabriel's tense grip.

Antonio admitted, "*Sí.*"

Gabriel's blind eyes turned toward the sound of Antonio's voice. He said nothing for a long moment. Then, thickly, "You should have let me die."

"Do not say that!" And despite his resolve to be gentle and patient, Antonio couldn't help the wave of anger that swept over him. Didn't the little fool *know*? Didn't he *understand*? "Never again say such a thing."

"Or what?" Gabriel sneered. "You won't like me anymore? We won't be pals? Fuck buddies? I've got news for you, we're not friends now, and just because you're feeling guilty —"

"I do not feel guilty," Antonio lied. "I could not have stopped what happened in the warehouse. Your cover was blown, and it played out from there. You knew the risks as did I."

"Oh, fuck you!" Gabriel sat up straight, hair disheveled, face flushed. "I don't need to be scolded on top of shot and blinded."

He tried to scramble off the far side of the bed, pulling wires and tubes in the process. Antonio was up and around the bed in a flash. Gabriel didn't get farther than having his heels over the edge of the mattress before Antonio grabbed him and moved him bodily back into place.

"Let go of me, you son of a bitch!" Gabriel twisted and thrashed, but Antonio gathered him up without effort, wrapping his arms firmly around the slighter man, ignoring his rage as he cradled him against his chest. "Get your fucking hands off me. Fucker! Goddamned son of a bitch. I don't want you. I don't need you. Let *go*!"

Antonio ignored the hate-filled words inspired by Gabriel's pain and terror.

"I know," he murmured. "I am sorry."

He repeated the soothing words over and over while Gabriel's struggles grew weaker and weaker. The burst of adrenaline faded, and Gabriel lay motionless against Antonio's broad chest.

For a moment Antonio rested his face in the silky soft hair. Gabriel smelled of sleep-sweat and antiseptic, of fear and much-laundered cotton.

"Hush," Antonio said softly.

"I hate you," Gabriel mumbled.

I love you, Antonio thought. He said calmly, "So? Nothing has changed."

Under the circumstances it was not the smartest thing he could have said. The words simply popped out.

Gabriel started fighting again, and this time he really did seem frantic to escape. "Nothing has changed? *Zurramato!* You goddamned filthy fucker. If I could see you, I'd kill you, you arrogant, selfish cocksucker —" He threw his head back and clipped Antonio on the underside of his jaw.

t hurt like hell — and from the way Gabriel shut up, it couldn't have felt good on the administering side of it either. Antonio ignored the sensation of getting socked on the jaw and firmly tucked Gabriel's head between his chin and shoulder.

"All right. Enough." He spoke sternly over the other man's exhausted panting. "We have established that you hate me and do not want me here. But I am not going away, so you may as well get used to me."

A nurse uneasily poked her head inside the cubicle and mouthed a question. Antonio nodded reassuringly at her, and she ducked back out.

"Fucker." It was little more than a whispered mumble. Gabriel had melted against him, exhausted, frightened and lost. Antonio realized that Gabriel could not even know where he was sitting. A lifetime of proud independence had exploded and disappeared like grains of white powder on the wind.

Settling back against the headboard, Antonio altered his embrace so that Gabriel was cradled lovingly rather than restrained forcibly. "Later perhaps. When you are more yourself. Right now the nurses are watching."

There was a blank silence and then Gabriel laughed, a shaky, angry laugh, but his body relaxed into Antonio's hold. "Asshole."

"*Si.*" Antonio kissed his hot, sweaty temple. He could see Gabriel was fighting tears. He said tenderly, "Let go, *gatito*. Mourn and then move on. Your life is not over. Not by any means. So let the tears fall for the past and then we will speak of the future."

He felt Gabriel begin to tremble, and then a racking sob tore out of his throat. It was followed by another.

"That's it, my little one," Antonio whispered in the shiny black hair. "Let go. I have you safe now. It's alright for brave men to cry on days like these…"

He held Gabriel while the young man cried and daylight bled slowly into night.

CHAPTER THIRTEEN

Gabriel spent a restless night, his nervous system kicking off the sedatives surprisingly fast. Antonio had not wanted to leave him for even a short time. Instead, he'd spent the long night in the hard plastic chair, speaking quietly to Gabriel each time he jerked awake after brief spells of uneasy sleep. Antonio allowed himself to doze only when he knew Gabriel had once more slipped into restive sleep.

With morning, the bustling hospital routine began. Gabriel was edgy, tensing at sudden sounds, and borderline hostile to Antonio. It was difficult, but Antonio had expected nothing else.

"Do you live here or something?" Gabriel asked irritably.

Antonio answered calmly, "No. In fact, if you're alright for a few hours, I have things I must see to."

Gabriel swallowed hard. "Don't let me keep you," he said indifferently.

Antonio rose, catching the little flinch Gabriel gave as the chair scraped on linoleum. He bent over the bed, brushing his knuckles against Gabriel's bristly cheek. "I'll be back soon, eh? And help you shave."

The fixed pupils stared up at his face. Gabriel's pretty mouth firmed with an effort. "Take your time," he said coolly.

If Gabriel were still sighted, it would have been different. Antonio would have kissed him hard, punishing and teasing, but now…now he felt strongly that he must not overwhelm Gabriel, must not cross that fine line between reassurance and bullying. Antonio feared that he was out of his depth, but he knew he mustn't make Gabriel feel that he had no choice or that he was forced into something for which he might not be ready.

Something that he might not want.

Yes, it had to be faced.

"Behave yourself, Sandalini," he said with a briskness he did not feel, and he left the cubicle. But he paused a moment outside the room, looking through the long windows. Gabriel was leaning back against the pillows, staring at the ceiling. The bitter hopelessness of his expression made walking away one of the hardest things Antonio had ever done.

After calling Captain O'Brien and letting him know Gabriel had recovered consciousness, Antonio headed back to his townhouse. He showered, treated himself to the first real, hot breakfast he had enjoyed in many weeks, sorted quickly through a stack of what was almost entirely junk mail. He packed a change of clothes for the hospital and sat down to write one of his brief monthly letters to his family.

When that was done and he had run out of reasonable excuses, he finally called Assistant Director Hall at the Bureau.

Hall, predictably, was interested only in the possibility that Gabriel might have some useful information for helping to track down Sanchez and Gina Botelli. That Gabriel was physically and emotionally as fragile as eggshell meant nothing to him.

"Then when *will* he be well enough to be debriefed?" he questioned sharply in answer to Antonio's insistence that fighting Gabriel's doctors for access would be pointless.

"Not for a few days, certainly," Antonio replied. "I'm with him all the time. I'll know when he's ready."

"That's another thing," Hall said. "As soon as Sandalini is debriefed, I've got a case for you back in New Jersey. We've got a drug trafficking ring under investigation, and your…expertise is required."

The slight inflection on *expertise* raised Antonio's hackles, but he kept his voice even. "This is another undercover operation?"

And Hall laughed — a hard, cold sound like an icicle snapping from roof overhang. "I think your undercover days are over, don't you? Your face was splashed all over the news after the fiasco with Operation Tequila Sunset."

There had been two photographs. One of Antonio leaving the hospital on one of his infrequent trips from Gabriel's side, the other of his arriving at the courthouse to testify in front of the grand jury. Together they didn't exactly add up to an exposé, but Hall was right — a bastard, but right. Antonio's usefulness undercover was compromised for the foreseeable future on the west coast.

But New Jersey? The other side of the country? That last image of Gabriel's silent despair was etched on his memory. He couldn't contemplate leaving him at such a time.

"I would have to refuse the case," he said.

"I don't think I heard you correctly," Hall said. The frost in his voice told Antonio that his boss had heard quite clearly.

"I do not wish to transfer to another field office. I do not wish to work a case on the other side of the country right now," he replied.

"I don't recall asking. You're being transferred. Your usefulness on the west coast is over."

This was monumental bullshit, and they both knew it. Antonio was an experienced and respected field agent. This was payback for putting the life of an SFPD officer above the needs of the FBI. Hall had had a lot riding on that high profile bust.

"There is a death threat against Sandalini from the Sanchez organization."

"I'm well aware of it," Hall said. "And it's SFPD's problem, not ours. Sandalini is not one of ours. You on the other hand, *are* — assuming you're still willing to follow orders and do your job."

Antonio opened his mouth to tell Hall calmly and precisely what he could do with his job, but thought better of it. His resignation now would mean someone else from the Bureau would debrief Gabriel — someone unlikely to be as careful with him as Antonio would be. It might even mean that Antonio no longer had any legitimate reason for sticking by Gabriel's side, and the next time the young fool threw a fit it might result in getting Antonio kicked out of the hospital.

So Antonio curbed his temper, and said composedly, "Very well. When I've debriefed Sandalini, I'll book my flight."

"You do that," Hall said, and rang off.

Antonio replaced the phone thoughtfully and stared at it.

Picking up his bag, he left the townhouse and drove back to General Hospital — where he found the parking lot full of police cars.

Heart pounding, he left his car and made his way — flashing his ID — through the cops milling outside and made it to the security booth inside the hospital entrance. O'Brien was there, and he waved Antonio over immediately.

"What's happened?" Antonio's mouth was dry with something he only dimly recognized as fear.

"Someone made a try for Sandalini," O'Brien said grimly.

Antonio gripped the older man's arm. "Is he all right?"

"Sandalini's fine. He has no idea what happened. He was asleep the whole time. The shooter never made it past the second floor."

"Where is he?"

"Got away."

Antonio swore. "But you have identified him?"

"Oh, yeah. Ramon Olmo. We spotted him right away coming into the building. I guess he thought we weren't keeping a watch on Gabe. Or maybe he thought *you* were the guard. Or maybe it was just coincidence."

"I don't believe in coincidence."

"Me neither," O'Brien agreed. "The kid's not well enough to move yet, is he?"

"No." Antonio thought a moment. "I have orders to debrief him, and then I'm being transferred back East."

"Oh, hell," O'Brien said. "Are you —?"

Antonio shook his head. "No. I must play along of course, until Gabriel's well enough to leave here, but I'll never leave him unless he sends me away — and truly means it."

O'Brien blinked. After a pause he said, "Uh, I hope he appreciates everything you're doing for him. You're talking about throwing away your career, you know."

"The thought had occurred to me." Antonio felt grim. "But I am not doing it for Gabriel's appreciation. This is something I must do."

He nodded to O'Brien, who still looked doubtful, and then made his way to the elevators.

The uniformed cop outside Gabriel's room grimaced when he spotted Antonio and said, "He's awake. Hope you're wearing your flak jacket."

Antonio raised his eyebrows.

"He was a real charmer all morning. Had one of the nurses in tears — and threw his lunch tray on the floor."

"Ah. He must have ordered the chicken," Antonio said. "I had a similar reaction to it."

The cop snickered and Antonio stepped inside Gabriel's cubicle.

White-faced and breathing heavily, Gabriel was hobbling back to bed with the help of a nurse.

"The bed is at twelve o'clock, the nightstand at one —"

Gabriel held his hands straight out, feeling impatiently in front of him. This mark of helplessness twisted Antonio's guts.

"That's right," the nurse said cheerfully. "You're doing fine."

He climbed back into bed, and the nurse fussed around rehooking him to the various monitors and machines. Gabriel sank back against the pillows, his face gleaming with perspiration.

"Agent Lorenzo is back," the nurse informed him.

"Fuckin' A," Gabriel muttered, but he was too whipped to inject much venom into it.

The nurse met Antonio's eyes. Gabriel didn't know about the threat against him. The last few moments had confirmed for him that Gabriel already had his hands full dealing with getting back on his feet. The last thing he needed was to know someone was trying to kill him.

The nurse left them, and Antonio pulled the chair over to the bed.

"I hear you've been terrorizing the nursing staff," he said.

Gabriel made a face. "They're treating me like a child. Or a moron."

"So you threw your lunch on the floor to prove you were an intelligent grown up. Interesting strategy, Sandalini."

"Fuck off," Gabriel said wearily.

Antonio tilted his head, studying him. "Would you like to talk?"

"No."

Antonio was obligingly silent and after a few moments Gabriel raised his head. "Are you staring at me?"

Antonio could hear the edge in his voice. He said, "I am watching the intensive care ward through the window. It is most interesting."

"Glad we can provide a little reality TV for you, asshole."

Antonio sighed.

"Don't do that," Gabriel said tightly.

"Do what?"

He heaved a huge sigh, mimicking Antonio. "Don't give me that fucking long-suffering act. Like you're too noble — or too sorry for me — to say what you think."

"I think you're behaving like a shit," Antonio said.

Gabriel raised his head, glared past Antonio. This further sign of vulnerability caught at Antonio's heart. But he said, "We have all worked very hard to keep you alive. A little gratitude would become you."

"*Gratitude?*" And Gabriel spluttered for an instant. "You think I should be grateful for —"

"For being alive?" Antonio cut in. "Yes, I do. I am sorry you are blind, but blind and alive is still better than under thirty and dead. You will soon be stronger, and you will realize the truth of what I'm saying."

"Christ," Gabriel said, sounding truly amazed. "Do you ever have *any* doubts that you know best? Has it ever occurred to you that you *might* be wrong about something?"

"I am not wrong about this," Antonio said with finality. "And when you are stronger and more yourself, you will see -"

"No, I *won't* see," Gabriel broke in. "That's the goddamned point. I'll never see anything again. I'm —" He broke off sharply and struggled visibly for control.

Antonio covered one white-knuckled hand with his own, and, to his surprise, Gabriel's fingers twisted within his grasp, lacing with his own. It was a surprisingly fierce grip.

"It will be alright," Antonio told him.

"It will never be alright again," Gabriel replied, but he did not let go.

"Tell me again, everything that happened," Gabriel requested. He was having trouble sleeping despite the drugs they continued to pump into him. He had declined television, music, and being read to. Nor had he seemed to have interest in talking until he suddenly broke his brooding silence. "You know, after I...I went down. Did the seizures start right away?"

Antonio grimaced. He didn't like to encourage this morbid train of thought. Still, Gabriel's need to know was natural.

He said placidly, "*Sí.* Almost immediately." He didn't tell Gabriel about what he had gone through during these long weeks while Gabriel had lain wasting away in his coma hooked to breathing machines, wrapped in special blankets, with tubes running out of his chest, monitors ringing as his frail body suffered almost daily seizures. Antonio did not tell him how many times his heart had nearly stopped or how many times he had hovered near death.

"Will I have more seizures?"

"I don't know," Antonio admitted. "It is two weeks since the last one."

Gabriel's mouth tightened. "What else?"

Antonio said reluctantly, eyeing that white knuckled grip on the bed railing, "These are questions for your doctor, Sandalini."

"What else?" Gabriel repeated tersely.

"Your lung was collapsed for many days. The doctor said once that happens, it can happen again very easily. No more smoking."

And no extreme exertion — but you did not tell this to a young man facing what Gabriel was.

"Oh, bullshit," Gabriel said irritably. "Doctors always say that. I'm not going to be an invalid even if I'm…"

"Blind," Antonio finished calmly. "You must accept that your life's changed now. There are adjustments you must make, whether you wish it or not."

"I'm not accepting anything," Gabriel said truculently. "I haven't even had a second opinion. I don't believe…" he swallowed on the words, but he recovered instantly. "I'm not going to take *your* word for anything."

Antonio saw the childish rudeness for what it was — fear and anger and frustration. He said, "Why are you angry with me? What possible motive would I have for lying to you? You've asked me, and I've told you. Your doctors will explain it to you much more clearly than I can. And if you wish a second opinion — or a third or even a fourth — I will arrange it for you."

Gabriel's chest rose and fell in agitation as he listened. Antonio watched him fight for control, watched the scared grip on the bed railing gradually loosen as the younger man consciously forced himself to relax.

"You'll arrange it?" he asked finally. "Why should *you*…arrange anything?"

"You know why," Antonio said simply.

"You're feeling guilty about what happened to me."

"No."

Gabriel's mouth curved maliciously. "Yes, you are. I can hear it in your voice. And you're sorry for me."

Antonio said quietly, "You're speaking of guilt and pity. I'm speaking of something entirely different."

The smile faded from Gabriel's gaunt face. He turned his head, the silky hair hiding his profile. He said roughly, "You're confusing sex with something else, hombre."

"I think I am old enough to know the difference."

"You think I'm not?" Gabriel turned his head and Antonio's heart caught painfully at those huge black eyes — wide and dark like a fawn's — but limpid and blank.

"You are old enough to know the difference," Antonio admitted.

"You think a couple of fucks are the basis for…what?" Gabriel's jeering voice was at odds with those enormous helpless eyes.

"I do not know. Maybe…friendship. Maybe something more. In time."

Gabriel's face twisted. "I haven't even got used to thinking of you being on the same side as me. And you want to be *friends*?"

Antonio said, "Do you have so many friends you can't use another?"

Silence.

The silence stretched — and stretched. Antonio began to wonder if he had gone too far. He opened his mouth to retract or soften his last comment. He knew only too well how very much alone in the world Gabriel was.

Gabriel licked his lips. "There's a cop posted to my room. Why?"

And now it was Antonio's turn to be caught off guard. He had underestimated how alert Gabriel was, how quickly he could put two and two together without the aid of his sight.

Even a portion of the truth would be terrifying for a man who could no longer see his enemies coming. He said carefully, "It's possible that Sanchez may wish to retaliate for the destruction of his plans for West Coast expansion."

Gabriel took this calmly, although he blinked a couple of times, straining to see in the darkness surrounding him. "Retaliate? You mean he wants revenge?"

"It's possible."

"Against me?"

"Against both of us perhaps."

Gabriel nodded, but his hands twisted nervously in the well-worn blankets.

"I've spoken to your Captain O'Brien," Antonio said. "When you're strong enough, when your doctors give permission, we'll go away for a time."

"Go…away?"

"To some place quiet where you can recover your strength in peace."

"Protective custody?"

Yes, despite the drugs, Gabriel was much more alert than Antonio had imagined. He said, "Have I said so? You just need time to recover…and adjust."

"To being blind," Gabriel said bitterly.

"To being blind," Antonio agreed.

Gabriel's Adam's apple jumped in his thin throat. "What if I don't want to go away with you?"

"If there's somewhere else you prefer to stay during your rehabilitation, we'll make those arrangements for you," Antonio said. He kept his tone unemotional, but it wasn't easy. Gabriel could very easily call his bluff, and then he would have to admit the whole story and risk destroying whatever fragile trust was growing between them.

Gabriel said nothing for a long moment. Then, unexpectedly, he yawned widely offering a glimpse of white teeth and pink tonsils. He was blinking again, but it was with tiredness now.

"I guess it doesn't matter," he said.

"You flatter me," Antonio said gravely, and Gabriel gave a sleepy grin, moving carefully onto his side, wincing a little at the pull of IV and catheters.

"Hey, you don't want to build a relationship on lies, do you?"

Antonio's heart jumped. He kept his voice smooth with an effort.

"Are we building a relationship?"

"I don't know. Maybe." Gabriel's eyes closed. He sounded drugged with weariness. "Friends is good. Are you staying the night?"

"Yes."

Gabriel's mouth curved in a faint smile. His hand moved on the blanket, feeling its way, and Antonio reached through the bars to clasp it in his own large one.

"Sleep well, *gatito*," he said softly.

"Sweet dreams," Gabriel mumbled.

Antonio smiled grimly. His dreams were sweet indeed, but sadly, dreams were all he had.

CHAPTER FOURTEEN

"Three steps up to the landing of the front porch. Then six feet to the front door."

Thin fingers sinking into muscle, Gabriel gripped Antonio's upper arm as he climbed the three steps to the beach house. His gait was halting and slow, but he made it up to the porch without incident. Which was more than he had managed in the hospital parking lot, stumbling over an uneven join in the sidewalk, and nearly falling flat on his face. All that had saved him were Antonio's quick reflexes and strong arms, and it had shaken his already rocky confidence.

"*Si.* Exactly. *Bueno*, Sandalini." Gabriel threw him a quick, wary look. Antonio felt a rueful smile spread across his own face.

Gabriel depended on him, but he resented that dependence — as any man would. Antonio could only imagine how unnerving this must be for one such as Gabriel, a man who had chosen a career of protecting and helping others, now helpless and in need of someone to do the protecting and caring.

It was a difficult situation for Antonio — feeling as he did. He was a little surprised to find himself so willing to shoulder the role of caretaker. He'd never had much patience for helpless or clingy lovers. Gabriel's strength and smartass attitude had challenged and amused him. And it wasn't as though he and Gabriel had had time to build the foundation of a real relationship. A couple of highly memorable fucks hardly made for Happy Ever After.

Still, he very much feared for the first time in his life he was truly, deeply, irrevocably in love.

And the hell of it was that it was completely one-sided.

Gabriel's touch was cold where his fingers and palm rested on Antonio's arm. Antonio covered the thin hand with his own larger one, pleased when Gabriel leaned a little into his side. He was very tired, of course, and already exhausted by the long drive from the hospital to this private and secluded house up the coast.

"Six feet straight ahead," Antonio said briskly, managing not to show how touched he was by this rare turning to him for support.

"Six feet," Gabriel muttered. "Great. Like I can tell what six feet looks like." He moved away from Antonio, took a shuffling step, one hand in front of him feeling for some landmark. Antonio watched him like a hawk, ready to scoop him up if he stumbled, but he kept his voice unmoved, crisp. Gabriel did not react well to sympathy.

One step, then another. One more hesitant slide and Gabriel halted.

"You wear a size nine shoe, Sandalini. Each step you take is not quite a foot. March it out, or the first time you walk out here on your own you'll fall down the steps."

"You mean you might let me out on my own someday?" Gabriel scoffed.

"You are not a prisoner," Antonio said shortly

"No?"

Blind or no, still an aggravating little shit.

It had taken two weeks for Gabriel to gain sufficient strength to be discharged into Antonio's care. His other option had been a rehab facility for the blind. He'd fought the notion of institutional care as fiercely as he'd fought the idea of being delivered into Antonio's keeping. But even if he'd been well enough to avoid rehab and eventual placement in an assisted living facility…he had no family, no parents or partner or lover to look after him. He didn't even have a home. The pathetic little room that he'd rented as Giovanni Contadino had also been home for Gabriel Sandalini.

When the truth of it hit him, Gabriel had grown surlier and more morose than ever. With great difficulty, Antonio had left him to it — or appeared to. In reality, he'd gone on making plans for Gabriel's care and protection.

He viewed many houses, finally settling on one located on the shore — quiet and private and close to good medical facilities. He wound up his own business affairs and began incrementally vanishing without a trace, transferring bank accounts and moving the things into storage. With O'Brien's help, he did the same for Gabriel. Within days, anyone looking for Gabriel Sandalini had trouble finding any sign of him in San Francisco — trouble finding any sign he had ever existed at all.

After two days away, he had returned to General Hospital to find a quiet and strangely subdued Gabriel.

"Have you been behaving yourself, *amigo*?" he had asked, pulling up a chair and preparing for the resumption of hostilities. Instead, Gabriel just stared up at him with those wide, black eyes in his drawn face.

"Yeah."

"And…they are treating you alright?"

Gabriel shrugged.

Antonio was at a loss. Gabriel lay quietly, responding when Antonio spoke to him but otherwise silent, seemingly lost in his thoughts. It worried Antonio, this strange, almost polite distance. When Gabriel fell asleep, Antonio sought answers. A nurse confided that Officer Sandalini hadn't slept well or eaten much the entire time Antonio was gone. The few times Gabriel had dozed off he woke more restless and anxious than ever. He had asked for Antonio twice.

And Antonio had felt an unworthy spark of happiness because surely that meant Gabriel was, if nothing else, coming to rely on his friendship.

He returned to Gabriel's private room — he had been moved from the intensive care unit the previous week — and waited patiently for Gabriel to awaken. When Gabriel had opened his eyes at last, turning his head on the pillow and concentrating…listening… Antonio had said casually, "So, Sandalini, have you thought much about where you will be staying when you leave here?"

Antonio didn't miss the flicker of relief that crossed Gabriel's face.

"Yeah." Gabriel had swallowed. "Is the…is your offer still open?"

"Of course," Antonio said. "Everything is arranged — if this is what you wish."

Gabriel lifted a shoulder. "If it's all arranged," he said indifferently, but Antonio didn't miss the almost imperceptible relaxation. Within the hour, Gabriel was responding to Antonio in his inimitable, obnoxious style.

He stood now a couple of feet from Antonio, his face angled, listening. The dark glasses he insisted on wearing concealed much of his face, but there was a small, irritating smile on his pretty mouth. Antonio knew he was enjoying once again getting under Antonio's skin.

"Not a prisoner? That's exactly how it feels to *me, amigo*," he said.

"I did not kidnap you, although apparently it amuses you to think so."

"Kidnapping? Hey, kinky," mocked Gabriel, but Antonio could see the tension vibrating through his slight frame. Antonio understood that it was easier for Gabriel to bait him than to deal with the terror of walking six feet across a strange porch.

So Antonio moved to the door, unlocked it, pushed it wide. He reached his hand back and said, "Yes, very kinky. I am a wild and crazy guy. Come and check out our new bachelor pad."

Gabriel snickered and reached. Antonio's hand closed around his, drawing him forward. "Five and six. Six steps."

"Six steps," Gabriel repeated.

Again, Antonio felt the tiny tremors moving through Gabriel's body. He was tired, exhausted from the long drive and the unaccustomed walking.

He closed the door behind them and said, "This is the front room. The path from the front door to the hallway —"

"I can smell the ocean," Gabriel interrupted. He dropped his hold on Antonio's arm, feeling his way through the chairs and sofas grouped in the center of the large room, finding his way to the large picture windows. He rested his hand on the glass. "It's warm. What time is it?"

Antonio glanced at his watch. "Two thirty."

Gabriel turned back to the window. "I can hear the waves," he said.

"We are very close to the water."

"And the seagulls."

"*Sí.*" He came up behind Gabriel, resting his hands on the slender shoulders. "Time to rest, I think." He squeezed gently, careful of the healing bullet wounds.

He was surprised when Gabriel leaned back against his chest, and after a moment he closed his arms about the slim body in a loose embrace. It was the first time that Gabriel had made any move toward him — any move that could be construed as even remotely sexual.

"You move quietly," Gabriel said. "It's hard to hear you."

With great daring, Antonio touched his lips to Gabriel's temple. "I will try to make more noise," he said softly.

Seriously, Gabriel said, "I like the quiet. It's easier to…follow what's happening when it's quiet."

"It will get easier as you grow accustomed…" His voice trailed.

Gabriel didn't answer.

Antonio said gently, "You're asleep on your feet, *gatito.*"

He wanted nothing more than to lead Gabriel off to bed and offer him the comfort and reassurance of sex. But Gabriel had previously relied on anonymous, casual sex to relax, and Antonio could no longer give him that. If they had sex now, it would not be fucking. For Antonio it would be making love. And Gabriel wasn't ready for that.

All the same, when Gabriel angled his mouth up for a kiss, Antonio brushed that soft mouth with his own, the kiss chaste and brief. Gabriel tasted like coffee and mints and something faintly metallic, probably from his recent dose of medications.

Gabriel sucked in a deep, surprised breath. "You taste like color."

"What color?" Antonio asked curiously. He tucked a strand of black hair behind Gabriel's ear.

Gabriel was shaking his head slowly. "I don't know it. I never saw it before. Sort of gold and brown…" His voice trailed a little, his body leaning more heavily into Antonio's. "I'm tired."

"Come." His arm around Gabriel's shoulders, Antonio guided him through the long, bright room. The formal tour could wait. Gabriel was practically sleepwalking. Antonio led him past the giant windows looking over white beach and blue ocean, over polished wood floors, and under high open-beamed ceilings, and among a few pieces of good furniture. The rooms were spacious and clean, done in a sparse beach cottage décor that was decidedly masculine. The house smelled like salt air, fresh and clean.

"How did you pick this place?" Gabriel felt for a wall as they walked, trailing his left hand along the white plaster — broken by occasional spaces of empty air as they passed open doorways.

"It belongs to a friend."

That woke him up. Gabriel halted in his tracks, turning his head from side to side, listening. "Are we staying with someone?"

Antonio was quick to reassure. "It's just the two of us. No one will bother us. The cottage is owned by the father of a sister-in-law. We are leasing it from him. He lives mostly in his other house in Colorado."

"Must be nice."

"Cheryl is married to my older brother, Armando. They have graciously offered this summer home to us for as long as we need it."

"That wasn't true what you told me in Mexico, was it? About not keeping in touch with your family."

"I don't see them as much as I would wish," Antonio hedged. He'd been undercover. Of course he'd lied. That Gabriel had revealed so many truths as Giovanni Contadino was more about their different styles of concealment than…what? Trust? There had been no trust between them then. Attraction, yes. Lust, yes. Even…caring. On Antonio's part anyway.

Gabriel frowned behind the dark glasses. Antonio urged him forward, guiding him into the master bedroom. The large room had a small patio through a pair of French doors, and an attached bath that would be most convenient for Gabriel.

"We will go over the layout of the rest of the cottage later. This is the bedroom. The bath —"

"Where's the bed?"

"To your right." Antonio guided him till Gabriel bumped against the side of the king-size mattress. Gabriel sat on the edge of the bed. Antonio knelt before him, deftly removing his shoes.

"So you're rich?" Gabriel asked shortly.

Antonio tried to judge his tone. He said cautiously, "My family is comfortably off. I live on my salary as an FBI agent."

"You don't have a salary. You quit the bureau."

That had been the last thing Antonio did before taking Gabriel out of the city. He suspected Assistant Director Hall was still screaming. Gabriel has also had a few choice things to say about that decision.

He said now, edgily, "So…what? Being an FBI agent was just a hobby for you?"

"Of course not."

"What are you not telling me?"

"Rest now," Antonio said. "We'll talk when you've slept."

Gabriel brushed that off. "Why are we here? Why a beach house in the middle of nowhere?"

"Because it has everything you require — fresh air, warm sunshine, and miles of sand to walk so you can regain your strength."

"Oh, is that everything I require?"

"Your injured lung must have the right environment to heal." Antonio rose. "Lie back." He slipped the dark glasses off Gabriel's nose. "The bed is very large. Room for three of you. You can stretch out." He set the glasses on the bedside table.

Gabriel scooted back, feeling for the pillows. He grabbed one and lay flat. Antonio unfolded the soft quilt from the foot of the bed, spreading it over the thin hips and shoulders.

"Tucking me in?" Gabriel scoffed. "Are you going to give me a kiss goodnight?"

Antonio bent down and found his mouth, delivering a quick hard kiss — catching him off guard.

"I will tell you a secret," he said.

Gabriel's sightless eyes stared past him. "What?"

"The real reason I chose this house is there is a hot tub on the back deck. Completely private."

Gabriel blinked. Then a reluctant, tired grin tweaked his mouth. He rolled onto his side and closed his eyes.

When Antonio had finished ordering groceries from the local market he returned to the master bedroom. He'd become good at judging how long Gabriel slept at any one time — never long enough, safe to say.

For a moment he stood in the doorway observing the man on the bed. Gabriel's fingers twitched in sleep, his head moving uneasily on the pillow. Another nightmare. Antonio pushed away from the doorframe and went to sit on the side of the bed.

"What?" Gabriel woke with a start. He sucked in a long breath and reached out, fingers stretching for the side rails of a hospital bed.

"Here." Antonio captured the questing hand in a warm vice. Gabriel's hand gripped back hard. For a few moments he lay there breathing hard.

"Goddamn it to hell," he snarled finally. "I hate waking up like a scared six-year-old." Despite the anger in his voice, he continued to hold tight to Antonio.

"But it is getting better, no?"

Gabriel said bitterly, "I don't wake up screaming anymore if that's what you mean."

"You must be patient with yourself, *gatito*."

"That stupid name." His mouth curved sardonically. Antonio watched him, watched the nostrils of the delicately chiseled nose flare as he took stock of his surroundings. What did he smell? Antonio closed his eyes for a moment trying to experience the world as Gabriel now knew it.

It would be very different from the hospital — the only world Gabriel had known since he'd been blinded. No rubber-soled footsteps on hard linoleum floors, no rumbling carts or loudspeaker calls. The smell was different, too. From down the hall, the scent of supper cooking. And closer, cool air with the scent of wood — the paneling and beams of the cottage — and salt. Sea air.

"One good thing," Gabriel said, and Antonio opened his eyes. "At least I won't have to worry about some shit-for-brains moron moving the wastebasket or a chair so that I fall over when I try to maneuver around on my own"

No, he would be safe from that. Safe from prying eyes and curious stares. Safe from pity. And safe from Sanchez' vengeance.

He pulled his hand free, and Antonio let him go reluctantly. "What time is it?"

"Past midnight."

"You're kidding!"

"You needed the rest."

Annoyance flickered across the mobile features. Gabriel hated any and all reminders that he was still unwell. He asked shortly, "And did you sit here the whole time watching me?"

"Of course not," Antonio said, amused — although frankly there was nothing he would have enjoyed more. "I had many things to attend to."

Gabriel was silent for a moment. Then he said, "But you didn't want me to wake alone in a strange room."

His perceptivity surprised Antonio. Gabriel was — not unreasonably — preoccupied with himself these days. That he had noticed Antonio's efforts to cushion his rocky awakenings signaled that he was beginning to regain his awareness of others.

"True," Antonio said. "And of course you are right. I enjoy watching you sleep."

"You'd think you'd had enough of that." Gabriel sat up. "Jesus. This bed is as big as a raft." He felt around himself impatiently.

"This way. To your left," Antonio said, rising from the mattress.

Gabriel followed, standing beside him uncertainly. "Where's the john?"

"This way." Antonio tapped the back of his hand against Gabriel's, and Gabriel immediately grasped Antonio's arm just above the elbow.

Walking one step ahead, Antonio led the way to the large, open bathroom. He was quiet, knowing Gabriel was counting the steps. He counted as well. Nine steps before the carpet gave way to chill granite.

Four more steps and Gabriel's jeans-clad legs were snug against the toilet. He widened his stance, letting his calves mold around the bowl the way the hospital staff had shown him. He unzipped, sighing with relief when the sound of urine hitting water told him he had hit his target.

Glancing over his shoulder, he said, "Are you watching me, you perv?"

"I was merely making sure you're not peeing on the floor," Antonio said with great dignity.

Gabriel laughed. He finished and tucked himself away, zipping up again.

"To your right." Antonio advised.

They had been through this routine many times at the hospital and Gabriel understood that he was being directed to the sink. A side step and a moment of fumbling for the tap handles got him clean hands and a chance to splash some water on his face to wipe away the remnants of sleep. A large soft towel hung to his right, which he found on the first wave of his hand.

"Very good. The shower is to the left of the toilet." Antonio tapped Gabriel's hand again and Gabriel latched on. "The laundry hamper is behind you. Make sure you use it." His tone was pretend stern. "I cook, but I do *not* pick up after the slovenly."

"Great. I'm trapped with Felix Unger," Gabriel said.

Antonio was not exactly sure who Felix Unger was, but he knew it was not a flattering reference. Gabriel was not one for compliments. In fact, Antonio thought if he ever managed to win a genuine compliment from Gabriel Sandalini, he would faint from the shock of it.

"This way," he said, guiding Gabriel back to the bedroom. "You must be hungry by now."

Except that Gabriel was never hungry.

"Nah. It's too late to cook." The protest was lame, and Antonio treated accordingly. There were no clocks and no schedules in their lives now.

"Dinner is made. All it needs is to be warmed and someone to eat it. Come. ¡*Vamos*!" To his amusement, Gabriel's stomach growled loudly enough for them both to hear it.

"Shut up, you," Gabriel said to his belly, and this indication of a returning sense of humor seemed another good sign to Antonio.

He said gravely, "Embarrassing that your gut is smarter than you are, *sí*?"

Gabriel's mouth pursed in a sour little smile, but he didn't rise to the bait. Antonio led him to the kitchen, aware that Gabriel was again counting steps. Gabriel was desperate to be independent and self-sufficient again, and Antonio wanted this for him, but at the same time it was a little painful to realize how much Gabriel longed to be free of him.

Antonio stopped beside the table and took Gabriel's hand, placing it on the back of the chair. "The chair is at the end of a long oblong table."

Gabriel nodded, felt his way down to the seat, lowering himself with an awkwardness that suggested he suspected the chair might drop out from under him.

Antonio moved to the stove, again very much aware of all that Gabriel would be experiencing. A cool, gentle breeze blew in from his left, carrying the smell of the ocean and the spicy scent of tacos. It swirled around his bare feet, licked at the exposed skin of his neck above his polo shirt. He glanced over at Gabriel. He looked delicious, cheeks flushed, hair ruffled, altogether a little rumpled in his soft jeans and sleep-wrinkled T-shirt. The sea breeze made the hair on his arms stand up as gooseflesh rippled over them. He shivered.

Antonio moved immediately to the window, closing it, and Gabriel turned his head attentively.

"What are you doing? I like the fresh air."

"It is too cold in here for you."

Gabriel's voice was tight. "I said I *like* the fresh air."

"And I said it is too cold for you. If you were to catch pneumonia —"

"Goddamn it!" Gabriel was on his feet, his chair knocked to the floor. "Quit treating me like I'm some fucking invalid — or a baby."

"Listen to me, you are still —" Antonio broke off as headlights flashed across the living room windows. A car was approaching up the long drive.

He moved swiftly, grabbing Gabriel, who was angrily stumbling back toward the hallway.

To his astonishment, Gabriel swung at him, fist connecting hard with the side of Antonio's head. He blinked, shook it off, grabbing Gabriel and bodily moving him to the recess between the refrigerator and the end of the granite-topped counter.

"Stay there."

Instead, Gabriel hit out, knocking the cookie jar off the counter and shattering it on the floor. He struck out again, and Antonio ducked back, grabbed his hand, and slapped him once across his face.

It was not a hard blow, Antonio pulled it even as his hand connected with Gabriel's cheek, but instantly Gabriel went stone still, staring rigidly before him, lips parted in shock.

"Be still. Listen," Antonio said urgently, "there is a car coming up the drive. Stay there. Don't move. I will be back in a moment." He was already checking his Glock, which he had left on the counter while he cooked their supper.

Visitors at one thirty in the morning were unlikely to be good things. He was already running through strategies in his mind as he strode through to the living room where someone was banging on the door.

Antonio stood to the side of the door. "Yes?"

"Pizza delivery!"

Pizza delivery. The oldest ploy in the world. He turned on the porch light but said nothing.

"Uh…large with everything on it?" The voice cracked, indicating…fear perhaps?

Antonio darted to the window overlooking the front yard. He poked his head around the window frame. There was indeed a Volkswagen with a ridiculous giant slice of plastic pizza on top. He could just make out the driver in the yellow porch light, a tall, gangly, pimply-faced adolescent. He was holding a large square box wrapped in one of those black thermal bags. There was no one else in sight.

As Antonio watched, the kid sighed and looked up at the sky as though asking for divine intervention. "Hello?"

Not the behavior of one who believed himself under threat of violence. Antonio moved back to the door and opened it a crack. "You have the wrong house."

Eyes peered nearsightedly at him from behind glasses. "Huh? This is eighty-three Oasis Lane, right?"

"Eighty-eight. You passed it."

"Crap. I mean…thanks. Hey, sorry if I woke you. Half the houses here don't even have numbers on them and the other half you can't see in the dark."

"Understandable. You should hurry before it gets cold."

"They make me pay for it if I'm late. Crap…"

Antonio closed the door, watching through the window as the kid scurried back to his car. The car door slammed, the engine started up, loud in the still night. The Volkswagen backed up in a large erratic arc, nearly taking out the birdhouse in the grassy square of lawn beside the shell-covered drive. Red taillights vanished down the road.

Antonio closed the blinds — which he should have done earlier. He moved methodically around the room shutting up everything, double-checking the locks. He verified that the security system was set, and returned to the kitchen.

Gabriel had moved from the safety of the recess next to the refrigerator and was sitting at the table. He turned when Antonio entered the kitchen and the red mark of Antonio's hand stood out sharply on his bone white face.

"I apologize for striking you," Antonio said, taking the chair next to him. He reached for Gabriel's hand. "There wasn't time to explain —"

Gabriel jerked free. "You want to tell me what the fuck is going on?" His voice was cold.

Antonio made sure his tone was right before he answered. "I suppose I am jumpy. Old habits die hard and we are rather…isolated out here."

Gabriel said tersely, "I heard you crack open your piece. Who the fuck comes heavy to a beach house?"

"Habit," Antonio insisted. "You of all people can understand that."

"Bullshit. What's going on?"

Antonio took too long to answer.

"I'm calling O'Brien in the morning," Gabriel said. "I'm going back to town."

"No," Antonio said quickly.

Gabriel's face tightened. "Why not?"

"It would not be…wise."

"You lied to me in the hospital, didn't you?"

"I did not lie."

"No? Well, you sure as shit left a few things out. There's more than some vague threat against the two of us. There's something specific, right? Some specific threat. Against me."

Reluctantly, Antonio said, "It is possible that…someone is looking for you."

Gabriel was silent, seeming to think this over. At last — and the steadiness of his voice was a relief to Antonio — "Who? Botelli's dead, Rizzi's dead. Scarborough would probably give me a medal for clearing the field for him."

"We believe Sanchez has placed the hit."

"Placed…the…hit?" Gabriel repeated, dazed. "There's a contract out on me?"

Antonio covered the hand nervously twisting on the tabletop — and this time he would not be shaken off. Gabriel's skin was ice cold. "There's no need for concern, nothing for you to fear. We are perfectly safe here. I promise you."

"Really? Ten minutes ago you were ready to blow the head off a pizza delivery guy. Seems to me you thought there was some cause for concern."

There was no real answer to that, but Antonio tried. "I am out of the habit of responding like a civilian, that's all."

Gabriel thought it over. Finally, he said, "When were you going to tell me about this? Huh? How long are you planning to hide out here with me?"

Forever, Antonio thought. *For as long as you let me stay by your side.* He said calmly, "Our people are working to extradite Sanchez. A few months, perhaps less, and you will have nothing to fear."

"You son of a bitch!" Gabriel lunged forward and he slugged Antonio with his free hand, his fist connecting with bone-jarring strength on the other man's jaw. Antonio's head rocked back and he let go of Gabriel's hand, nearly falling out of his chair.

"Who the fuck do you think you *are*?" Gabriel yelled, his face red with rage. "How the fuck do you have the balls — the right — to make these decisions for me? You don't even fucking consult me? You don't even *tell* me?"

He hadn't thought Gabriel had that kind of strength, but fury fueled the younger man. Antonio shook off the dizziness, recovering and grabbing Gabriel, pulling him close. He was careful, but he was unstoppable as he grabbed Gabriel's hands, holding the smaller man against him. Gabriel continued to wrestle him, though.

"Listen to me," Antonio cried urgently, "you are exhausting yourself for nothing. You are angry with me. Very well, be angry. But my only concern is for your safety, your welfare."

"*Goddamn you!*"

"This is all I care about since…practically since the first time, but certainly since Mexico."

"Let me go!" Gabriel was fighting him so fiercely, Antonio had to let go or risk accidentally harming him. Gabriel fell to his knees. He began to crawl across wooden floor toward the hallway.

"*Gatito*…Gabriel!" Antonio rose, hovering over the crawling man, stepping out of range as Gabriel lashed out at him. "At least let me help you."

"You've helped me enough!" Gabriel reached the wall and used it to pull himself up.

He stood there shaking with rage, and despite his helplessness he had a strange heart-wrenching dignity. Antonio longed to take him into his arms, reassure him that he would be protected, safe — that he would give his life to spare him further pain. But it was only too obvious that this was the last thing Gabriel wished to hear from him.

"I'm going to my room." He pointed a finger in Antonio's face. Despite the high emotions, Antonio noted that Gabriel was getting better and better at pinpointing by sound. "Back off."

"At least let me —"

"What part of *stay the fuck away from me* do you not get, Lorenzo? I don't want your help. I don't want you anywhere near me. I'll manage on my own for one goddamned night."

He turned and just missed walking into the wall. Antonio sucked in a breath but managed to say nothing. Hand outstretched, Gabriel made his way down the hallway. He found the master bedroom, fumbled with the door and slammed it shut violently.

Antonio woke to the sound of the security alarm going off.

Instantly he was on his feet, reaching for the pistol on his nightstand, shaking off the fog of exhausted sleep. To his astonishment it was already daylight. Bright sunshine illuminated his room and through the window he could see waves crashing against the beach — already high tide.

How long had he slept?

He was already moving swiftly down the hallway toward Gabriel's room. The baby monitor next to his bed had given no indication that Gabriel was in any danger — or even awake yet —

The door to Gabriel's room was open and he burst through the doorway prepared for…anything.

Except what he found — which was Gabriel sitting on the little patio outside his bedroom. The French doors stood wide open and the scent and sound of waves flooded the room. Gabriel, wearing swim trunks, was leaning back in a wooden deck chair, face tilted up to the sun. He looked very tired, but calm.

Antonio's heart, which had been in overdrive, slammed to a screeching halt — colliding with the thoughts still speeding to catch up. He realized he was shaking with adrenaline and alarm. His knees actually went weak with relief that there was apparently no threat.

Gabriel turned his head toward him and said clearly — raising his voice enough to be heard over the clamor of the alarm, "You want to turn that thing off, Lorenzo?"

Turning, Antonio went back into the house and switched off the alarm system. He had not slept well. At least, it had taken him a very long time to fall asleep the night before. He had lain in bed listening through the static of the baby monitor hooked up to Gabriel's room to the sound of the other man pacing, moving restlessly around his quarters.

Gabriel's furious words had struck home, and Antonio's wounded heart had ached. He was not much used to second-guessing himself, but last night he had questioned his own motivations harshly. Had it truly been in Gabriel's best interests to make all these decisions on his behalf without consulting him? Was it only because he wished to keep Gabriel safe, or was it partly a selfish attempt to lay the foundation for a future together?

He wasn't sure. He wasn't sure of anything anymore except that he might have destroyed any chance for a relationship with Gabriel by his domineering attitude and arrogance. The more he'd analyzed his behavior during the long hours of listening to Gabriel's distressed pacing, the more disgusted he'd grown with his actions and attitudes. Gabriel wasn't a child, and he wasn't stupid. Yet this was how Antonio, in his attempts to protect and cherish, had treated him.

He returned to his room, put down the gun, pulled on his jeans, and went back to the patio. As he reached the doorway, Gabriel turned his head, and Antonio recognized again that Gabriel was already learning to compensate for the loss of his eyes.

He took the other deck chair, although he sat stiffly, his hands braced on his jean-clad legs.

"You didn't tell me there was a security system," Gabriel said.

"Er…no," Antonio admitted. "I was going to go over all that today."

"Yeah, well we need to talk," Gabriel said flatly.

He was going to say he wanted to go back to town, that he preferred to go into a school for the blind than stay with someone who treated him like a helpless halfwit, and Antonio could not marshal the arguments to convince him otherwise. Every mistake he had made, he had made out of his love for Gabriel. He had never felt like this for anyone, and it was throwing him off balance, causing him to make foolish mistakes. But if he admitted this, he would only make it all worse. It was obvious Gabriel did not feel the same.

And at this rate was unlikely to.

He said, striving for some neutral topic of conversation — and because the idea scared the hell out of him, "You did not…attempt to swim on your own, *amigo*?"

"No," Gabriel said curtly. "Despite what you think, I'm not a fucking jamook."

Antonio clenched his jaw against his first angry defense. Gabriel was the only person who could get under his skin like this — with just a few casual words. He said, "I do not think you are a jamook, an imbecile. I think you are…sometimes reckless. The first night we met…"

"I don't want to talk about the first night we met," Gabriel jerked out.

"Very well. What did you wish to talk about?"

Gabriel seemed to struggle for the right words. He said at last, "Okay. Maybe you're right. Maybe I am — was — a little reckless." He added bitterly, "An adrenaline junkie."

Maybe? But Antonio held his tongue.

Gabriel again seemed to have to fight for the right words. Antonio's heart warmed cautiously. If Gabriel just wanted to leave, he would say so. He was struggling for words because he was trying not to end it all between them by choosing the wrong words.

"Everything has changed for me," Gabriel said. His chin quivered, but he managed to control it. "I don't feel like taking stupid risks, okay? I'm…scared. All the time. I can't see what's coming at me. I don't know what's out there."

Antonio's throat closed, and he couldn't speak.

Gabriel drew a long, shaky breath. "The only thing I have — the only person I can rely on — is you." And his voice broke. He reached up quickly and swiped at the tears trickling from behind the black shades. "Okay?" he said a little harshly. "You're like…my lifeline. You're like the bridge between who I was and…this." Impatiently, he rubbed at his face again. "I have to be able to trust you, Lorenzo. And I can't trust you if you're going to tell me lies or keep things from me because you think I'm not strong enough — not man enough —"

"No!" Antonio said quickly, and he was on his knees beside Gabriel's chair, taking the cold-knotted hands in his. "Listen, Gabriel. You were so ill for so long. That is all. You had enough to deal with. I wouldn't —"

"Yeah, but you did," Gabriel interrupted.

"Yes, but I won't do it again." Antonio heard the childish echo of his words with faint surprise. Was he going to beg? A proud son of Spain? *Yes.* Yes, he was going to beg if that's what it took because nothing on Earth was going to separate him from Gabriel Sandalini. Not even Gabriel Sandalini.

Only death would stop Antonio now.

Maybe Gabriel sensed some of his tumultuous thoughts because he said wryly, "The hell you won't, you fucking conquistador. It's your nature. I know you that well. But I'm warning you…" he swallowed. "If you want something…between us…then…"

"Between us?" Antonio repeated before he had time to bite back the words. But he was alight with hope. He wished he could see Gabriel's face without those horrible black glasses.

Gabriel nodded curtly. "It's gotta be equals, Lorenzo. All the way."

"Very well," Antonio said sturdily. "Equals." He would try. Gabriel was much frailer than he realized, but Antonio would not again insult him by treating him like a child. He would discuss…what he could with him. He would not allow Gabriel's health to suffer with undue worry or insecurity, but he would be more careful about consulting him when it came to his own protection. That only made sense.

He said huskily, "You know, Gabriel, my name is Antonio."

Gabriel's mouth curved into an unexpectedly sweet smile. "I know," he said. "It's a nice name."

CHAPTER FIFTEEN

"I want to start carrying my gun again."

"You are joking of course."

"The hell I am." Gabriel rolled and sprang to his feet.

Watching critically, Antonio observed how Gabriel found his center of balance and took a defensive stance. He tilted his head, listening to the shuffle of Antonio's feet, trying to track his movements on the protective mat where they wrestled.

Antonio was rightfully proud of his athletic prowess. He knew how to move fast and quietly, but Gabriel was getting better and better at anticipating him. His hearing was increasingly acute, too. Antonio knew by the flicker that crossed his still too thin face that he heard the air compressed out of the plastic covered pads by Antonio's shifting weight.

It had taken Gabriel many weeks to get to this point. Many bumps and bruises too, although Antonio suspected he felt Gabriel's aches and pains even more than Gabriel did. Gabriel shrugged off the hard falls and sore muscles. His sole focus was on getting back his strength and independence. Sometimes that ferocious single-mindedness was a little daunting to Antonio, but he was committed to doing what was best for Gabriel — and being able to take care of himself was clearly best.

Arming him, though? Probably not.

He said mildly, "They do not normally give gun permits to blind men, you know."

"I wasn't thinking of applying for a permit."

"And you, an ex-police officer." Antonio was teasing, but he was uneasy. When Gabriel took something into that stubborn head of his, it was nearly impossible to shake loose. "What were you thinking of then?"

He circled Gabriel, watching how Gabriel instinctively adjusted his position to face him. Arms loose, concentration focused, Gabriel cocked his head to capture the sounds of

Antonio's breathing and movements, ready for a new assault. Yes, he was getting much better.

At everything.

Antonio needed to give Gabriel clues to where he was — fleeting touches, a cleared throat, a soft cough, even a casual *here*. That simple word had become a signal between them, a way for Gabriel to orient himself when he was overwhelmed or in strange surroundings. Just that little bit of reassurance lessened the younger man's tension the few times they had gone into public. In truth, Antonio was learning to deal with Gabriel's blindness as much as Gabriel was.

Antonio had observed how anxiety lessened in Gabriel's face and body language the moment he knew where Antonio was, and it sent a warm thrill through him. As much as he wanted Gabriel's independence and self-confidence returned to him, Antonio liked being needed. Wanted. He could not help the pleasure he took in knowing Gabriel felt safer with him near. It called to the ingrained protector in his traditional Old World upbringing. Gabriel was a man, but he was Antonio's man, to be cared for, cherished and sheltered. No matter how reluctant Gabriel had been to resume their relationship, Antonio had been committed to winning Gabriel's heart from the moment he knew Gabriel was a cop.

Perhaps…even before that.

And now, *madre dios,* Gabriel finally appeared ready to accept all that Antonio longed to give. That relinquishing of control so recklessly handed over that first night at the Club Madrone was finally proving to be the cornerstone of a bigger, more genuine intimacy and, as far as Antonio was concerned, true love.

Gabriel said, "You just got done pinning my ass to the floor four out of five matches — and I'm not sure you didn't let me win that one. I'm at a disadvantage in hand-to-hand combat. That means I need to nail the fuckers before they get close to me."

"No one is going to get close to you," Antonio said and he couldn't keep the hardness out of his voice. Anyone who came after Gabriel was dead. End of story.

Gabriel made a face. "Yeah, yeah. They'll have to go through you first. Well, what if they do? Not to be rude, hombre, but what if they nail your hide to the door? What happens to me then?"

It was blunt, but that was Gabriel. And it was not as though the thought had never occurred to Antonio.

"What is it that you want?"

"I want you to help me learn to shoot again."

Antonio darted in and moved back out of range. Gabriel tensed, but he didn't fall for the feint.

"Just like that, eh?"

Gabriel said dourly, "No, not *just like that*. I know it won't be easy. But you said yourself I've gotten damn good at judging distances and movement."

"True," Antonio agreed, "But you know shooting an unwilling target is difficult under ordinary circumstances. Even if I believed you could master handling a firearm again, I...don't think this would be a wise idea."

Gabriel's face tightened with anger. "Is that so?"

"Yes, that is so. You said you wished me to be honest with you. I think this is a foolish idea."

Gabriel dived for him. It wasn't a surprise. He could still be angered into recklessness, despite his endearing belief that he'd become the model of prudent behavior.

Their bodies collided, and Antonio winced as those fine bones and still healing muscles slammed into his hard length. He tackled Gabriel at waist level, lifted him into the air. Oxygen oofed from his lungs as Gabriel landed a knee to Antonio's middle before he wrestled him to the mat, pinning him with his own two hundred and some pounds.

"Fuck!" Gabriel gasped as the air was knocked out of him. He wheezed, "Up, up! My chest hurts!"

Antonio jumped up instantly, bending over him in concern. Gabriel's leg swept out, catching him on the side of his calf — hard.

His leg gave way, and Antonio tumbled forward. Gabriel rolled out of the way, legs scissoring to catch Antonio in his midriff and send him flying over Gabriel. Antonio slammed down on the mat with a grunt, momentarily too surprised to react.

The next instant Gabriel was on top of him, forearm pressing threateningly against Antonio's throat.

"Sucker."

"Cheater," Antonio choked out. The really distracting thing was the feel of Gabriel's slim body lying down the length of his own. The last thing he wanted to do was throw him off, but he heaved up, slipping an arm around Gabriel's waist and flipping them both over — pinning Gabriel beneath him.

Gabriel's breath left him in a pained whoosh. Antonio could see by the way his face lost color that he was hurting. The bullet-scarred lung ached when the air was too cold or too dry — or two hundred pounds landed on it.

He lifted half off the slighter man, saying, "The men who want you dead are cheaters, too."

"That's why I need a gun."

Gabriel closed his eyes, taking a cautious breath. He looked very young, very vulnerable like this. Antonio couldn't help reaching out to trace one silky dark eyebrow. It quirked inquiringly at his touch.

"You are alright?" Antonio asked sternly.

Gabriel's mouth curved. "Yeah."

He was telling the truth, his cock was stirring against Antonio's groin. And he wasn't the only one noticing his companion's arousal. Antonio heard his own gulp as he swallowed. He'd been trying like hell to keep everything low-key and unthreatening.

It hadn't been easy. Gabriel had needed a lot of help at first — bathing, showering, swimming in the ocean. They'd spent a lot of time together half-naked, sorely testing Antonio's restraint. But, he was nothing if not patient, and he wasn't about to risk the future by grabbing greedily at the present.

"Nobody smells like you," Gabriel murmured, eyes still closed.

"We've been working out," Antonio said haughtily. He surreptitiously sniffed at his underarm. "Of course I'm...fragrant."

Gabriel gave a funny gurgle of laughter and opened his eyes. Antonio felt that catch in his chest as those wide, innocently empty eyes stared up without focus.

"I don't mean you stink. I mean I can recognize you by your scent. Lime...bay rum...soap...something musky..." He closed his eyes. "Come to think of it, you *do* stink."

Antonio couldn't help it. He kissed him. It was just a tiny kiss, a graze of lips on eyelid. Gabriel started, but then lay still, and Antonio's mouth trailed to the other eye, kissing the bridge of Gabriel's nose as his lips traveled.

He was careful to keep it all gentle and unthreatening. Though Gabriel had liked to be dominated sexually before he had been blinded, that dynamic was liable to no longer appeal to him — whereas this — Antonio could feel the hard prod of Gabriel's cock. Yes, Gabriel did seem to be all right with this so far.

Very much all right. His hands slid up Antonio's broad back and raked through Antonio's hair.

He paused, and Antonio stopped too, his mouth hovering uncertainly over Gabriel's, aching to touch those lips with his own, but fearing to make the wrong move that would spoil everything. He didn't even dare speak.

Tentatively, Gabriel began to explore with both hands, tracing the ridge of Antonio's eyebrows down the curve of the bone around the heavy eyelids to feather across the rise of sharp cheekbone. Antonio held very still, barely breathing.

Gabriel's touch was gentle but curious as he mapped the long crest of Antonio's nose. He smiled and said, "I remember the way your nostrils flare when you're pissed off."

"No one has ever been better at pissing me off than you, Sandalini," Antonio whispered. His lips stilled as Gabriel delicately traced the outline of his mouth. Then his fingertips moved away, rounding the end of Antonio's nose, caressing the dip between nose and lips.

Antonio stared down at Gabriel's absorbed face. His own breath stirred Gabriel's hair, and Gabriel's lips parted as his fingers returned to Antonio's mouth. Antonio firmed his lips at the tickle of that ghosting touch, and then he gave into temptation and kissed the fingertips touching his lower lip.

"Ah," said Gabriel. "Say something."

"What shall I say?" Antonio said softly against the fingers pressed to his mouth.

"Whatever you want. I can feel…your lips are moist and your voice vibrates against my fingertips…I can feel it all the way to the center of my chest…all the way to my cock."

"*Madre mios*," Antonio murmured. "That mouth of yours."

"Say something else," Gabriel ordered.

"I want to kiss you," Antonio said against those thin, warm fingers. "I want to fuck you."

Gabriel's mouth twitched in a grin. "Go on."

"I never tire of kissing you. The taste of your skin is like sunlight and honey."

"Jesus, the shit you talk, Antonio. Go on."

"You are an angelic demon. Beautiful on the outside. Passion, rage, and chaos on the inside. You burn my heart. You have since that first night. You haunt my dreams and when you died in my arms, I thought my soul would die with you."

Gabriel shivered. "Go on. Tell me how you want to fuck me."

Antonio could feel the poke of Gabriel's cock through the thin shorts, feel the hard full thrust, the dampness leaking from the head, needy and ready, begging to be cared for the way Gabriel longed to be cared for.

"I want to take your cock into my mouth and suck you, devour you, taste and pleasure you…"

"But what if I don't want you, Antonio?" Gabriel said breathlessly. "What if I tell you no?"

Antonio hesitated. If he was wrong he was about to make a fatal mistake and undo weeks of careful building of trust.

He whispered, "I will not…" his voice gave for a moment and he saw something die out of Gabriel's rapt face. He said fiercely, "I will not let you tell me no. You belong to me now, *gatito.* You are mine."

"Prove it," Gabriel challenged him.

They left a trail of clothing through the house, and when they reached the bedroom, both were naked — brown and lithe from weeks spent on the beach swimming and sunning and running together.

Gabriel sprawled on the wide bed, waiting, face attentively turned to Antonio. Antonio stood over him, warning himself not to rush, not to overwhelm. It would be different for Gabriel — he could not know how different — for now he was truly helpless. Truly at Antonio's mercy.

Slowly, Antonio climbed onto the bed to sit tucked close to Gabriel's side, thigh pressed to Gabriel's ribcage.

"You are so beautiful." Leaning over him, Antonio kissed Gabriel's neck, trailing a path down his sternum, then rubbed his hand over Gabriel's chest, teasing the swollen dusky nubs with his thumb in passing, mapping out the smooth hairless planes of the lean chest, then trailing his palm down to play in the thin line of dark hair that connected belly button to groin.

"Still?" Gabriel said with a hint of rare insecurity. "Even with the scars? Even with my eyes like this?"

"Very beautiful. Lean. Strong. You have the face of an angel."

Gabriel snorted, and Antonio said, "A wicked angel, true enough."

He slid his hand lower to cup Gabriel's balls, and Gabriel relaxed his legs, letting them fall open, allowing him better access. Antonio shifted so that he could kiss the tip of Gabriel's swollen cock, licking the bead of precum out of the dark slit with a slow swipe of his tongue.

Gabriel gasped and stiffened, a tiny sound of need vibrating in his throat.

"Beautiful and delicious." Antonio sucked Gabriel down, mouthing the smooth crown, teasing the underside with the firm tip of his tongue and swirling the rough, broad flat of it over the sensitive tip. He could feel how tense, ready and on edge Gabriel was. Months of healing and building a mutual trust had been good for their complex relationship, but hell on their libido.

The narrow hips arched. "Fuck! God, your mouth! Jesus-fucking-Christ!" Gabriel's hands clenched in Antonio's hair, his back arched, his hips moving in a dance of desperation.

Antonio worked the shaft, sucking and bobbing his head to a rapid beat, teasing and stroking, pushing Gabriel to a rapid climax. He swallowed, pressing his tongue to the pulsing length, enjoying the sensation of Gabriel's cock swelling against the roof of his mouth. Gripping Gabriel's jerking hips, he pinned them to the bed, setting his own pace, forcing Gabriel to take only what Antonio gave.

Gabriel's fingers yanked convulsively on Antonio's hair, and he began that mewling, whimpering his desperate need to be taken and controlled. It set Antonio on fire to hear that hoarse voice pleading for more, begging him for everything.

Yes, it was going to be alright. He was going to give Gabriel exactly what he needed — and more. Antonio tugged on Gabriel's tight sac, massaging the round glands with a heavy hand, sucking just a little harder and faster. Gabriel's restless hands left Antonio's head to pound the sheets.

He felt the wave of orgasm roll through the slight frame and Gabriel went off like a firecracker, burning hot and loud. "Holy shit. So long…I can't…oh, fuck! *Antonio*!"

Cum splashed over Antonio's tongue, the bittersweet tang of creamy smoothness mixing with the salty sweat of Gabriel's skin and the musky scent of his groin. Wrapping his arms around Gabriel's raised hips, he forced Gabriel as far down his throat as he could take him. He held him in place, sweaty smooth groin to his face, firm, tight lips sucking the base of the slender cock. He swallowed again and again, slowly milking the shaft even after it had spilled its load.

At long last he felt Gabriel's fingers fumbling at him. He swallowed twice more and then eased away, closely observing Gabriel's labored, shallow breathing, and weakly fluttering hands.

The moment he moved away, Gabriel was tossing restlessly, reaching for him, pulling him near. Antonio came willingly, moving up the length of Gabriel's body to kiss his sweaty forehead.

"That was to be sure you could lie still long enough for us to do this right. Regain your breath, *gatito*. I want you completely relaxed."

The unfocused black velvet eyes stared blankly just past his chin. The gorgeous hazel irises were all but swallowed by Gabriel's permanently dilated pupils, and yet Antonio still found Gabriel's eyes beautiful — just as he found his battered and scarred body beautiful. Perhaps more beautiful after all his lover had suffered — beautiful because Gabriel had survived.

"Where are you going?" Gabriel's hand tightened, his closely clipped nails digging into Antonio's shoulder. Antonio rubbed Gabriel's arm and gently disengaged his grip, squeezing the restless fingers before pressing them to the sheets.

"I'll be right back. I have planned for this moment for a very long time." He lingered for an instant, drinking in the sight of his lover's lean body, now grown trim and hard again, flushed with arousal, and throbbing eagerly with need and passion. "Don't move a muscle…"

Gabriel was smiling drowsily when Antonio returned to the master bedroom. He said tenderly, "You find something amusing, *gatito*?"

The mattress dipped beneath him as he crawled back next to Gabriel, lying beside him.

Gabriel chuckled. "I was thinking about your woody." Sliding his hand down Antonio's abdomen he rubbed the head of his man's stiff erection. Antonio closed his eyes for a moment, straining against him, wanting to feel more of that casual touch. Gabriel said huskily, "Is it oak? Spanish Oak?"

"Ah, we are in a playful mood, *sí*?" Antonio humped Gabriel's hand for a few strokes.

"Oh, yeah. Play with me some more like you did before." Tracing a path up Antonio's chest and neck, Gabriel grabbed a handful of hair and pulled him down into a kiss. Antonio allowed him a few moments of control before taking charge of him once more, and Gabriel subsided with a sigh of pleasure.

So wild and rebellious out of bed, so sweet and submissive between the sheets. Well, sometimes. Antonio thought of that night in Mexico when the game of *Espera* had not turned out at all the way he had hoped. The many contradictions of Gabriel Sandalini. He hoped to become familiar with them all.

He used his weight to hold Gabriel down, pushing him into the mattress, covering him with heat and muscle. Gabriel quivered with tense anticipation. Antonio gripped one lean hip, and Gabriel's hand covered his as though he wanted to be held tighter still. Antonio cupped his chin and plundered his panting mouth, and Gabriel made weak acquiescent sounds that excited them both.

The sweet wet mouth opened wider and Antonio felt Gabriel's kiss go from needy to passionate to voracious. It sent a ripple of fire down his nerves like flames following a trail of lamp oil, burning bright, consuming the air around them. His stomach flipped and he was left panting, hungry for more, needing more, always more, from this slight young man.

Gabriel reached for one of his hands, lacing his fingers through Antonio's fingers. "So big," he murmured. "So strong."

It hadn't been lost on Antonio that Gabriel liked his hands. He used them now to speak to Gabriel in their sign language — long strokes and firm grips, gentle pressure and teasing rubs.

Sliding a leg between Gabriel's, Antonio rubbed a hot, hard thigh against Gabriel's balls, his knee pressing on the sensitive strip of flesh between sac and opening. Gabriel moaned and wriggled against the mattress as though trying to spread himself wider.

Antonio's hand slowly kneaded Gabriel's satiny flesh, working up his flank, his waist, ribs and chest, exploring in massaging strokes that changed from firm to gentle and back again. Gabriel squirmed when the pressure stayed gentle for too long, craving the heavier, demanding grip from his lover.

Antonio kissed him again, sealing their mouths together, claiming Gabriel with a fierce possessive strength that sent the smaller man's heart hammering against his rib cage. Instantly

Antonio eased up, gentling mouth and hands, drawing back a little, and Gabriel made a choked, anxious sound. His cock was thrusting up, throbbing, leaking, clearly aching for release. Antonio had never seen anything so desirable.

He smiled. "Now that I have your attention..."

Antonio slipped away, the bed springs groaning at the loss.

"*Twice?* Come back here you bastard," Gabriel swore.

"One momento. *Espera, gatito.*"

Gabriel moaned. "Not that fucking game again? Please tell me we aren't going to play that stupid, goddamned..."

He was still bitching as Antonio finished setting up his tableau and climbed back on the bed. Instantly he reached out, one hot fist wrapping around Antonio's jutting cock. Antonio gulped, but managed to remove the slim fingers without doing either of them injury.

He straddled Gabriel's waist and Gabriel's cock snuggled against Antonio, riding the crease between the two mounds of ass cheeks. Antonio clenched his butt cheeks tightly.

"Control freak..." Gabriel was saying, and then he broke off. "*Jesus*, what are you doing?"

"You tell me," Antonio teased.

Absently, Gabriel said, "I'm not in the mood for games, and I refuse to do shots for sex. At least...not right now." He fell silent again, focusing on the grip Antonio had on his cock. Antonio focused on his slow deliberate pumping action — and the use of his secret weapon. He knew from his own experience exactly what Gabriel was feeling. Each upward stroke ended in a pinch of the cock head and a swipe of fingertips around the crown with a resulting sensation like having a thousand smooth-tipped needles run over his cock.

Gabriel's breath caught. "Holy shit. Do that again."

"Tell me what you feel."

"What I...feel? I feel...it feels weird. Good weird." He gasped again as he arched up into Antonio's prickly grip.

"No. I mean, what do you think I am doing to you?"

Gabriel laughed unsteadily. "I think you're...I think you've got a cactus up your butt or something."

It nearly undid Antonio but he managed to hang on to his grip and his dignity.

"Street urchin. Think. Listen." He moved the soft netting next to Gabriel's ear, crinkling it. Gabriel flinched a little — his hearing was much more acute now — then he relaxed. He shook his head.

"I don't know."

"Remember, *gatito*? The night we shared in Mexico."

Gabriel spluttered, "Christ! *Mexico*? Do you know how drunk I was in Mexico? Not to mention concussed? Not to mention…" he changed that, and Antonio knew why. It brought no happiness to remember the betrayal they had planned for each other back then. Gabriel said, "I wasn't taking notes on anything we did. I just…did it."

Antonio brushed the netting lightly over Gabriel's parted lips.

"What the fuck?"

"Wrong. Describe it."

Gabriel said obediently, "It feels like some kind of…fabric. Tight weave. Strong." To Antonio's surprise, he bit at it and his teeth snagged in the small openings. Antonio held still and Gabriel spit the netting out again.

Antonio sighed. "You are truly crazy, you know that?"

But Gabriel said, "Empty shot glasses! Pulque. Limes. It's the netting you buy limes in!"

"*Sí.*"

Gabriel laughed. "*I'm* crazy? You're jacking me off with a vegetable bag!"

"It feels good, no?"

"It feels good, yeah," Gabriel said tersely. There was brightness glinting in his eyes. He said, "It would feel a hell of a lot better if you'd just fuck me, though."

"As you wish, *gatito*."

He lifted his leg over Gabriel, pausing when Gabriel said a little bitterly, "Always as I wish. You made one convincing bad man, Lorenzo. I thought you were the real deal."

"And I, you. But it did not stop me from falling in love with you."

"Love?" Gabriel said the word slowly, as though it were new to his vocabulary. "How the hell can someone like you be in love with someone like me?"

"How the hell could someone like me *not* be in love with someone like you?" Antonio said simply. "You are smart and brave and beautiful — although you do not have much sense of humor. And your manners…*ai yi yi*!"

Gabriel tried to slug him, and Antonio caught his fist and kissed it.

"What are you doing? That tickles."

"What tickles?"

Gabriel huffed out an impatient sigh. "You know what."

"No. You tell me. What does it feel like?" Antonio murmured, fascinated by the twitches of smooth brown skin beneath his assiduous ministrations.

"Goddamn it, Antonio! Can we just fuck once in a while without the whole side show routine?"

Antonio moved out of the way as Gabriel tossed irritably on the pillows.

"Patience," Antonio said, and he chuckled at the growl Gabriel gave. "Describe what you feel." He added with sudden inspiration, "It turns me on."

Gabriel turned his head, astonished. "You're kidding."

"No. I am not a…kidder. This…er…sideshow routine gets me…er…hot."

Gabriel burst out laughing. He mimicked, "*Gets me*…how you say eet?…*hot*."

"I didn't say *how you say it*," Antonio remarked, a little hurt. "I merely said…"

"I know, I know." And Gabriel slung an arm around his neck and kissed him quickly — if crookedly — on his cheekbone. He dropped back in the nest of pillows and said with a sigh, "Okay. It tickles. It's…wispy. Light. It's not hot. It's not cold. Oh. My. God. *Antonio*, could it be *a feather*?"

"You can be a real shit," Antonio remarked evenly. He moved on to the next thing, watching with satisfaction as the smirk died on Gabriel's face. "So?"

Gabriel shivered lightly as Antonio traced the small piece of ice down his tanned, scarred chest, gliding to circle the flat belly button, and then skating along the crease where thigh met his groin.

"Ice, you bastard."

"Of course it is ice, but what does it feel like to you?"

Gabriel hesitated, as though fearful Antonio might laugh — although Antonio was not the one who mocked or made fun. It was just a defense mechanism, of course, but sometimes Antonio wished Gabriel would let his guard down for more than a few seconds at a time.

Gabriel said, "I kind of imagine it as sharp, tiny beads of silver jumping up and down on my skin. It's…nice. Kind of lingers even after you stop."

"Good. Now this?"

The shock of ice on his nipples nearly sent Gabriel to the ceiling. "Jesus Christ!" Fascinated, Antonio watched the small brown nipples crinkle into tight pebbles. Gooseflesh broke over Gabriel's entire sleek body. "Fucking *warn* a guy next time!"

"That mouth of yours." Antonio's mouth twitched with evil humor. He turned away. "Perhaps this will sweeten you up." He dribbled liquid, thick and sweet, over Gabriel's groin.

Gabriel's jaw dropped. "Did you just pour maple syrup on my dick?"

"Does it smell like maple syrup?"

"It smells like…" Gabriel paused. "Very kinky, Pooh Bear. I won't be able to dress for a week."

These occasional reminders of the child Gabriel had once been never failed to melt Antonio's heart. It had not been a happy childhood. A small and sickly child, he had been loved — adored even — by his mother, but the stepfather had been a bully and a brute. No wonder he was slow to lower his defenses.

"I will clean you. Tell me what it feels like?" Antonio invited huskily.

"Like sunshine melting into me, like a warm golden river oozing…" More prosaically, he added, "You left it in the sun, didn't you? It's a little runny…"

He broke off as Antonio gripped his narrow hips and steadied him. Antonio bent and applied his tongue to the sticky sweet cock and groin.

"Delicious," Antonio murmured. "Oh…yes. You are a delectable morsel, Gabriel Sandalini." He buried his face in the honey-scented heat of Gabriel's crotch, taking his time licking the sweet flesh, the broad wet back of his tongue lapping at the side of Gabriel's rock hard dick as he cleaned away the honey around the base.

He could feel Gabriel trembling with pleasure and excitement, but then…

…then something changed. Antonio felt the tenor of Gabriel's breath alter and a sob tear out of his chest.

Aghast, Antonio was up and bending over the younger man, hand to his face, examining the tear streaks.

"What is it?" He felt breathless with a kind of terror. "Did I hurt you? But surely…This did not embarrass you? Anger you?"

Gabriel shook his head, trying to roll away.

Antonio would not let him go. "Tell me! What have I done?"

Eyes brilliant with tears stared up. "I…just…"

"What? *Madre mios. What?*"

"How long till I can't remember what you look like?"

Antonio felt paralyzed.

Gabriel was still speaking through tears, eyes drowning, wet glistening beneath his nostrils. "I'm already forgetting. So many things are fading, messed up in my memory. I didn't know you that long before this happened. I'm not going to —" He swallowed the words and that naked gulp shattered Antonio.

"*Gatito*, shush, *mi amante*. Ssshhh, it will be all right." He tried to gather Gabriel up against him, but Gabriel shoved him away.

"No, actually it won't. Don't say shit like that. Don't patronize me."

238 Baumbach and Lanyon

"I'm sorry," Antonio said humbly. "What can I say? I'm here. I'm not going anywhere. I would do anything for you…" He broke off as Gabriel covered his mouth in a kiss. It was not so much hard as desperate.

Wet eyelashes, wet nose, wet mouth, and then Gabriel was pulling away, talking to him. "Then do this for me, Antonio. Stop the games and the talking. Stop me from thinking."

He moved to kiss Antonio again, hungry and frantic. But Antonio took control, gentling him with his own strength and experience, and the exploration of mouths became something slow and sweet.

"You taste like honey," Gabriel said softly, when their lips parted at last.

"You taste like life," Antonio whispered back. "You are everything to me."

Gabriel shook his head. "Don't say that. Don't…depend on me for happiness. No one should mean that much to anyone else."

"That's what love is, Gabriel. That's what love means."

Gabriel's jaw quivered with emotion, but this time he controlled it, joining his mouth to Antonio's again. And Antonio met that urgency with his own controlled hunger, probing at Gabriel's soft lips until they opened to his tongue. Antonio kissed him deeply, passionately, then withdrew to trail kisses along Gabriel's lips to the corners of his mouth, tiny chaste touches, teasing the nerves in that thin skin. Antonio's lips grazed Gabriel's jaw, traveled to his nose and then pressing lovingly over the closed eyelids.

"Can I touch you?"

Antonio drew back, surprised. "Of course."

"I need to…want to…memorize you." Gabriel seemed to make an effort to firm his voice, although his fingers were not quite steady as they smoothed Antonio's skin.

"You have already touched my soul, *gatito*. My face is a small thing in comparison."

Gabriel made a pained expression, but said nothing as Antonio's lips moved under his fingertips. His fingers were thin, the bones of his hands and wrists much smaller than Antonio's — although he had a wiry and unexpected strength. His touch was light, his expression thoughtful as he traced his way over Antonio's mouth, running a finger along the edge of Antonio's teeth. Antonio pretended to bite him, and that drew a faint smile, although he continued to feel his way to the hard line of Antonio's jaw, almost fluttering over ears and then moving up to cheekbones, eyes, brows and forehead.

"Good looking bastard, aren't you?" he said at last, lying back.

"*Si*," Antonio said smugly.

"I wish I could." But he sounded wry, no longer distraught.

Antonio kissed him. Gabriel responded eagerly, and words again became unnecessary. Antonio tore himself away from the scent of Gabriel's skin, the taste of his mouth only long enough to prepare his young lover's hot little hole with plenty of lubricant before plunging deep into that lithe, accommodating body.

"Yes. Fuck. Finally. *Yes*," Gabriel cried.

Antonio thrust into him possessively and Gabriel responded with needy grunts, squirming on his belly, his skin brown against the white sheets. Antonio fastened his hands on those slender humping hips and took charge in the way he knew Gabriel longed for, understanding that the emptiness inside his lover was more than physical.

He parted Gabriel's ass cheeks wide, stuffing himself into that narrow channel, wringing a moan from Gabriel. Antonio echoed that cry as the slick heat of Gabriel's body wrapped snuggly around his slow, stroking cock, each velvet thrust measured, long and deep, Antonio imagining that he was lancing through the protective shield around Gabriel's heart.

Perspiration glistened on their bodies. Gabriel's hands moved restlessly, blindly across the pale expanse of bed linens, and Antonio pinned his wrists, forcing him to be still and simply receive. Gabriel twisted, testing rather than resisting, relaxing when he found himself claimed and mastered. He pushed his ass up to receive the long, hard thrusts Antonio delivered, trying to take him in deeper, and Antonio shivered at that blazing clutch of muscle and nerves. He angled his thrusts to hit the swollen nub inside Gabriel's tensed body.

The feel of Gabriel's stretched, clutching channel sliding over his thick cock was a dizzying delight, mapping every pulsing blood vessel and bulging ridge. Fire blazed at the core of his lower abdomen, an electric buzz of slow building blissful ecstasy, all bright lights behind his eyelids and constricted muscles in his chest and belly.

Gabriel was starting to make that crazy cat sound again, his *gatito* going mad with pleasure. That wild sound set something alight in Antonio and the growing buzz of mounting orgasm crept up his spine, bleeding into every part of his body, setting every cell vibrating.

Antonio arched and stiffened, plunging his cock deeply, fiercely into Gabriel's now lax body — dimly he recognized that Gabriel had already come — and fireworks exploded in Antonio's head, star bursts of yellow and white light timed somehow with the pulse beats of his emptying cock. He collapsed, unmoving, unseeing. The orgasm was so intense, so explosive that for a few seconds afterwards everything was blank and black in Antonio's mind. A sort of whirling velvet emptiness.

Was this how it was for Gabriel?

Lips found his, sweet but salty. Tears? Antonio forced open his eyes. Gabriel's face rested against his own. He could not see his features but the scent and taste of him was everything.

Gabriel's lips moved against his skin, and Antonio listened carefully. His heart moved at the halting words — more precious perhaps because they were in his own tongue.

"*Te amo*, too."

CHAPTER SIXTEEN

"You are very quiet tonight."

Gabriel, warmly wrapped in an Amish quilt over his jeans and sweater, glanced up. "Thinking."

They sat out on the open redwood deck that looked over the ocean. The salty night was chilly with approaching autumn, and unusually dark. No moon, no stars in the heavy sky. The waves tumbled over themselves in an endless black shine of foam and water. Somewhere out on the open sea a storm was brewing.

"About what?" Antonio reached for his coffee, watching Gabriel's shadowy outline as he sipped the warm liquid.

"About Gina."

"I am sure she's all right," Antonio reassured. "She was a survivor, that one. And Sanchez…as much as he is capable of love, he loved the *signorina*."

Gabriel's look turned to him, and in this light it was easy to forget he was blind. "You haven't heard anything? In six months?"

"I would tell you if I had," Antonio said.

"Maybe," Gabriel said.

"I would tell you," Antonio insisted.

"If you didn't think it would upset me too much. Or set back my recovery."

Antonio said simply, "You are as recovered as you will ever be, Gabriel."

They were both silent for a moment in the face of that truth. Gabriel had made huge gains, but he was never going to be strong. The injured lung made him susceptible to pneumonia and infection, the damage to his optic nerves caused migraines, and his eating habits — or lack of them — aggravated all his other problems. And there was the blindness.

Overall Gabriel had adjusted well, but sometimes… Antonio tried to understand and support rather than humor Gabriel in his quest for independence. He'd helped him learn to shoot again — against his own instinct — and he allowed him to walk by himself on the beach, although he watched him the entire time through binoculars (information he didn't share with Gabriel).

"Who phoned today?"

Antonio stared at Gabriel's faceless form. He didn't understand the tension he felt emanating from his lover. But there were many things he didn't understand about Gabriel. For someone like Antonio, who came from a large, warm, and loving family, Gabriel's reserve and defensiveness were alien and even painful.

He said, "My sister-in-law —"

"Your sister-in-law!" Gabriel sounded as though the idea of extended family was something that only happened on other planets. "Then why didn't you say something? Why didn't you say she'd called?"

"I—" Why hadn't he mentioned it? Antonio wasn't sure. Partly because he was still thinking through the phone call himself, partly because it was deeply ingrained in him by now to do or say nothing that might rock Gabriel's fragile equilibrium. He temporized, "I didn't know you heard the phone call. It was nothing important."

Gabriel had been lying down earlier with one of his migraines. Usually when one of his headaches sent him to bed, an atomic explosion couldn't wake him. The medication was quite strong.

"So you weren't going to tell me unless I asked?"

Suddenly, there was a minefield before Antonio. He said, "Gabriel, you have never given much indication you were interested in my family."

The only sound was the rush and roar of the waves beneath them.

Much more quietly, Gabriel said, "What did your sister-in-law want? Is someone ill?"

"No." Antonio decided to admit the truth. "My family is asking that we come home for Christmas."

"Christmas."

"*Sí.*"

"That's three months away."

"*Sí.*"

The silence lasted so long this time Antonio thought Gabriel had finished with the conversation. He had a way of turning off when he was bored or annoyed.

At last Gabriel said, "Does your family know about me?"

Cautiously, Antonio said, "They know there is someone in my life now."

"They're okay with you being gay?"

"Being gay is not the life they wish for me, but they have come to accept it. More or less." Antonio sipped his coffee and added honestly, "Luckily, I'm not the eldest son."

"That would make a difference?"

Antonio could feel Gabriel's alert curiosity from across the table. "Very much so. My family is very traditional, strongly rooted in the Old World. My mother is Californios, but my father was born and spent much of his life in Spain. Fortunately for me, I have older brothers with lovely, fruitful wives to give them many grandchildren. They have six already between the two brothers that are married."

"*Six!* Christ." The horror in Gabriel's voice was actually rather funny, but Antonio understood that children would be alarming to a blind man. Especially one as highly strung as Gabriel.

"They are nice children." Antonio shrugged.

Gabriel pulled the quilt more tightly about himself. "Do you — did you — want children?"

"The life of an FBI undercover agent is not conducive to raising a family."

Impatiently, Gabriel said, "You're not an FBI agent anymore. You could have a family if you wanted."

"I have what I want," Antonio said quietly. "I have you. And I have never wanted anything so much as I wanted — and will always want — you."

"Jesus, Antonio," Gabriel said shakily. "You just *say* these things right out loud."

"I say what is in my heart."

Gabriel's hand moved up and scratched his nose. He said finally, "Do you want to go there for Christmas?"

Antonio did. It had been nearly four years since he'd been home for a holiday — home for more than a fleeting visit. He loved and missed his big rambunctious and loving clan. But such a trip would be exhausting and terrifying for Gabriel. He still hated going out in public, still found crowds — strangers — confusing, nerve-wracking.

Antonio could not put him through such a trial. Perhaps a few years down the line when Gabriel was more comfortable, more confident with his blindness — and their own relationship.

"It doesn't matter," he said, and he thought he did a good job of sounding indifferent.

"The hell it doesn't," Gabriel said. "If that's what you want…" He took a deep breath. "We could do that. Spend Christmas with your…folks."

This uncharacteristic unselfishness caught Antonio right in his solar plexus. He opened his mouth to speak, but the phone rang from inside the house, the sound — because it was so rare — making them both jump.

Neither moved. In six months they had received six calls — two of them in one day.

The phone continued to ring, shrilling through the empty house.

"Did you want me to get that?" Gabriel asked dryly.

Recalled to himself, Antonio rose and strode inside the house, snatching the receiver off the wall.

"Yes?"

The phone crackled and faded then a deep male voice with a Texas drawl spoke. "Tony?"

The voice was as known to him as family, and yet it took Antonio a moment to place it. "Jake?"

Ten years his senior, Jake Philips had been Antonio's mentor and partner when he first joined the FBI. Thirty years of work with law enforcement agencies had left Jake with a jaundiced worldview, but he was still one of the best cops in the business. For twenty years he had also been one of Antonio's closest friends — and one of the only people Antonio had told about Gabriel and the isolated beach house on the Northern California coast.

"That's right, *amigo*. And this is a secure line, in case you're wondering."

The static rose and then faded out again. Jake's voice was softer, more distant — but the words hit Antonio like a sledgehammer. "I got some bad news — news you need to act on right away. SFPD has a leak. The word is out that your — Sandalini — is still alive."

Antonio swore, then lowered his voice, glancing sharply at the kitchen window and the deck outside.

"How?"

"No one slipped up, if that's what you're thinking. It turns out Rocky Scarborough had a man on the inside. He was trying to build an alliance with Sanchez, and apparently Sanchez has been actively seeking word on your boy ever since he went down."

Antonio's jaw ached. He realized he was clenching it — clenching every muscle in his body in an effort to contain his rage — and fear for Gabriel.

Jake was still talking, and he made himself focus. "Word is Scarborough's faction was responsible for lacing that heroin with the shit that blinded Sandalini. Scarborough had a lot of ambition for a little punk, and it looks like he was bound and determined to crawl into bed with Sanchez."

"Had? Was?"

"Scarborough's dead."

"*What?*"

Jake's laugh was humorless. "You heard right. Rocky Scarborough was hit yesterday. Apparently Sanchez wasn't grateful enough for the information on Sandalini to forget about the disaster at that warehouse six months ago."

"You're saying Sanchez had Scarborough hit after Scarborough gave him a lead on Gabriel?"

"That's about the size of it. No honor among murdering drug dealing scum, huh?"

"It seems not."

Something flashed at the window, and Antonio turned. Gabriel was on his feet, moving across the deck toward the kitchen door. He swore inwardly. He did not want Gabriel to hear this conversation, did not want him worried.

"Is our location compromised?" he asked Jake crisply.

"I don't know. How many people know about the beach house?"

"I can count them on one hand," Antonio said. "And two of them are on the phone talking."

Jake was quiet, then he said, "Yeah, but you know as well as I do when it comes to secrets, that's still four people too many."

Yes, and in fact though Gabriel Sandalini had all but vanished from the face of the planet, Antonio Lorenzo had been forced to stay in limited contact with the world. If the people looking for Gabriel knew about Antonio — and how could they not — it was only a matter of time. And probably not a lot of time at that.

The screen door opened and Gabriel stepped inside. He walked across the kitchen, tossed the quilt unerringly over one of the chairs at the table, and came to join Antonio. If an observer hadn't known differently, there'd have been no clue that he was blind.

Antonio wrapped an arm around his shoulders and hugged him close. Gabriel let himself be hugged, leaning into Antonio comfortably, but Antonio could tell he was listening to Jake's voice, small but distinct through the handset.

"There are two bright spots," Jake was saying.

"Yes?"

"Anyone coming after your boy is not expecting trouble. The official word is he's in bad shape, pretty much a vegetable." Gabriel straightened, and Antonio felt stress vibrating through his slender frame. He hugged him tighter. "Nothing in his file gave away the fact that he's living with an ex-FBI agent, let alone that you're one of the toughest sonsofbitches around."

"We can't rely on that," Antonio said. "We must assume that they do know about me."

"What you can rely on," Jake said, "is they don't know you've got word they're coming. They won't be expecting trouble. Odds are they think they're coming after an invalid and his male nurse."

That would mean three or four goons. Perhaps fewer. Hopefully fewer.

"I think, given the hit on Scarborough, that they'll be coming your way fast, but you should still have time to phone the locals. If that's what you want."

"If that's what we want?"

Jake said casually, "Dead men tell no tales, *amigo*."

He felt the stillness wash through Gabriel as understanding hit him. Antonio smoothed a reassuring hand up his back.

"I don't know why Sanchez wants your boy so bad, but you better send a clear message back to him. Either that or you better think about WPP for yourself and Sandalini."

Witness Protection Program. So much for going home for Christmas.

"No fucking way," Gabriel said tightly.

Antonio gave him a little silencing squeeze.

"Thank you for the heads up, *amigo*. I owe you."

"*De nada*," Jake said. "Take care of yourself, *compadre*."

Before Antonio hung up the phone, Gabriel was ranting.

"No, goddamned way am I going into the Witness Protection Program. You can fuck that shit right now."

"Have I suggested such a thing?" Antonio said, exasperated, staring at Gabriel's furious face.

"Yeah, but you're thinking it. I know you, Lorenzo. You're thinking it's the only way to keep me safe, to protect me, like I'm some goddamned helpless baby cripple —"

"*Baby cripple*," murmured Antonio. "*Madre mios* —"

"Don't laugh at me!" Gabriel flung away from him, but Antonio noted that he didn't crash into anything, didn't lose his balance. Angry though he was, he wasn't losing his bearings, and that was the best news Antonio had had all night.

"We don't have time to laugh," he said. "We must plan our strategy."

Gabriel quieted. "What do you mean?"

"We have three options. The WPP — which neither of us wishes."

"I'm not going into hiding for the rest of my life. I lost my fucking eyesight, I'm not losing my identity, too." The words were curt, but Gabriel reached out his hand. Antonio took it immediately. Beneath the fierce determination on Gabriel's pale face he saw fear. Gabriel knew only too well his limitations, and he would be doubly anxious that his stubbornness did not cost Antonio his life. But a man could only give up so much and still retain his manhood.

"We can request police protection, move to another safe house."

Gabriel bit his lip, his grip tightening on Antonio's. "Is that what you want to do?"

Yes. But Antonio did not say it. He knew if they ran now it would only be the beginning — and they would only be postponing the inevitable. Sooner or later it would come to a showdown. Jake had a point. Right now they had two advantages. Their enemies didn't know that Gabriel was far from being a helpless victim, and they didn't know their attack was anticipated. They didn't offer a huge edge, but it might be enough.

And if they could decisively win this battle, it would send a very clear message to Don Sanchez, who was unlikely to waste money and manpower on pursuing one insignificant ex-cop.

"Or," he said slowly, reluctantly, "we could take them on here — on our terms."

Color flooded back into Gabriel's face. He actually relaxed, and Antonio realized that this was indeed the right decision. Choosing to run would have damaged Gabriel's returning confidence and shaken his faith in both Antonio and himself.

"Yes. Jesus, *yes*. Let's find a way to end this."

Gabriel moved to him, putting his arms out, and Antonio pulled him into a rough hug. He held him tight, feeling the tension, the excitement coursing through that thin, hard body. His throat closed, but he managed to force out the words, "If you are sure this is what you want?"

Gabriel nodded, his head pressing hard into Antonio's shoulder. "Yes. Here. Now. Let's face it. Together."

Gabriel gave a soft grunt as Antonio's arms drew him closer still.

"Together," Antonio agreed. "Always."

The waiting got to Gabriel, as Antonio had feared it would. He controlled it, of course, did his best to hide it from Antonio, but his appetite — never robust — dwindled to nothing, and his sleep grew restless and dream-haunted again.

Antonio watched him and worried, but he managed to keep from voicing concerns that would only have irritated Gabriel and undermined his confidence. The only time he spoke up was when Gabriel attempted to order cigarettes from the local market. *That* had not been a pretty scene.

"Goddamn it, you're not my father — or my doctor!" Gabriel had raged.

"No, I am your lover, and I am not going to stand silently by and watch you destroy your health."

"*What* health?" Gabriel had retorted. "You act like I'll die of pneumonia if a breeze hits me. I swear to Christ my own mama never nagged me about eating vegetables the way you do. No wonder you don't want kids. You think you *have* one with me. You should have been a woman, Antonio!"

Gabriel had no notion how to argue like a civilized person. He didn't understand that every disagreement didn't need to end in the total annihilation of the one who had angered you. He said cruel, stupid things — anticipating, perhaps, a coming assault. Antonio understood that this was mostly about fear and the early betrayals of Gabriel's young life, but if he were a less strong and confident man, Gabriel's heedless and hurtful words might have damaged the love and respect growing daily between them.

As it was, Antonio ignored the antagonizing words and stayed focused on the real argument. "No cigarettes. No smoking. You wish to keep swimming and running then give some thought to that damaged lung of yours."

"Yeah, well I'm *not* swimming or running am I?" Gabriel had said, pacing nervously up and down the long living room. "I can't go outside in case some asshole picks me off with a long range rifle. I mean, what the fuck does it matter about my lung when any moment I'm probably going to wind up with a bullet in my brain?"

Antonio had gone to him then, pulling him into a rough embrace, not allowing Gabriel to shove him away, relentlessly gentle, growling tender words into deaf ears until at last Gabriel had stopped struggling, and he listened calmly.

"Is it too much, Gabriel? The waiting? I can make a phone call and you will be safe again."

For a time. And then it would all begin again.

Weary, Gabriel had shaken his head. "No. I just want it over."

They both just wanted it to be over. But it seemed that Sanchez' men were having trouble finding them. Antonio had done a good job covering their tracks.

He wondered who Sanchez would send. Don Jesus had lost some of his best men in that San Francisco warehouse. Perhaps these would be men unknown to Antonio; new men, men who did not know what to expect from the man who had called himself Miguel Ortega. Assuming they even knew he was still with Gabriel. That Gabriel's "nurse" was in fact, an ex-FBI agent — and Don Jesus' former underboss.

And Antonio wondered about why Sanchez was so bent on taking revenge on Gabriel. True, he had disliked the young *cugine* intensely, had resented Gina Botelli's interest and attraction, but Gabriel was no longer a romantic rival, and he was certainly no kind of threat. And one thing Sanchez was, was supremely practical. He was a ruthless enemy — destroying anything that got in his way — but once a threat had been eliminated, he forgot about it. He was not one for regrets or revenge.

So why had he targeted Gabriel?

And why *not* target Antonio Lorenzo?

If anyone could take credit for stopping — or at least delaying — Sanchez' West Coast expansion, it was the FBI and Antonio. And Antonio was the man who had personally betrayed Don Jesus' trust. It could not be any lingering affection or friendship on Sanchez' part. He would never forgive that kind of treachery. And yet all the intelligence confirmed that Gabriel was the target. There was no threat to Antonio unless he placed himself between Gabriel and those who wished him dead.

Furthermore, as far as Sanchez knew — as far as anyone but those closest to Antonio knew — Gabriel was hopelessly brain damaged. To go after someone described as a vegetable would offend Sanchez' macho pride. He would feel no compassion, no pity. It would be all about a target unworthy of his time and attention.

The only possible reason for wanting Gabriel dead would be if Doña Sanchez, the former Signorina Botelli, still had feelings for Gabriel. If Sanchez still saw Gabriel as a romantic rival…

But that was unlikely. If Gina knew that Gabriel was still alive, she would have the story they all had — brain damaged, crippled. Even if she had truly fallen for Gabriel, she was not the type who would see herself in the role of a Florence Nightingale. She was unlikely to waste time mooning over the young man who had been destroyed trying to bring down her brother…

Trying to bring down her brother.

Antonio stared across at Gabriel asleep on the long leather sofa, the headphones he'd been wearing knocked askew. Even asleep, his fingers twitched restlessly, his foot moved now and then feeling for a step that wasn't there.

Hell hath no fury like a woman scorned.

And if Gina Botelli had placed the contract on Gabriel's head, that made much more sense. And it gave Antonio hope, because if this hit failed — and it would, it must — Gina would

252 Baumbach and Lanyon

be unlikely to go on trying. Sanchez would not allow her to waste his men and money — or her own — attracting the attention of American law enforcement. In fact, odds were good that Sanchez had no idea what his little darling was up to. But if the hit failed, he would most certainly know. And then Gina would have bigger problems than how Gabriel was spending his retirement.

Eight long days.

Antonio had lived through longer days — the twenty-one days he'd waited in hospital for Gabriel to regain consciousness were the longest of his life — but these eight days dragged.

They'd taken to sleeping in the front room. It offered several escape routes and gave them ideal vantage for hearing or seeing any approach from the road. The most likely scenario was that they would be hit at night, and if that was the case, Antonio was sure the bedrooms would be the point of attack. Hit fast and hit hard. That was the Sanchez MO.

Then, the eighth night, Antonio woke to the feel of Gabriel's hand on his arm. Instantly alert, he opened his eyes to see Gabriel sitting on the sofa-bed next to him.

"What is it?" He spoke so softly the words were barely audible.

Gabriel's voice was equally muted. "Someone coming up the road…"

Antonio pushed up on elbow listening. He heard nothing. There were no lights, no purr of an engine in the night to indicate someone approaching the house.

"Are you sure?" He stroked Gabriel's arm reassuringly. Gabriel's nerves were shot. In fact, Antonio had already made the decision that he would call for backup the next day. No one could live under this kind of strain indefinitely.

Gabriel replied with quiet certainty, "They're on foot. Two. Maybe more. It's hard to tell."

Hard to tell? How the hell could he hear anything? Antonio could make out little beyond the low thunder of the waves hitting the cliff outside the beach house, the night sounds of crickets, and the screens rattling against the windows.

Gabriel threw aside the tangle of sheets and blankets, rising and going toward the window. "Turn off the power."

Antonio hesitated, and then he heard it — the rattle of pebbles down the road. And once alerted to the sound, to that swift approaching presence, he wondered how he had missed it. Boots pounding on the earth, men running up the dirt track toward the house.

Scrambling out of bed, he caught Gabriel, hands on his shoulders. "Remember — don't step in front of the windows."

Gabriel nodded. He pulled away, moving to the table beside the couch, picking up his pistol.

"Jesus, don't shoot me — or yourself," Antonio couldn't help saying. They had been over this a dozen times. Allowing Gabriel to shoot at a stationary target on an empty beach was not remotely the same thing, but Gabriel had insisted — and finally pled — that if it came down to a last stand, he would need every possible advantage.

He had a steady hand and one hell of an ear. Even so…

Gabriel whispered indignantly, "I used to be a cop, Lorenzo. I do know a couple things about gun safety. Turn the fucking electricity off!"

Antonio grabbed his flashlight, his pistol, and went.

They had planned it and reviewed the plan many times during the past week, but even so…there was no telling what would happen once bullets started flying. He moved quickly and quietly down the hall. He didn't need the flashlight. Moonlight through the kitchen window was bright enough to guide him. He unfastened the back door, stepped out onto the enclosed side porch, and found his way to the fuse box.

When the power went off, the security alarm would silently notify the monitoring service, who would then call the house. And if they did not receive confirmation by phone that all was well, they were to contact the sheriffs. This was the arrangement Antonio had set up — and hopefully the security company would abide by it.

He threw the main switch and heard the freezer on the back porch rumble into silence. He made his way back to the kitchen, now strangely silent. No lights on the microwave or answering machine, no rattle from the fridge. The only sound was the loud click as the hands on the battery operated wall clock changed position.

If all went according to plan — and clockwork — the sheriff's department should arrive fifteen to twenty minutes after the power had gone. Of course, it could — and very likely would — be long over by then.

Pausing by the sink, Antonio stared out at the night, his heart skipping as two gray figures stepped out of the shadows and mist at the top of the road, moving like ghosts toward the house. Two hundred feet from the house they split apart, one moving toward the little patio that led onto the master bedroom. The second figure headed for the back deck.

The window before Antonio blasted apart, sending glass to sting his face, and the bullet passed so close to his forehead that he felt the burn. The sound of the shot deafened him for seconds.

He dropped behind the sink as more shots were pumped into the kitchen, slamming into the walls, sending dishes and cups crashing out of splintered cupboards.

"*Hijo de mil putas*," Antonio muttered, drawing his pistol. He hadn't spotted this third man, and there might be still more out there.

"Antonio!" yelled Gabriel, and Antonio's heart rocketed into overdrive.

Even if he had been able to answer without giving away the fact that he was still alive, he would have gone unheard as the other gunmen opened fire from their positions. He heard the French doors on the master bedroom go, and the crash of something that sounded like the front door being kicked in. The glass door leading from the deck shattered.

Jesús, Maria y José. Four soldiers? Who did these bastards think they were hunting? Praying fervently, Antonio silently begged Gabriel to stay cool, stick to the plan.

The lull that he expected came, and Antonio jumped up, firing point blank into the face of the man who had foolishly come to the window to see his handiwork. No time for the assassin to do more than gurgle and die as he fell back from the broken window.

"Here!" Antonio yelled. Partly it was to reassure Gabriel who would be going loco wondering if he was still alive, and partly it was to draw the attention of the other shooters.

Even as he called out, Antonio was moving to the recess between the fridge and counter, and sure enough the would-be assassin who'd taken out the glass door on the deck leaned into the kitchen firing. He laid down a very nice and very deadly grouping in the wall where Antonio had been kneeling thirty seconds earlier — and turned himself into an excellent target in doing so.

Antonio brought his Glock up and put two rounds into the shooter's head. The man crashed back into the pantry cupboard. Antonio was taking no prisoners tonight.

Then…then his blood turned cold as he heard the unmistakable bang of Gabriel's Walther P99.

Bang. Bang. Bang.

Followed by a dull thud like a bag of wet cement slopping onto the floor.

"Gabriel!" Antonio shouted, and all the terror he felt was there in his voice. Gabriel at the mercy of these animals, firing blindly in the night, and every flash of gun muzzle making him a target for the men after him.

"Here," Gabriel called. He sounded breathless, but there was no panic in his voice — and he had made it to the hallway as they had planned. From the sound of it, he was in position, a handy escape route down the pitch black hallway if he needed it, a sturdy wall at his back — and anyone approaching him had to walk up the hallway like a duck gliding along a shooting gallery.

Pride in Gabriel outweighed Antonio's fear, and he stepped into the hallway. Because he knew what he was looking for, he could just make out Gabriel crouched in the middle of the hallway, and a few feet beyond him the dark outline of a body sprawled in the doorway leading from the front room into the hall.

Gabriel whipped around, aiming at Antonio, and Antonio knew a moment of genuine fright. He knew Gabriel was going to shoot him before he could speak. He opened his mouth, but the shot took him high in the right shoulder. He heard the blast as he spun sideways and fell against the wall. Only then he realized dimly that the shot had come from behind him.

Not Gabriel.

Gabriel, still holding fire, cried, "*Antonio?*" More afraid of accidentally shooting Antonio than being shot himself.

"Here," Antonio got out, muffled, and Gabriel fired over him.

The killer behind Antonio was firing too, bullets splintering floorboards, thumping into walls, sending plaster and paneling flying — but he was more blind than Gabriel in this setting. And Gabriel kept shooting, the Walther's muzzle flaring in the darkness.

Antonio was trying to get himself out of the way — his right arm was not working well — when a falling tree landed on him.

At least that was how it felt, something heavy crashing down on him out of the darkness. He was knocked back down on the floor, and the numbness in his shoulder gave way to a burst of pain.

The gunman had stopped firing. He was lying atop Antonio, his blood soaking into Antonio's back. He was still breathing, hoarse and hot in Antonio's ear, still moving feebly.

Antonio got control of himself and awkwardly kicked the shooter's gun away toward Gabriel. He tried to push the body off.

The house was suddenly and shatteringly silent but for the hard breathing of the men in the hall and the slow and steady banging of the back porch door. Beneath his ear, Antonio could hear the distant roar of the ocean hitting against the cliffs. It sounded much louder lying on the floor. Like listening to water rushing through an underground cavern.

"Antonio?"

Through the blur of sweat and tears of pain, Antonio saw the silhouette that was Gabriel moving toward him, scooting down the hallway, one hand feeling its way, the other still clutching his pistol.

"All right, *gatito*?" he managed.

The next moment Gabriel's hands, smelling of gun powder and perspiration, were feeling their way over his face and hair, moving down to his shoulders.

"Jesus, you're hit." Gabriel's voice was tight with suppressed emotion. "How bad?"

"Ouch!" Antonio gasped as the groping hands found the injury.

He swore in Spanish, and Gabriel said shakily, "*Madre mios*, that gutter mouth of yours, Lorenzo." He began tugging at the man on top of Antonio.

"Listen to me," Antonio said, "are you sure there are no more of them?"

"I think we'd know by now," Gabriel said. "Two teams. I guess I should be flattered."

He managed to roll the shooter off Antonio. The stranger swore weakly before subsiding back into unconsciousness.

Antonio struggled to push himself up, and Gabriel moved back to help him.

"You shouldn't move. I can't tell how…" his voice cracked and Antonio made shushing sounds, reaching out with his good arm and pulling Gabriel to him.

Gabriel leaned into him, tremors shaking his lean frame. Antonio bent his face to his hair, finding his ear and kissing it, whispering soothing Spanish words.

After a short time the shaking stopped, and Gabriel sat up, mopping his face. "Christ, you're fucking dying here, and I —"

"I'm not dying, Gabriel. But if I was I do not expect to see any angels in heaven as beautiful as —"

But he was speaking to an empty hallway. Gabriel had already gone to use the phone.

Antonio closed his eyes. Somewhere in the night a siren wailed

"I don't believe it."

Antonio said calmly, "It is true, nonetheless. The wounded man confirms it. Gina Botelli ordered the hit on you."

Gabriel felt his way from the foot of Antonio's hospital bed to the chair next to it, and sat down heavily, still emotionally and physically wearied by the previous night's attack. The sheriffs had arrested the surviving shooter and handed him over to the feds. Antonio had received an early morning phone call — confirming his suspicion — that Gina was behind the price on Gabriel's head.

"But why?" Gabriel looked wan in the artificial light. He hated hospitals and he was lost without Antonio. He'd had permission to spend the previous night in the empty bed next to Antonio. But Antonio was making damned sure that he'd be released within hours that afternoon so he could get his lover home, back on familiar ground.

"Why?" he repeated. "Because she blamed you for her brother's death And, I think, you broke her heart."

Gabriel flushed. "I never did."

Antonio chuckled and the flush deepened.

"I never laid a hand on her!" Gabriel said heatedly.

"Perhaps that is what she can't forgive."

Gabriel brooded over this awhile. Then he said, "So what now?"

"Well," Antonio said, "to begin with, our government will try to arrange with the Mexican government to have Gina extradited. I don't know how successful they will be since they've not made any headway on getting Sanchez himself back here."

"Great."

"There is a bright side to this."

"Yeah?"

Antonio reached out, wrapped a hand around Gabriel's wrist and tugged him to the bed. Gabriel came gingerly, sitting on the edge of the mattress. "I don't believe there'll be more attempts on your life. I know Sanchez and his organization well. He'll not allow her to pursue this vendetta. She's bringing too much attention to him, and he'll not permit that."

Behind the dark glasses, Gabriel's face was unreadable. "So what does that mean?"

"For one thing, it means we no longer have to hide like a pair of outlaws."

"Great." Gabriel's tone said it was anything but great.

"It means life can go back to normal."

"Which means what?" Gabriel asked shortly. "You go back to the FBI and I… what? Go hang out at the Braille Institute?"

"What are you talking about?" Antonio studied the hard lines in Gabriel's thin face.

"What's normal?" Gabriel questioned. "We've never had normal. For all I know —"

He didn't finish it, and Antonio was surprised to find himself getting rather angry. "For all you know *what?*"

Gabriel seemed to have trouble controlling his face. He said aggressively, "Well, for one thing, are we going to stay together?"

Antonio felt his jaw gape. "I hope you're joking," he said sternly. "What do you imagine these six months have been about?"

Gabriel shrugged. "Guilt. Honor. Chivalry. You've got a lot of Old World hang-ups, hombre. For all I know —"

"Yes," Antonio cut in, "for all you know — because you know very little of these things, do you, Gabriel? I have been telling you for *six months* — no, I have been telling you since a long ago night in the backroom of a place neither of us should have been — what I feel for you. What part of *I love you* do you not understand?"

"All of it," Gabriel replied simply, taking Antonio's breath away. "I don't understand any part of it. I don't understand how you can —"

Antonio shut him up in the best way possible, pulling Gabriel to him for a deep kiss that quickly changed from exasperation to tenderness. When he let him up at last, Gabriel's glasses were crooked and his face pink.

"You're going to get me thrown out of here," he muttered.

"I want us both thrown out of here as soon as possible," Antonio informed him. "You wish to know what the future holds? I'll tell you what it holds. It holds whatever you wish it to, *sí?*"

"*Sí*," Gabriel said sheepishly.

Antonio pulled him back down saying softly, "Always as you wish, *gatito*. Always as you wish."

End

ABOUT THE AUTHORS

LAURA BAUMBACH is an award-winning author of erotic romance and fiction. Named best M/M writer of 2006, she captured 3 Top Ten Preditors & Editors spots in 3 different categories for 2006 and her scifi adventure romance is nominated for an EPPIE award for best GLBT novel of 2006. Her favorite genre to work in is manlove or gay erotic romances. Manlove is not traditional gay fiction, but erotic romances written specifically for the romantic-minded reader, male or female. Author of numerous novels, screenplays, and short stoies including Alyson Books' Ultimate Gay Erotica 2007, Laura has also written erotic stories for several magazines.

Laura's action/adventure/erotic romance **The Lost Temple of Karttikeya**, #9 in the *Collector Series* with LooseId won the coveted EPPIE Award for best GLBT novel of 2008. You can visit Laura at her website: www.laurabaumbach.com.

JOSH LANYON is the author of numerous novellas and short stories as well as the critically praised Adrien English mystery series. THE HELL YOU SAY was shortlisted for a Lambda Literary Award and is the winner of the 2006 USABookNews awards for GLBT fiction. In 2008, Josh released MAN, OH MAN: WRITING M/M FICTION FOR KINKS AND CA$H, the definitive guide to writing for the m/m or gay romance market. Josh lives in Los Angeles, California, and is currently at work on the fifth book in the Adrien English series. You can visit Josh at his website: www.joshlanyon.com.

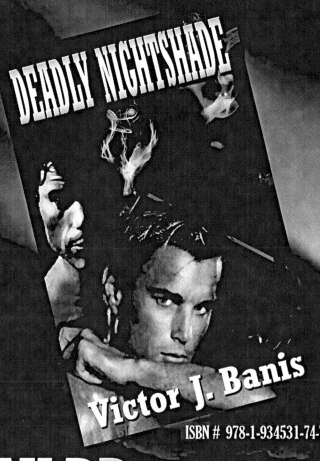

Printed in the United States
220177BV00001B/2/P